T Shape of Justice

By Phil Webberley

The Shape of Justice

A Crime Story

Contents

Characters

Principal Character
Robert (Bob) Shape
Company Boss & Father

Josh
son

Lynda
daughter

Julie
secretary

Dave
friend of Bob

The Cocaine King And the *Shape* of things to come

The 'Cocaine King' - also sometimes named the 'Drug Baron' by the media in times past - the very same man who had smirked when he was sent down knowing his money was safely hidden away - came out of his home from a side door adjoining the garage; he realised he would always be a marked man now and knew the many enemies he had made in his life before going to jail, so he took all steps to reduce his exposure when venturing out following release from prison; and with no gang of 'minders' now in tow, you could never be too cautious.

How much easier life had been before he was incarcerated; he would have conveniently left his car in the drive by the front door; lazy really. But back then he was all-powerful - no one messed with him. No one *wanted* to mess with him: they knew the penalty. These days however, he kept his motor out of sight in the garage so that without exposure, he could leave his house and drive straight out using the remote.

Having already been out earlier, and making an exception, on his return had left his car close by - he was going to use it yet again...going out for a round of golf and to continue to play 'catch-up' with his business. And there was certainly plenty to catch-up on.

His obvious, accumulated wealth from his past activities and the extensive drug empire he'd built, was manifestly evident in the large house and sprawling, but well-tended gardens which ensured a high level of privacy, courtesy of the only person he ever trusted and who he had now re-employed...his old gardener friend.

He'd had problems with the paparazzi in his past so liked his seclusion and wanted to keep it that way.

However, his large garden - and you could describe it as a veritable jungle in parts, not only afforded him his desired seclusion from prying eyes. but also provided excellent cover to anybody who might have gained access to the garden and its surrounds 'by other means', they too would be hidden; the advantage worked both ways. This is what a certain man, a man who shouldn't have been there, was banking upon.

***

As the ex-con came out of his house towards his Jaguar he looked around. He always did, just a well-ingrained habit and caution. Now he just wanted to enjoy his freedom and wealth...in peace.

The car's lights blinked as he approached, before putting his extensive and expensive golfing equipment in the boot. It was a warm day and he'd left the driver's window down. With the door open, and as he reached out to the roof with one arm and to the door with the other to steady himself, he slowly sank in towards his lovely soft leather seat, savouring the essence, the comforting whiff of the material...of luxury.

Just then he may have briefly heard just a whisper, a hiss, who knows...the hiss of a projectile travelling extremely fast towards him that had emanated from within his own territory. It slammed into his body just under his outstretched arm, under his armpit. He didn't even have time to utter a sound - only time to register the worst pain he'd ever felt in his now dwindling life. He wanted to scream but could not physically draw breath. For several seconds he struggled in agony as his door closed by itself as he sank into that lovely leather seat; then darkness arrived.

And so ended the life of one who dealt in, and peddled, misery.

The man responsible was satisfied...another one down. He then disappeared into an adjacent copse via the 'jungle' and onto the street.

**

It was the trusted gardener who found his now lifeless boss.

As thoroughly as they had searched, the police were unsuccessful in finding any trace of the murder weapon. They simply could not understand how a bullet that went into a body while the victim was sat in the car left no traces either in the body, the car, or in the yard by the house. Nothing.

"Another one bites the dust." Such words were used in the police stations in the area and yet... and although he was a villain, a high-profile one at that, the law must go through the motions, the boss...the Inspector, did not like anybody, no matter who they were being killed on his patch.

A Nice Joint

'It was like this Josh...the old couple were always rowing, arguing and shouting at each other; however, the man told the police that while they were watching TV in the front room, a burglar had brazenly nipped through the back kitchen door - that his wife had said 'she had heard a noise' and going to the kitchen quietly to investigate, had disturbed this burglar who was as surprised as she was - and who had hit her hard during his mad scramble to escape back out of the house.

'...with something heavy,' the police had reported; her skull was caved in. There she was...face down on the kitchen floor with blood pooled beneath her.

The argument had occurred as the evening meal was being planned and prepared; he had simply lost his cool and the frozen leg of lamb, just removed from the freezer, fitted beautifully within his grasp. He had bludgeoned his wife to death with it during the very heated argument. Straight after he had dispatched the 'old dragon', as he was wont to call her..her with a barbed tongue, he defrosted the joint in the microwave then popped it into the oven - 200 degrees C for a couple of hours. All the veg had previously been prepared, places laid at the kitchen table...just for the two of them. When the meat was 10 minutes 'on its way' he dialled 999 for help and to report a devastating crime.

When the law arrived the house was of course turned into a Crime Scene. One of the officers, after initial investigations had taken place, and the 'scene' made good, had commented on the wonderful aroma in the kitchen; the lamb had been left cooking and was now done.

'You are welcome to take the joint with you,' the old man offered between sniffles, 'otherwise it'll be binned - I have no appetite as you can imagine....please take it away, it'll just be a reminder if you don't,' he said between more sobs.

They never did find the murder weapon...or the murderer.

The police canteen served up a great dish for the night shift later that evening.

***

'So Josh, an unlikely story eh?' Robert Shape was telling his son of the nuances of crime and relating an old yarn he'd heard before, from the mists of time - what lengths some people will go to, or of flashes of anger and what steps they take to avoid discovery. 'Difficult of course if there's no body Josh, and equally difficult of course if you can't find the murder weapon. Always helpful if you find the weapon from which you can obtain prints, blood groups and gun details - from cartridges and bullets.'

'I like that dad...so cool, did this actually happen? Was it English or New Zealand lamb?' Bob laughed, typical of his son - the way he was with his Aspergers... Even he thought the yarn amusing, a neat idea. 'Well if the joint did a dance first, then it would have been New Zealand...boom boom! But actually son, the story, or tale - I believe it originated from one of our famous authors who sadly is no longer with us.'

He reflected upon it from time to time - the frozen joint. It was one of those tales that stuck in his mind...and of a solid weapon that disappears.

You may recall this later, reader...

The Business And some Lab Trouble

His office and the building was quiet, unusually quiet for a Thursday morning.

Then he felt it rather than heard it...a rumble; the office shook a little.

'What the hell was that?' asked Robert Shape as he leaned towards his squawk-box, his direct link to the lab. 'What's happened?'

'It's okay boss,' came the excited reply, '- the pressure-test cabinet blew - given up the ghost. It's okay, nobody hurt - just a bit of a mess down here.'

'No one hurt...? Bob persisted, 'Are you sure...everybody okay? Who is that...is that you Roger?'

'It's Keith here – Keith Woods, lab-rat No 2; all okay, really, but the cabinet's come off the wall. I think the
door latch wasn't engaged properly. It's played up before if you remember.'

'I'm coming over.' Bob said as he picked up his coat and walked out the office. 'Won't be too long I hope,' he mumbled over his shoulder to his secretary Julie, who nodded - and who had also 'felt the noise'.

***

Bob Shape was the owner of a company that he had set up and named 'IBBIIK Materials' a few years ago on the outskirts of North London, an outfit with niche skills in materials such as shape-memory alloys, plastics. You name it, he produced or provided it. He'd actually started out with a ramshackle workshop and then moved to where he now was as his business grew. And right now they were working on gossamers. But if you were to ask him what had 'IBBIIK' stood for when he had started up, he would return a sympathetic, even meek smile and say:- 'I be buggered if I know.' And he would laugh. 'Well, I've always been interested in engineering and chemistry so when I started the company, I really didn't have a clue for a name at the time - so 'I be buggered if I knew' what to call it...and that's what it stood for...back then.' But not now.

You could see the looks on visitor's faces as they mentally worked that out. However, as the company' grew along with its prowess and reputation, Bob realised that a proper and professional name was required; now it was called **Shape Materials.**

***

The building in question from which the explosion was both heard and felt sat away from the main business but linked by an open corridor with the usual security measures in place. **SM** wasn't a big company but nor was it a two-man band - it had enough facility and capability to support three labs, both a plastic and metal workshop and because of its niche know-how, had good and established connections with a couple of universities, the Police, and a government agency. Occasional queries would also come in from the MoD.

***

He set off to find out if this current 'mishap' involved work on one of the external contracts or on one of their own speculative research initiatives. Thankfully, it turned out to be the latter.

As he ventured into the lab it was not apparent anything abnormal had happened, at least not near the entrance until he saw the other end of the lab...glass and plastic strewn around. A mess, but the explosion, because it was in an excluded part of the room, had not caused much damage...or any injuries.

'Was this work on the current programme - in fact where exactly *are we* on the current programme?' Bob asked Keith, the lab-rat who had been at the other end of the squawk line.

'We were on the shape-memory thingy Bob - the programme involving plastics...along with some of the metal alloys when we can...and we have a promising line with a couple of metals which should be of interest to you soon.'

'Okay...you know what you need to do as soon as you can Keith, a Report, what the delay is etc. I'll leave you to it and get out of your hair...and keep Vince up to speed please.'

***

Back in his office later, Bob had called his trouble-shooter and right-hand man Vince, to talk about clean-up and to re-plan the programmes...if needed.

'First the cabinet blows up, what next? A bad day so far.'

Julie spoke up, 'Bob...not all bad news; two orders have just come in, one from MoD and the other from a training establishment associate with the Health services.'

'MoD? Health service? Hmm, two in one day; perhaps the day's not going to be *all* bad,' said Bob.

'Small mercies,' added Vince.

Julie went on, 'And Bob, your friend...the policeman Dave...he'll be at his usual place later on he said.' Bob nodded. 'He must have a cold - he sounded different,' Julie added. Bob nodded again.

***

Bob didn't want to keep Vince behind too long as he was aware that his colleague was itching to get home to sort out his wife's crash-for-cash incident; she had fallen victim to an unscrupulous gang operating in the area who deliberately inserted themselves in-front of an unsuspecting victim's vehicle, usually on a roundabout - and then slam on the brakes.

'Shower of bastards. If I get my hands on them...' he said to Bob as he moved the edge of his hand across his throat. The incident had turned his wife sick with worry. Fortunately for Vince, there was a witness who spotted the scam from another vehicle.

'Go get 'em Vince,' said Bob, who could sympathise; there were some real idiots about, intermingled with violent and vicious-minded, ignorant thugs...many quite young and totally irresponsible.

But the next day brought *not* encouraging news from Vince...some smart-ass lawyer used some 'technicality' to delay Vince's wife's claim; he was fuming about it.

The Shape

Robert Shape. If you knew him...you would both see and discover about him an approachability, a man who had a rather whimsical outlook on life and always with a readiness of wit, a dry wit. He was just over medium height; his age? Perhaps middle forties but his figure still preserved the grace of youth as did his countenance which was interesting in a rather infantile way...smooth of contours, free from lines. His movements and carriage argued that much youth still lingered within him, considering his age.

He was also one to like the unusual, quirky aspects of life and its mysteries, but also exasperated on its less savoury aspects, therefore and quite often, he was wont to contemplate the world at times like this with disapproval, thinking he was born either on the wrong planet...or at the wrong time, and Vince's woes were a reminder, as was Bob's recall of an incident quite recently of some young lout...and an old man with his shopping trolley; it had happened by the local supermarket...I digress for a moment...

***

Bob had seen the old man a few times before who was in the habit of collecting returnable bottles and cans on the newly introduced local deposit scheme, which Bob applauded because he always made a point himself, whenever out and about, to pick up a minimum of two pieces of garbage, no matter what...he just could not abide litter, mess and untidy streets.

On this occasion, the old man had a trolley-full. It wouldn't have amounted to much really, just pennies, but the old man happily shuffled along only this time there was a small group of youngsters with time on their hands, but not much of anything between the ears, who thought they could make sport with the old geezer.

Just for a laugh, and after flicking a fag-end towards the road...which did not go down well with Mr Shape at all, they approached the old man, muscled in, slowly back-slapping each other and laughing, taking the trolley away from him to claim the money, the old man too bewildered or too late to understand what was going on.

'Oi...' The old man protested...in vain.

But Bob had spotted their game; he knew a 'wrong' when he saw it and had moved in and stood in front of the trolley, blocking its progress. The young lads paused.

'Okay sunshine, that's far enough - give it back,' instructed Bob. The skinny, mean-looking, shrivelled little fellow, a ginger-haired lad, hesitated at first, but one of his mates began to pull him away. Realising he had no choice, he mouthed an obscenity or two for the benefit of his mates which included a couple of sloppy, gum-chewing girls, and moved on, but not before Mr Shape said... 'Hey *Buggerlugs*...and where the hell do you think you're going?! Come back here and pick up that fag-end;

go on!' he commanded with a menacing look, while advancing. The other timid lad, realising that this man brooked no nonsense - and was much bigger and uglier than them, quickly scrambled to pick up the still smouldering butt, then scarpered.

The old man thanked Bob before disappearing inside. Bob hung around just in case, until everybody had cleared off.

It was mindless incidents like these that both baffled and dismayed Bob.

'Must be drugs,' he muttered. '...and their bloody parents; maybe they're on drugs too...'

***

Bob left work late in the evening after a business meeting with Vince. On the way home he looked forward to a weekend of watching his lad Josh play in the usual Saturday morning soccer match.

No player himself, his adopted son was something else when it came to pure enjoyment and enthusiasm where soccer was concerned, even if he eventually kept tripping over the ball; he was definitely not cut out for physical and sporty endeavours, but Bob just loved the look on his lad's face as he joined in and played. You see reader, his boy Josh was one of those that had been 'touched' by Asperger's Syndrome that resulted, in Josh's case, with a physical awkwardness and coordination that amazingly, enabled him to play as if the ball was tied to his feet...and yet, he'd forget in which direction goal was, either goal - which also totally confused the opposition; he was hardly going to be a star player in most things physical...he'd simply get lost. As for his manner...he was gifted with humour that delighted the most surly and disarmed the most envious among those around him.

But his mind? Now *that* was something else. It was special...

***

Certainly not a mind totally enclosed as some minds can be at one end of the autism range; no, his mind was sharp and unusual. Actually, it was quite simply amazing. It was here that the real power abode, a very unusual power.

'What day was it on Dec 13th, 1878?'

'Friday,' he would answer without any hesitation, no thinking about it, no outward signs of his brain clanking into action, no number-crunching looks on his youthful, boyish features. Nor was he ever wrong...and he couldn't tell Bob how he did it. *He just did it*. Then he would take on a jigsaw puzzle that was upside down - and with *no picture*, put the pieces in place!

'How wonderful and strange the mind can be,' Robert Shape had remarked to his wife Sarah. However, on social issues, Josh was slightly odd-ball. It's the way he was...some liken it to being a 'Savant' but Bob thought Josh's quirky life and feelings were just as valid as anybody's.

***

In his early years it had been difficult for Sarah and Bob when they realised his upbringing might differ from normality...they often wept together with the frustrations and barriers they came up against; Josh didn't fit into any slot as regards education either, however - and much to their relief, Josh thankfully seemed to 'pick up' and progressed more or less towards normal lines.

But they had always been worried; in the back of their minds they knew that odd-ball kids not unlike their Josh – and kids being kids, could be picked upon mercifully by their peers - classmates hiding pencils and then watching as the odd-ball kid flew into rage trying to find them...or hiding the school cap and descending into fits of laughter as they observed the frantic efforts of odd-ball trying to find it – because he definitely, absolutely, could not go out wearing his blazer WITHOUT WEARING A CAP! That's how odd-balls were sometimes.

They often asked themselves as well as the doctors and specialists what had made him like he was but answers were thin on the ground – no one really knew.

But Josh's parents need not have worried because as he grew, the lad had discovered *that* magic link - that critical link that was part of his chemistry that enabled him to by-pass the darkness within people...as a dog might see the good in its owner. It seemed the lad's thinking was always along the lines of ignoring 'bad' - that the 'bad' was somehow just a momentary departure from goodness, soon to be corrected. So his parents began to worry less about Josh - and what was supposedly 'normal', or worrying about whether he could become, or 'made' normal again to be like other children. In fact they began to avoid the word *normal* because as far as they were concerned, he was.

And Josh was loved – loved absolutely by his parents.

***

Bob and Sarah had adopted Josh as a baby when all normal methods to start a family had failed, but hey-ho, as luck would have it, Sarah, after all previous failures, fell pregnant a year after they had brought Josh home...and along came Lynda. They were ecstatic...absolutely delighted.

He remembered as if it was yesterday the look on their newborn's shrivelled little face that screamed 'What's happening - what am I doing here?!' Now they had one of each, and quite close in age, both at school with Josh just nearly two years older than his sister.

As they both grew older, she too enjoyed watching Josh play soccer, shouting from the sidelines along with her dad. The two children took absolute delight in playing together and although taking on their own independent traits as they grew, Bob and Sarah considered that their children's attunement with each other was very much like the way twins behaved...a very strong bond.

***

Bob recalled all this on his way back. Then tragedy...because he was in truth, still coming to terms with the loss of his wife Sarah a few years ago...he struggled and cried with the loneliness for weeks after she had gone, due to a heart problem that she never knew she had until it was too late, Bob usually retiring to his shed or mini-workshop that he had equipped as his hobby.

How bitter life could be...his wife cruelly snatched away. He had wept...and wept.

As had his wonderful Josh.

And his lovely Lynda.

A family in mourning.

He would make absolutely sure nothing was going to harm or threaten the remainder of his family.

The Workshop

Bob spent many hours in this workshop. It was his comfort-zone, his sanctuary; he loved 'fiddling and tinkering' with things because what Bob couldn't fashion with metals wasn't worth doing. He could make practically anything, so this is to where he would retire - to his shed, which was really more than a simple shed, being almost an extension of his business.

It was equipped with 'machine-shop tools and equipment, he would answer if asked - lathes, drills, ovens etc. with extensive work-tops including a big-ass China sink; he'd spend hours here. But it wasn't just about building and constructing for the hell of it - he took great delight looking at current designs then seeing if he could put them either to alternative uses, or to use them for something unexpected and yes, although he wouldn't admit it, he played at being a kind of 'Q' from the Bond films but nothing too serious; he just liked to dabble. Often he would see an object, any object - from a piece of plastic or some interesting gadget, and his mind would start churning...

'If I did that, changed the angle here, added some...' and away his mind would go. Or he'd see an old design, probably decades old that had failed, or hadn't quite worked back then because the technology hadn't been available at the time...

'Now if had been made of CFC instead of...' Once again he'd be away. It had passed the time and soon became a hobby...especially concerning two of his promising lines of thinking upon which he would definitely concentrate his efforts.

***

Bob Shape also had useful contacts, one of them a long-standing acquaintance, no more than that, Dave Carradine who was a policeman, a detective - Bob Shape was never quite sure, but who was a like-minded fellow, a kindred spirit who was always interested in, apart from cars and motorbikes, technology and gadgets generally. Bob was sure they'd attended the same college at the same time when he first struck up the friendship - he just looked familiar. However, that's not how the pair became friends, became closer - it was because of a Technology Fair that had arrived in town.

Having looked in on the fair, Bob Shape had stopped off at his favourite watering hole, *In Fine Spirits,* and took a seat outside in the sun. Someone else, a not unfamiliar face, had the same idea, someone of similar age to Bob and who'd also attended the fair. This was Dave. They soon struck up a conversation.

Bob often wondered how his enterprise could in some way bring elements of technology into the world of security and Law Enforcement; he thought they could so they would often get together over a pint and chew on ideas......and put the world 'to rights' of course.

Bob also found, to his obvious delight, whenever he had an idea or a thought that might be bugging him, Dave was always available, usually at the same watering hole to chew over ideas. And of course he would be at his favourite spot outside the pub, away from the crowds, a pint and a few packets of crisps becoming their usual fare.

'Don't ever bother phoning me Bob - you'll never get through; you know what police stations are like these days!'

Well Bob didn't really know about police stations, apart from the fact that there didn't seem to be many about, but took his word for it anyway and with a pint or two, always looked forward to their discussions, realising after a little time why Dave preferred to be outside...especially when they broached matters of law and order.

Julie

Bob remembered hiring Julie.

At the time, when he was struggling and busy setting up the company he was not really fussed on who would do the role of secretary, just somebody, anybody, who was half-way competent, who could look after an office, the paperwork and appointments. There were three people who were interviewed, two women and a man, all lacking in Bob's opinion. On a fourth attempt, a lady, a very quiet lady, walked in. Her name Julie. Nor was Julie as young as the others who had previously been interviewed.

There was a gentle, quiet dignity about Julie. The way she moved, softly, with an intriguing reserve about her. She was of medium height, a well-proportioned woman with an attractive countenance, an indirect gaze from unusual brown eyes; for all that she was well past the spring of life. However, he suspected that along with her capacity for coolness, the appearance of calm perhaps might hide hidden depths, a great deal more than met the eye, yet to be discovered.

Bob was surprised when looking at her resume, realising that hers made the other applicants look like a Witch-Doctor's - she was very well qualified...and also a few years older than himself. He didn't bother to interview anybody else afterwards, so taken was he with her steady, confident poise and demeanour. Whenever she moved it was with a leisurely grace - and he found himself taking pleasure in the contemplation of her movements.

When she had settled in and became more acquainted, these days they both laughed together at their attempts to thwart the encroaching effects of age...and greyness, his once fair hair, at the hand of time had scattered a little of that white dust that marks its passage, while Julie might visit the hairdresser to 'right a wrong' as she would say.

And whenever she left notes or post-its for Bob, her handwriting was always immaculate - always beautifully written in wonderfully exaggerated serifs and Italics, no matter how hurried or inconsequential the note or message might be; no hurried doctor's scribbles from Julie that's for sure.

***

Knowing only that he was a widower with two children, Julie would never ask her boss what had happened to his wife as she was sure he might volunteer the information one day, while Bob knew Julie was married and had wondered about her husband who she rarely mentioned, although he had bumped into her when in town one afternoon while out with Josh; she was with her husband whom she introduced, the first time Bob had met him. He came away unimpressed.

'Ah, the big boss,' her husband had responded to the introduction almost in a disinterested way. Julie had frowned slightly in displeasure at her husband's tone...was embarrassed. Bob saw this and suspected immediately that little warmth flowed between Julie and her partner...or perhaps they'd just recently quarrelled.

'Hopefully not too big,' Bob pleasantly countered with a chuckle. 'I have to keep working on it, desk-bound as I normally am as Julie will tell you.'

On the surface, Julie's husband seemed a robust character having the appearance of someone who'd had a life of 'hard knocks' but if he was in his 40s or 50s...Bob couldn't tell either way - he was wearing the years badly.

As his secretary, Bob thought Julie quite wonderful, but after this meeting, had an entirely different opinion of her husband...and felt sorry for her. From the few words he had uttered he gave the impression to Bob Shape that he was not an adorable person.

Julie, for her part could not fail to make a comparison between the two, her husband and her boss - and she would admit that secretly, when at work, she suffered her boss's occasional glances and gaze with some pleasure.

The Game

Bob, Josh and Lynda piled into the car and headed off to the grounds, a large area which comprised a mixture of soccer, rugby and hockey pitches, all grouped together alongside a slight railway cutting.

For some reason, and only Josh could tell you why, he always liked to take his own ball along with him so that he could kick around with 'dad' first before the real game started...and his ball was different, bright red infused with yellow flashes and very special to Josh - a birthday present from his dad and which he cherished dearly; it was this part that Bob enjoyed, watching Josh work himself up into a bundle of enthusiasm and anticipation for the game to come as they warmed up. And on occasion they would actually use Josh's ball for the game...fun matches played between local teams. Nothing too serious.

***

They threw their gear into the back of the goal, dad and Lynda going to the sidelines as Josh took up his position with the team, probably the *only* time in the whole 90 minutes of the match that Josh was where he was supposed to be. Bob knew of course that in a any game the team players would, should, play to their positions - if you are 'defence' you'd be at the back somewhere - if on 'attack', hopefully at the other end trying to score.

But not Josh.

He'd be everywhere...and his team-mates knew it...and made allowances for it because reader, his Asperger quirk had, as we have already noted, endowed him with the ability to absolutely dazzle when it came to dribbling – but on the other hand, had constrained this marvellous skill by inflicting Josh with an utter inability to retain any sense of direction on the pitch.

Bob likened Josh to watching old shots of the *Harlem Globetrotters* basketball team and the part where one of them, all on his own, takes on the opposition while his team-mates sit around playing cards for five minutes. Yes, you got it...this was Josh. 'Great!' Bob thought...they only needed three in the team - a goalie, Josh and one other for him to pass to occasionally...visions of the team playing bridge or poker on the sidelines while Josh won the game for them single-handedly.

He was truly magnificent. He really enjoyed it, loved it. Trouble was, and as we know already, he'd get lost - not looking up, going the wrong way...giggling, laughing as he went and when he got the ball, he'd hang onto it for ages wandering all over the pitch surrounded by half of the other side trying to get the ball off him.

Nobody can be that good his dad and his friends thought – as they watched as he disappeared once more in the wrong direction.

'This way Josh! Over here Josh!' the team would shout to him - including Bob....and Lynda. The audience, and there seemed to be about thirty or forty others watching usually, would laugh.

When like this, Josh was a showman; when it came to football he'd probably play until he was 90; although happy in anything else he did, as long as he could play or was promised a game now and then, he was *really* happy. It was his drug.

Off the field, he never responded to any behaviour other than with a mature, adult, but innocent ego, no macho from Josh, nor could he ever get 'wound up' from any barbs...they simply bounced off – he'd laugh in response. Josh was truly neutral off-pitch. His personality was one that didn't need probing, empathising with or listening to, for he was truly gifted in happy, inoffensive neutrality - with humour that delighted the most surly and disarmed the most envious among his colleagues.

Thus Josh.

"Another game next weekend Josh?".

That was all his motivation and aspiration - next week's game. Bob often reflected...as a dad, wasn't he lucky...or what? And real proud.

On this occasion however, the high spirits, the amazing skills that Josh effortlessly displayed with the sheer enjoyment writ large on his boyish features as he dribbled and laughed, had also drawn some attention, perhaps envy, from one particular group who were watching on the sidelines...and who had mischief on their minds.

***

Half time and it was one each...Josh had been his usual exotic self. To his delight, the ref allowed his ball to be used for the second half. They had retrieved their kit and Josh's ball from one goal and moved it to the centre.

As before he dribbles here and dribbles there, laughing as he goes, plainly having fun while brilliantly keeping the opposition at bay much to their discomfiture...completely oblivious of all else...and as always in which direction he is supposed to be going?

Nobody knew? Spectators on the sidelines are entertained once more.

But in this half, his genius at holding onto the ball - coupled with his look of sheer rapture beaming from his face, did not go down well with one family watching the game and who - if truth be known - had designs on his bright red and yellow fancy ball amongst other things, perhaps a family who didn't like somebody else having more fun and enjoyment than they were accustomed to...an element of envy involved because it did not help matters when one of this family dashed onto the pitch to prove that 'happy' Josh wasn't so good as he thought he was at dribbling - to show him up in other words - while attempting to lay his hands on that attractive, fancy ball - only to fall flat on his bony derriere as Josh easily waltzed past and away from him, still laughing as he went, which of course would rub salt into the wound.

Naturally, it was a humiliation that did not go down well at all with the watching family, a family known to be steeped in general criminal activities and also known to resort to wanton and mindless violence when it suited them...especially when humiliated.

Of all this, our modern day Stanley Matthews - our 'Ronaldo' - was oblivious as he dribbled and sashayed his way around the pitch during the game. However...

On this occasion the patriarch of the family who were now watching the game - usually a restraining influence on the younger and generally more irresponsible idiots of his brood - was temporarily absent. Had he been present that day, the lives of many at the game would have turned out differently.

***

Josh had a whale of a time rushing around as he confounded the opposition and everybody was happy with the result. By the time the final whistle blew, the score was two-all. All tired but happy, they trudged off the pitch. When they came to collect the kit, the red and yellow ball was nowhere to be seen at first...until Josh piped up:- 'I can see it, those lads have got it, over there...I'll go get it - won't be a mo,' he said as Lynda and Bob moved towards the car.

Those lads actually belonged to that family who'd been taking an interest in the game which included the lad who had been embarrassed earlier. A minute or two later Bob looked over...and sensed trouble. Josh had his ball but there other lads all over him trying to wrestle it away and Bob could see that this was no friendly tussle. Then punches were thrown bringing Josh to the ground where a few kicks followed. Bob ran over to Josh who by now had a bloody nose.

'Stop it! Get away from him you animals!' Bob shouted, as he pulled off one of boys who was on top of Josh. 'What's the hell's matter with you eh? That's his ball!' The lad who had been pulled off fell over, snarling and spitting at Bob and shouting obscenities; nor had the other lads given up trying to get the ball either, but Bob held them off.

'What's the matter with you people? And *you* - just stay away,' Bob warned the first lad...who he then recognised, 'Well well, I might have guessed, it's the young foul-mouthed lout from the supermarket. Bugger off!' he exclaimed out loud. His mate stood close by but was now hesitating to join in.

That's as far he got before an arm grabbed him from behind and a gruff voice saying, 'Or what?'

Bob momentarily struggled with the unknown assailant turning him round to his front before there was an explosion between his legs - a massive kick from behind by someone else, yet another assailant that propelled Bob head-first into the turf before crumpling into a heap.

'That should stop him!' said the other. More voices joined in the melee. Bob was collapsed on the floor in sheer agony, unable to breath, curled up in a ball, probably feinted. More punishment followed with attacks all over including kicks to the head. But amongst all the attacks as he lay there, his only concern was for Josh. He remembered being hauled to his feet but initially, being unable to walk, only hearing maniacal laughter, more shouting, more kicks - the sound of a passing train clattering nearby and screams from the direction of the railway track, a girl's voice amongst them. That voice sounded like Lynda's.

Then blue flashing lights – then darkness.

***

When he came round he was perched in the back of an ambulance, a paramedic asking;- 'Are you the father - is this your son?' Lynda was crying in the background.

It was only then he realised that the other medic was tending to a young lad...it was Josh. This realisation suddenly brought Bob back to his senses and faculties.

'Yes, yes, I am. What's happened to him - what's happened? Bloody animals,' he shouted, repeating the words as he moved closer to Josh laying in a stretcher in the vehicle; Josh appeared unconscious, his face bleeding, some darkness around his features. Then he suddenly remembered the fracas as he looked over at his son.

'Okay, let's move - and fast,' shouted the paramedic to the driver, an urgency in his instruction. Both Bob and Lynda, who was crying, were going along with the ride.

***

Again, 'So tell me what happened?' this time from the medic.

Lynda, between sobs tried to recount to both her dad and the ambulance crew... 'They threw him on the railway line during the fight...there was a big flash...' she descended into tears once more.

His injuries might be burns!? Bob reasoned. 'Bloody animals!' He was horrified and could not stop weeping during the journey - he wanted to know how, from a happy, innocent soccer match, they were now in the back of an ambulance headed rapidly to A&E as Bob kept asking if his son would be alright.

And who did it? he had asked, to which there was no answer except to tell him the police were also now involved.

The Long Journey Made longer

It transpired, from information gleaned from Lynda, another family and from some other bystanders who were also watching, that a group of young men decided that they were going to take Josh's yellow ball home with them, which prompted a fight when Josh asked for it back, quite nicely apparently...with a *please,* Josh always being polite.

However, it also transpired that for the sake of bloody-mindedness, they had booted it over the fence onto the railway track which was part of the Underground, one of the few sections above ground on the network. But they had failed to kick it far enough and being thwarted - and at how easily Josh had retrieved it, the group pounced once more and took the struggling Josh back through the fence, as another group of onlookers attempted to intervene, and flung the ball back onto the track, pushing Josh after it. He stumbled and fell; the yobs ran off as soon as the flash occurred. Someone had dialled 999.

All this he he was told later, because when he tried to rescue his son, he too was attacked; some say by the father of one of the trouble-makers. Bob remembered little else, having been briefly knocked out. When he had looked back on the incident he was horrified, horrified at the casualness of the violence and total ignorance of the danger.

But surely, his son is going to live isn't he he kept asking himself? He can't die...he can't, not as a result of some silly soccer match. No, no...he can't. Not his wonderful Josh.

Now he just longed for the vehicle to quickly be at the A&E...his mind urging the driver for more speed.

***

In the ambulance Bob could only gaze and pray that his lovely boy was going to be alright, while at the same time building up a resentment and anger at the mindless, irresponsibility of it all. Why Josh? What had he done wrong? Nothing...just idiots, nasty idiots, hell-bent on mischief. Oh yes, he knew their faces; he would *remember* their faces, but now could only curse. And pray.

'Hang on in there Josh,' he shouted as the paramedics kept probing and assessing the lad's injuries.

***

However, fate was not yet done with Bob and his family. The jostling, bumpy journey suddenly came to a halt, the ambulance had stopped. Along with the siren, voices were heard...the driver was conversing with a policeman who was trying to explain that due to some demonstration – a protest, several bridges across the river were actually closed on the very route they needed to take to get to the hospital, one that dealt with burns, and that diversions were set up, prolonging the time. He'd forgotten all about his own injuries, the pain from which was beginning to register.

'What the bloody hell's going on?' shouted Bob to the world as they all sat there, helpless, waiting. Stuck. The medics tried to pacify and calm him. All Bob was worried about was Josh...and getting him to that hospital. Fast.

He raged. He cursed. When told by the medics why they were stationary, he raged some more, that they were actually held up by some protest.

'Who are these people holding us up? *Why* are they? Who are they?' From inside the vehicle all he could hear was the noise of rabble.

Eddie Sankey - And the seeds of Revenge

Bob Shape would never forget *that* journey on that fateful, horrible day. The hospital said it was 'touch and go' with Josh when he was admitted, however, the staff had been magnificent.

As it was, Josh spent nearly a month in the hospital including being in an induced coma, before he came home, a changed lad at first, quieter. Josh related the events as far as he could remember them but Bob told him not to worry.

'Don't worry lad, you're safe now...and I've marked their cards.' Bob had found out who the louts were including their parents, a nasty little gang known locally for their fondness for drugs and their involvement in violence and petty crime. He was also told that the father operated a garage.

'They'll get their comeuppance - one day Josh, I promise you,' he said touching his nose.

***

Already, Robert Shape was beginning to change. Yes, that day, the whole experience, the fraught journey - it had definitely changed him.

How was it allowable that hospitals, ambulances and other emergency services could be threatened in this manner with the police powerless to do anything, people possibly dying and other lives ruined by ego-driven pillocks? He didn't realise it at first but this incident and others that were to follow, was altering the trajectory of his life. In his mind, a little 'nasty' switch had activated.

***

Later, he had found out more about the delay the ambulance suffered due to the protest; he had watched a re-run of the news of the so-called protest-leader proudly boasting of causing mayhem each and every day of that week in the City. Nobody had been able to move in the area.

He told his son about this and that one day he too, the leader, would be 'sorted'. He would settle his score for what he had done, causing - by the delaying tactics - the death of his son...nearly. And still, this man was bragging, promising more mayhem.

***

He showed Josh the video recordings and news of the demo from that day a few weeks later.

'We all know who he is, I just need to find out where he hangs out, where he lives, probably a squat somewhere.'

'No Dad, not a squat; I know where he lives....' cut in Josh, '...he lives in Lincoln Park Road, No 21 - *Everglades*,' he said without any prompting. His name is Eddie Sankey.'

Silence followed as they looked at Josh.

'Eh? How do you know that...?' They already knew his name...

'I just do. It's true dad, that's where he lives.'

Bob was both shocked; then relieved, relieved that Josh had retained that quirkiness, that unfathomable and unique ability to do such things without explanations, as he did with dates and days. Then Josh shocked them more...

'If you like I can hack him as well.'

'Eh? How...you can do that too?'

'Yes, just like that kid in the papers the U.S. police want, who has been arrested for cracking the US Defence system.' Bob and Lynda looked at each other in wonder as if to say 'What has 'Our Josh' turned into?'

'Perhaps at another time Josh you can explain how you do it...eh? You don't by any chance have *Google Map* on tap in your head...?'

'Sort of Dad, it just pops into my mind...I see a face or read a name and it turns up in my head, some in more detail than others.'

'I was joking son, but bloody hell, hacking as well? Now that's got to be different,' Bob responded, cutting him off. 'And illegal..? But surely...what about VPNs – you can by-pass these...?'

Yes, indeed. It seemed he could - without knowing how. Whenever Bob Shape was on his business travels he made sure he always engaged his laptop VPN because hotels were notorious for being a target for hackers. He knew that the main purpose of a VPN was to hide your online activity, guarding against hackers and snoopers, but were also useful for hiding your IP address, browsing activity, and personal data on any Wi-Fi network - even at home. However, by-passing VPNs? That was something else entirely. In fact what Josh possessed was not a skill, but a power - a formidable one at that.

None of them knew, including Josh, that matters such as URLs, IP addresses and other 'computer niceties' simply fell into his lap; they were not hurdles or barriers to him and his mind - his quantum computer brain; and it seemed capable of being able to conjure up his own personal-generated Sat-Nav.

Bob was reminded of another young man featured on TV who, after giving a complicated structure or picture such as a cathedral a quick 'once over' no matter how many spires, windows or crevices it had, could reproduce it elsewhere down to the minutest detail, in a very short time, when traditional artists would take a whole day working next to their subject.

'Okay Josh, we'll park this for now, in the meantime let's have look at where this Mr Sankey lives...we'll do the Russian launch-codes some other time!'

'There is something that keeps flooding back to me Dad...from when I was in hospital...'

Josh went on to tell him that he remembered dreaming while full of drugs and apparently really 'out of it', a re-occurring dream, and that in the dream he was visited by... 'You Dad, Lynda and another young girl and that...well, you all came into my room, stood by my bed, said something then walked out. I felt utterly safe and comforted.'

'Another young girl you say...who? Anybody we know, maybe somebody else that was injured in the fracas perhaps?' They shook their heads. No idea...although his dearly beloved, but departed Sarah, did cross his mind.

***

Later...

'My God Dad, that's no squat, he's some posh git - one of those upper-class, well-off anarchists. Just look at his house, his address - definitely not hard up. He lives amongst all those celebs in south London. Huge house dad, look at it,' said Lynda looking over their shoulders.

Bob gazed at the picture for a few moments, 'Well, well. He gets to live in some nice pile down some leafy lane, gets up, goes out, causes mayhem on the streets... and my son's ambulance being held up is just collateral damage? Is that what we're saying? Who is he...who are *they*? And why is he laughing?! Look at him! Crowing at having caused mayhem while Josh was at death's door. Stuck in an ambulance.'

The TV screen showed a baying crowd with Sankey in the centre, on a platform as if he was conducting his audience, looking very pleased with himself as his mostly young followers gazed up at him, their idol.

Once more, Robert Shape was angry.

Thanks to Julie

When Josh was younger, Bob Shape had made sure that he would not miss out on the usual 'boy' activities, like riding a bike. It was difficult at first and Bob had, after trying out a normal bike, bought a tricycle for Josh which he soon learnt to master. But now the tricycle was only occasionally used although Lynda would take it out – she liked it; 'I feel safer on it,' she would say.

However, it now became a very useful means of transport while Josh was slowly recovering, both Bob and Lynda would ferry Josh about as he regained his strength. It was ideal. And Robert Shape being who he was soon adapted it to become a hybrid...a tricycle augmented by electrical power. Josh loved it, sat on the back seat - there were two back seats - like Lord Muck.

***

During the time Josh was recovering and before he knew any real details, Bob had been quietly taking stock on what to do if, and when the family returned to normal when Josh came home. At work Julie had cried on hearing about the soccer match and further sympathy came from Vince who was still trying to get justice for his own family, with little luck.

Julie had already met Josh and and thought him delightful, almost magnetic; it was then that Bob realised she and her husband had no children.

Julie was a rock during those dark days before Josh came round in hospital. Bob sent her a large bunch of flowers...

Julie - Many thanks for your concern - your help...and your shoulder.'
'Bob x'

When he came to see her at work to personally say a few words, he was told by his 'admin' that she was off sick few a few days. When she did return she was wearing large dark-tinted glasses...and was noticeably quieter.

'I suffer from migraines,' she explained. 'This time it was quite bad Bob - I'm sorry I left you in the lurch at a time like this,' she added.

When he was able to look at her more closely but without being intrusive, trying to guess what might be behind her dark glasses, he noticed some colour had faded from her cheeks and there were dark shadows, stains of suffering, the aftermath of sleeplessness and weeping under her brows and all about those gentle wistful eyes which he had always known to be more lively and bright...she looked fragile, slight and frail. Surely not he thought, so taking a middle road...

'Look Julie, please take some more time off if you need to...I'll manage.' He noticed her poise had lost a touch of its usual confidence and wanted to offer some help but thought it wise not to pry further but Bob felt guilty about his presumption.

'You just don't know what goes on in people's homes...' his policeman mate, Dave, had told him awhile back, '...probably best not to know.'

He didn't know it at the time but she had black misery in her heart.

It wasn't long after this incident when he was working on his own late in the evening that, lost in his own thoughts with Josh foremost amongst them, he began to weep himself when recalling that fateful day…when unexpectedly, Julie had returned to work.

'Oh sorry Bob, my phone…left it behind.' She was going to continue then realised that Bob - who was suddenly looking down into a drawer in an attempt to disguise his momentary loss of control of his emotions, his descent into personal sadness. 'Are you okay Bob?' guessing that he had probably been shedding a tear, something she hadn't seen him do before, even though he'd enough reasons for it with his son, for God's sake.

She was embarrassed to see him like this…wanting to offer him solace, some comfort for his troubled mind but could not find the words.

In Awe Once More

Following Josh's previous demonstration of his unique 'power', further evidence of his abilities were soon forthcoming. Bob had been glancing at a press clipping, an article of some notorious felon who had escaped custody and who was currently on the run. Josh was looking over his shoulder.

'Pankhurst Lane,' he suddenly announced. 'That's where he is right now, Pankhurst or Parkhurst.'

Bob looked up at him... 'What? Seriously, you are telling me that that's where he is...the whole of the UK looking for him - still looking for him without success and you say he's at Pankhurst Lane just by glancing at this article...?'

'Yes Dad, honest...or Parkhurst...'

'But where Josh, which Pankhurst Lane, eh son?' Josh shrugged his shoulders. 'There's going to be a few of those about in the whole country.' Bob was not one to ignore or question how, on the strength of a photo Josh could know such a thing.

'I just know dad...I just do.'

Josh didn't have a sixth sense, he had a seventh...perhaps even more. Bob was in awe but initially was loathe to offer the info to his mate Dave for fear of ridicule. If he told him, the law would want to know how Josh knew. What would he say?

***

Bob Shape had delved into 'Mediums' doing some further research on the matter; there was no doubt that the world was awash with charlatans claiming being able to predict 'this and that' or find lost treasures; and people, both dead or alive. The story of a *Peter Hurkos* intrigued him, a Dutchman who was apparently able to determine true identities of people just by touching objects or clothing that belonged to them; he was doing this in the 40s and 50s and allegedly solved a murder. If these stories were true then Josh was not alone.

***

Later...the next time they were together...crisps and drinks on the table...

'Dave, I have some info for you...your crook, your murderer who's in all the papers this week. Check out *Pankhurst* or *Parkhurst Lane*. That's where he is *right now.* Don't ask me *which Pankhurst* or *Parkhurst Lane* or which town or village Dave, but that's all I have...don't ask me how I know but better tell your bosses. And when this is all over, we'll have that meeting and I'll tell you a few things...a few things that will be of mutual benefit.'

Needless to say, the criminal was rounded up; the coppers had closed off a whole 'Pankhurst Street' in some Midlands town and systematically investigated all forty houses on it, one by one.

Now Bob was in awe once again. As was Dave.

'You know what Dave, I *will* explain to you and only you sometime soon, about certain things,' he said as he placed his finger on his nose.

Dave nodded, a grin on his face.

Later… with Dave

'Dave, this envelope suddenly appeared on my doorstep…some great but disturbing info in it too about those escaping justice. Thanks for that.'

'Eh, really; what envelope? Nothing to do with me mate.' Bob wasn't quite sure if he was serious or not.

'Anyway, why we are here; with respect to the incident that day after the soccer match when Josh was beaten up and the demo that jammed up London; any chance you would be able to find out how serious it was, the consequences, how many ops were cancelled or missed…did anyone croak as a result of the delays to the hospitals? That kind of stuff?'

Apart from a few one or two other topics, the discussion did not go beyond the ambulance journey and the incident, although Bob did say that Josh possessed a unique thinking capability and went as far as to relate the days / dates peculiarity. That's as much as he would confide in Dave…for now.

'Well I know it caused havoc with us, but as for the hospital, it caused big problems. Doctors and nurses - in fact all staff, could not get to work on time or park, but I'll see what I can dig out from the ambulance crews. I can't imagine how you must have felt on your way in with your son being held up like that.

'Thanks Dave. Now about that information you did, or didn't furnish for me in that envelope I happened upon.'

Dave smiled. 'And by the way, that old man with the shopping trolley…just thought I'd let you know. He was an old friend of my dad's…his name was 'Alfie'. My dad always used to pull his leg in years gone my with a rendering of 'Alfie'. Anyway, well done there, but sorry to tell you that the lovely family bunch of thugs who attacked you and Josh are all out-and-about...on bail. People's memories, witnesses, intimidation etc.'

Bob was warmed by Dave's information on 'Alfie'...it was a start, but thought it typical about the family being out on bail. How predictable...

Justice today? Things were wrong - and needed 'righting'.

'And talking of hospitals and doctors, I'm having a small op myself soon - shall be going in for a day or two, key-hole stuff, but I'll be alright.' Bob knew that Dave had complained of 'gut' problems more or less since he first knew him.

'All that beer and curries Dave...?' They often joked about it. It was at times like this that Bob realised he did not know a great deal about his friend and suspected that Dave was the kind of person who perhaps liked to keep it that way...a good casual friendship without going too deep but he seemed quite happy in his unspoken role of feeding information to Bob.

Fixing the world

The envelope Dave did, or didn't deliver, contained a considerable number of press extracts of those who seemed 'to put two fingers up' at the law and at the general public, cases that invited punishment or some kind of retribution at least from the authorities and yet, either through some technicality, some loop-hole...or simply because a judge 'took pity' on the poor malefactor... 'it was only his seventh conviction M'lord' cried the Defence Panel, these lowlifes were free once again to carry out another ten burglaries or to generally make life a misery for those around them, those that actually abided by the law.

'So we just look on and can do nothing Dave..to allow this...this...*bloody infamy* to continue?'

'That's about the size of it,' he admitted. 'How do you think I feel in my job and watching these louts go free,' he said rhetorically. 'There's things I'd *like* to do Bob but can't; *you* know that.'

'I had a quick look through those clippings...made my blood boil, especially after what happened to Josh; I know who did it - *we* know who did it and he's going to pay - *they* are going to pay, Christ, it could have gone either way with Josh thanks to Edward Sankey and his morons holding us up, so any dirt you can dig up will be much appreciated. Some of these buggers in these press extracts were caught red-handed too. Something is seriously wrong with the system we have in this country.'

'Well, they can get caught yet nothing happens, but we sneeze the wrong way or use the wrong pronoun and we get taken to the cleaners.'

'Yep, that's the trick Dave. Don't get caught.'

But...how *not to get caught?* How could he redress the balance - and *not get caught,* if he tried to put the world to rights?

'They' can and get away with it, but not us, the long-suffering public. I'm all for giving somebody a second chance, perhaps even a third...but 10 burglaries, 27 burglaries in one case, 58 in another and over a hundred in yet another!? Unbelievable! Who are the idiots in charge? Who is responsible? And yet, as you know, hundreds of police stations have been closed down so I suppose we shouldn't be surprised...no friendly Desk Sergeant at your local station that you can pop into, to see or complain to.

'Another factor in all this is that by closing down police stations and other hubs, we lost a valuable source of local intelligence, the bobbies knew what was going on locally and even knew where to lay a finger when something untoward cropped up. You lose all this when you close them.'

'Tell me about it,' Dave responded.

During their discussions they had recalled the story of some Russian politician, someone they would not normally call a natural ally who had boldly announced several years ago to his assembly, that he'd execute 10,000 criminals in order that the rest of the law-abiding population could live without fear from villains. They had laughed together, 'Probably need to be much more than just 10,000,' Dave had said. More laughter, but they both nodded...'I'm with that politician on this one,' they agreed, nodding.

'You and me both! Twenty-seven burglaries - and always let off; over one hundred...where do they find the bloody time? The mind boggles. It's not right...is it because they know they won't get caught, or if they do get caught, they won't get punished?'

'Yep, that's about the size of it my friend. Both.'

'Well I get heartily tired of it all...**I'm tired** of being told that drug addicts have a disease, and I must help support and treat them *and* pay for the damage they do. Did a giant germ rush out of a dark alley, grab them and stuff white powder up their noses or stick a needle in their arm while they tried to fight it off?' Dave laughed while nodding again. A silence descended upon them.

Then Bob Shape thought about Josh...and the Pankhurst Lane incident. He had an idea...

'What about fraud; you must get many calls from the public, or companies about being hacked and black-mailed...? It's in the papers nearly every day.'

'Yes, all the time, why?'

'I might be able to help...someone with special skills. If you have any company or a person facing these kind of difficulties, and I know it's time-consuming investigating them, then please 'let me in' - give me a transcript from these so-called anonymous mails...or let my specialist see them,' he said as he winked.

'Really - that good?'

'Well, we had a good result last time, remember?'

***

Dave brought the information the next day about the hospital....

'A lot of traffic was held up that day Bob as you know; one fatality in a waiting ambulance, another fatality possibly down to treatment not being administered in a timely fashion, but not confirmed. Six postponed operations - two of them urgent cancer victims. Two of our own men were held up for treatment, one a dislocated shoulder, the other a thrown bottle resulting in a head injury. I haven't got the figures for the following day but *do* know that there were at least three cancelled weddings/holidays ...planes missed etc.'

'Thanks Dave. Any names – any body I can talk to...?'

'You know I can't tell you that just yet, but to throw somebody on a railway track, well that defies any understanding, can't imagine how you must have felt; and did he know it was electrified? I bet he did. One hospital suffered from the fact that a main route to it was blocked by one man sitting in the middle of the road just across the bridge...one man! He just sat there, cross-legged, with some placard round his neck.'

'Didn't anyone shoot him...hopefully?' Bob just shook his head almost in disbelief. He thought back to *that* day...how it all started off, the thoughts in his mind now...

When a butterfly flaps its wings....

After a pause, 'Something else you should know Bob...the lout...yes, him, your favourite...'

'What about him?' Bob was looking at Dave expectantly, 'What's he done now?'

'He has been questioned in the past for, *allegedly,* molesting girls, harassment... 'touching them up' but we couldn't pin anything on him. Just make sure your daughter wasn't, well you know, when it 'all went down that day.'

'My God! What else *doesn't* he do?' Bob was getting more angry by the day each time he heard about the problem family. 'Who's supposed to be looking after us?' he mused. 'Doesn't look like the law that's for sure - not getting at you Dave, as you know.'

Dave told him that more than two thousand criminals under community supervision had appeared in court accused of crimes including murder and rape since four years ago. 'Probably more by now,' he added.

'The Probation Services have failed us Bob, just look at that serial rapist who raped at least ten women, the service missed many opportunities to prevent it. He was on cocaine.'

'Drugs again eh? But don't worry Dave, I'll calm down...a bit.'

***

Later, he carefully approached Lynda on the matter as soon as he found an appropriate opportunity. At first she was evasive but then admitted in a flood of tears that indeed, he and his accomplices were briefly diverted from chasing Josh and his ball by what seemed a more exciting sport - a girl...a not unattractive young girl, but she had swung and jabbed her umbrella successfully at them while enlisting help from other touch-line supporters.

'But did he or they actually touch you Lynda?'

She admitted, 'Almost dad, one of them touched my...you know..' she indicated by looking down at her chest, '...and tried to fondle me when we struggled but that was it.' She hadn't wanted to tell her dad or the coppers about this...it just seemed incidental compared to what Josh was suffering at the time.

And these people roam the streets. Another one for the scorecard.

Yes – we must keep a special scorecard for *knucklehead* and his gang. Definitely.

***

Robert Shape was definitely altering his view on 'Society' – and Law & Order, becoming more cynical – embittered even. He always considered himself a 'softy' to a large degree, but with a little part of him that was his hard edge - and he had a hard edge, usually kept under control, kept in the background. Now he found the soft part slinking away, the harder part of him increasingly in the ascent with each tale he heard from Dave...or saw in the media.

Mallock and The Dream

'Boss...that couple who bought a load of cocaine from us; both dead. Don't know how, but looks like an execution from what we're hearing.' Mallock, the boss, looked up.

' Eh? Somebody targeting our groups?' He wondered who it might be...there was always someone trying to muscle in.

'And *Fairy Boy*...remember him boss? Dropped down dead outside the *Sixes Club* just off The Avenue; they say OD'd.'

Yes, *Fairy Boy* was a regular buyer...Mallock remembered him well but thought him a 'careful' dope - if there really was such a thing.

***

Ed Mallock would brook no competition or threat to his little crooked empire, an 'empire to Mallock, a squalid little local enterprise to others that he had going on in town and in the adjacent, outlying villages; there was some sort of an understanding in the murky world of shifting drugs around to his customers and to the occasional ad-hoc buyer, so who is trying to mess things up he asked himself? Well okay, he did have his garage business that kept some cash coming in but it was only a bread and butter outfit; it was the drugs that brought in the real money.

His clientele? All of course, 'dopes', and there were more and more of them these days; poor saps. Oh yes, he knew what drugs eventually did to your mind....maybe not today, nor tomorrow or even next week, but ten years down the line. Some part of the brain goes short-circuit – goes haywire. Suddenly, no warning, brain circuitry not connecting, or connecting too well, resulting in an axe in the head of someone for no reason.

'If I ever catch you, son, taking any of this crap, I'll give you a bloody good hiding...got that!?' Thus Dad talking to his idiot, lay-about off-spring, named *'Penny'* - on account of the fact that he was both bad and bent, so everyone used the name that had stuck, his father being the only one who could control him. No, *Penny* hadn't liked his given name, *Boris*...too foreign-sounding he always thought. In truth he would have even preferred *Sue,* like in that Johnny Cash song; a sure-fire excuse to beat somebody up if they mocked him. But *Penny* was fine and resulted in quite a few scraps. He'd got used to it. Liked it.

'I know Dad...you don't have to worry on that score.' And he was right - *Penny* did indeed refrain from 'using'...other than alcohol. But his forte was violence, robbery, intimidation...just the pleasure of forcing his unfeeling, selfish muscle on those weaker than himself which included girls, women - even the vulnerable elderly. My God, weren't they easy targets! He didn't care. And Dad was there occasionally to back him up when circumstances did not work out, always mindful of the 'pigs', as the family called the law. And he had a few 'helpers' who looked up to him, followed him about which gave him satisfaction at his young age - the age of eighteen.

***

But according to feedback and word on the street, someone, somebody, was not enamoured by his activities and the whole cosy set-up. Mallock needed to find out what was going on...who was beginning to cause him grief, because, reader, he had a plan – a dream.

***

Some time ago one miserable January morning, a winter break beckoned - he had spotted a holiday advert. A spur of the moment decision followed; he went to Madeira for a long weekend with a lady companion. He knew nothing about the place, even had no clue where it was; it just sounded good. Everyone else seemed to be doing the Canaries. But Madeira? Sounded exotic, so he went.

He was impressed, not so much with his companion but with Madeira...it was January and it was warm - and not too far away with spectacular forest-covered mountains.

'I'm going to live here one day - all-year round warmth and not a million miles aqway,' he said to anyone who might be listening. He loved the place...especially its capital, Funchal; not too big, not too small. He even spotted the house, a house set back on a hill like most places there that he was definitely going to buy once he'd accumulated enough funds from his already developing business. Yes, he liked the island, never cold no matter when; never.

Even criminals like Mallock had a soft spot.

Two friends

Outside of work, Bob had two close friends and as we know reader, Dave was one of them. The other was a farmer whom he met in unusual circumstances; his name was Mal...Malcolm Munroe.

The unusual circumstance? While ambling down the High Street with Josh headed for a bookshop - this was sometime before the soccer match incident; an elderly lady walking in front of them had simply tripped over and fallen flat on her face on the pavement, literally right in front of Josh and his dad. Blood came gushing from her nose. In no time Josh and Bob were beside her and had taken care of immediate First Aid while calling 999.

Crowds gather round, all wondering if anybody's called for help when incidents like this occur in public but Josh played a starring role, making her comfortable and then happily chatting to her in his youthful, boyish manner and quickly they'd brought her a chair, courtesy of a nearby cafe. His cheerful chat began to make her both quite comfortable - and responsive.

In no time, a Land Rover pulled up. This was Malcolm Munroe, the unfortunate lady's son. He came rushing over but realised, agitated as he was, that she was already in good hands and became effusive and extremely thankful to both Bob and Josh.

'What a nice lad you have there,' when Mr Munroe realised later it was Josh that had kept his mum 'entertained' and comforted while they waited for the ambulance. It was from this incident that a friendship began and as a result, Josh was invited, at any time, to spend time on the farm, a handsome acknowledgment for his 'services' Bob thought. Josh was thrilled and Bob pleased too, knowing how his son loved animals.

'He's like my daughter, your Josh, animals and all that. They'll get on like a house on fire,' he'd said later to Bob Shape. Mal had been married, divorced and then remarried years ago – to a much younger woman than himself...this resulted in a daughter, Mandy.

***

The farm almost became a second home for Josh, who persuaded Lynda to go along with him on some visits. It only took one visit...she too became a fan and soon fell in love with all of the farmyard animals. And the busy life...there was always something that needed to be done.

1st Conversation

On occasion for his lunches and if he wasn't going to his u sual watering hole, he'd climb onto his trusty old steed, a Triumph, and motor around the country lanes for 20 minutes; it was an escape. But he would also - and usually this would be on Mondays, go and seek solace on one of the isolated park benches and spend half an hour catching up with *Technocrat Monthly*, knowing he'd be free from any disturbances - which is where he found himself on this particular Monday.

However, on this day, he was surprised by a presence...a rustle, to be suddenly joined on the bench by a young girl...or woman, he wasn't sure at first glance, but a complete stranger to him.

He nodded in acknowledgement as a 'hello' and not wanting to stare, sneaked a few side-way glances at her over his journal. He judged her to be an adolescent...and was that a school blazer she wore under her anorak? She had a pretty face and her light brown hair sported a pair of pigtails...not that common these days, and a winsome, engaging expression. Her build signalled to him that she was entering womanhood. However, the young girl caught him out when he had looked up...

'Hello...' she said with a beaming smile and obviously wanting to engage him in conversation; and what a conversation! There then followed an amazing dialogue - mostly one-sided, from the young girl. With bubbly expressions and a happy demeanour she talked about how nice the weather was...the flowers being pretty and what she was planning to do at the weekend. This girl was happy, very happy he felt. In fact she went on to talk about many things...as if she'd just found life. Bob had to find an opening...

'Where are you from?' he asked lamely, wondering what happened to the advice all kids surely received, about not talking to strangers.

'I come from over there...' she said pointing in a general direction. '...where they'll be waiting for me. We do all sorts of things to help...as you should, don't you think? You must watch what you do. I have to go now,' then stood up and walked off saying 'Bye, bye,' with a big smile.

And that was it.

He watched her go back along the street, astonished; how strange he mused. Young girls like her usually have their faces glued to their phones or have a pair of buds strapped around their heads and plugged into something. But not her, not this girl...she just wanted to chat, and to him of all people – a complete stranger to her! She had not told him her name. Silly; perhaps he should have asked but then thought that might come over as inappropriate, all things considered. He looked up just to catch another glimpse of her but she was nowhere to be seen now.

Bob could not shake off the memory of the occasion, her innocent, happy conversation and gaiety, her engaging and captivating friendliness towards a complete stranger – him, but most of all, he just could not forget...her. He had been completely bowled over by the young lady.

'I wonder who the hell she is?' he asked himself and also wondered, 'Did I just imagine it all?' It was almost akin to a dream.

Police Matters

'Please come in Adrian, take a seat,' invited the Superintendent. 'At the meeting I'm attending next week we will be discussing morale...no, not police morale Adrian, but the public's, viz-a-viz...is the public losing confidence in its police and Law & Order generally...at local level? Is it losing trust and are we concentrating on the wrong issues? Look at that headline yesterday - I have it here,' he said holding up the article. 'Here's another, a pensioner is burgled then beaten up in his own front room! What I'd like you to do is drill down, drill *right* down, down to beyond the 'Neighbourhood' Sergeants to Constable level in our sectors and get some feedback please, yes, from the rank and file. Ask them specifically if they *feel that the man, or woman, in the street feels let down*. Would also appreciate which particular crimes your force, your individuals, feel the public resent *not* being prevented or resolved - what sticks in the craw?'

'It will be subjective you realise but yes, indeed Chief, and on this issue, I frequently get the press on my back, I might add.' They chatted a little while longer. 'For when Sir?'

'By end of the month if you can manage it please Adrian.' Superintendent Hancock knew it wasn't a request, but an order.

***

At the lower level meeting, when given the tasks and when talking about a foreign criminal who kept turning up like a bent penny...this generated a great deal of discussion.

It was the Sgt. who followed up all the comments and replies from the Super and said, quite unabashed, 'Justice demanded that the man be gone from our shores; it's what Joe wants I suspect Sir, and probably a few of us too.'

'Joe? Who's Joe...which Joe?'

'Joe Public,' came the ready answer, followed by a few chuckles.

'May I remind you all,' said the Super, a hint more irritated than before, '...that we are here to uphold the law and if ever hear again one of my officers even hinting of any support for vigilantism as we often do hear, they'll be quickly out of a job. Do I make myself clear?' They all nodded. The Super was somewhat shocked and horrified at the mere suggestion of street justice.

***

I wasn't long before, via Dave, Bob heard of the meeting.

'Well, for Chrissake Dave, tell your bosses from me; in fact tell them about Josh and how that all kicked off; yes, I know, mum's the word and all that but this was registered - was in the local rag; can't miss it Dave.'

'I know, I know...he'll get to hear of this one I promise Bob.'

Progress At Work

At the weekly briefing Bob pointedly asked about the material they were looking at - last week's briefing had indicated promise in two lines of research; he was also swayed by the fact that on hearing of them and thinking longer-term, his own son's injuries might come into the equation. The lab assistant began...

'One material, which we call TC 2748 from our own material tables, could play a significant part in the treatment of injuries, skin problems and scars etc.'

This had made Bob look up. He sat there for an hour taking it all in but in truth reader, his mind was probably elsewhere; it kept returning to Josh's scars and his conversation with Dave.

'Let me see if I have this right in my mind,' he suddenly interjected, 'Am I correct in saying that the material we're looking at is not unlike the almost invisible elements we see, or can't see, in our heated windscreens on our cars?' As one they smiled at his half-joke.

'That's right Bob...'

'Except...and because it is a shape-memory alloy, you can make it change shape by applying some heat, a small voltage or current perhaps,' he continued...he was already way ahead of them. 'Could you 'train' a skin, someone's damaged human skin, by combining the new gossamer 'ultra' with this material, as part of a medical treatment – an implant?'

'Oh goodness!' someone piped up. Great idea.'
All of them around the table were all sympathetic towards the direction this was going, all aware of bob

and his son's traumatic event. But they also grasped the wider implications for other, new applications perhaps.

And the name Eddie Sankey popped into Bob's mind, as it often did nowadays with any reference to Josh, *that* delayed journey because of Mr Samkey - and medical possibilities for skin treatments.

'Hmm...interesting,' Vince chipped in. 'I like it.' Others nodded. He resumed, 'And with our medical connections we could put some feelers out quite soon.'

***

The company was also working on a special tape which could become a clean substitute for plasters and other sticky dressings.

'Please send me the details folks will you, including on the tape? We need to map out a strategy for these initiatives? They sound promising; Vince, can you pop in and see me please? And don't forget everyone, should any calls come through, just remember, we do specialised work and also work for the MoD, so if you get any sensitive calls, just refer anybody to me or Vince in the first instance, okay?'

Nods around the table.

Vince - Have patience

In Bob's office;-

'Did I hear right Vince - somebody posted faeces through your letter-box? You reckon it's the traffic scam people, or somebody connected to the traffic scam?'

'Yes, definitely...intimidation. My wife went bananas. She's now so paranoid about it all...and depressed. She wants to move!'

'Whoa...bit drastic? Look, hang on Vince...do me a favour; get me those pictures or photos of these people we saw. In fact I know someone else who can, even if you can't, and you probably know their names by now anyway?'

There were five occupants involved in the scam and Bob was pretty sure he'd get both photos or names one way or another...he had Dave - and Josh, which of course, Vince wouldn't know about either of them; he was not persuaded that anything would come of it that would make his missus happy but said he'd try and thanked Bob for his help.

***

Following the gossamer meeting Josh's injuries floated back into Bob's mind, reminding him of these materials and thought more about the shape memory possibilities and applications for treatments. But who would know...who could he speak to? He made an effort to contact the hospital they were taken to; this he managed, but it took an hour on the phone to get to 'somebody who knew somebody' who was there on that horrible day.

'You'll need to speak to our 'Mr Burns' as he's nick-named, for obvious reasons, his real name is Simpkins, Dr. Simpkins, but he's not in until this evening.' Bob left his details.

Mr 'Burns' eventually returned Bob's call....

'Yes, what you are saying about your company's work sounds exciting and interesting regarding skin treatment. Mr Shape, we must talk again and remain in contact. I'll speak to the Trust.'

Julie duly logged a future contact call.

Homeware Store - Pillows & Fibres

In not one of his normal shopping outlets, Bob idled amongst the shelves and goods on display. Lynda was after new bedding so here they were in a popular 'homeware' outlet. He casually scanned the notices that declared... 'free of this', 'free of that', or 'Of special fire-retardant material... blah, blah'. However, it was another notice, in smaller-print, that caught his eye... 'Contains hollow fibres' it announced quietly in reference to nearby pillows.

Now Bob, being tech-savy and always on the look-out for the unusual, was intrigued by this; yes, he knew a great deal about fibres, but these...what kind of fibres, he wondered? Fibres were already small enough...but hollow too? Bob bought the pillow. He bought it not because he necessarily wanted a good night's rest, but to look at the fibres...closely - very, very closely.

At home, and after stripping down the pillow and removing the innards he put the fibres under the microscope.

'Hmm- interesting...' he murmured. '....glass-fibres - and *hollow*. Never knew about being *hollow*.' Looking closer he estimated that they were about 10-12 microns wide, some wider, with a small hollow bore, possibly about 5 microns.

To you and me reader, that's small - a great deal smaller than a human hair, however if you are really interested, one micron is one millionth of a metre. And these fibres were hollow to boot! But what would, could be in the very, very small tube? Nothing or just air? He wondered...now what could we do with something like this?

Already his mind was churning.

***

After informing Vince about the fibres, the next time at work he dropped off his pillow sample to his favourite, forward-thinking, most open-minded technician.

'Please tell me 'Ace' what you might be able to do with this...and no, it's not so that you can have a nice kip in the afternoon...these are hollow fibres!'

They all called him *Ace* because at his job, he was. And he liked a challenge. 'Think fibre optics, only smaller, much smaller *Ace*; or perhaps you could put some Gucci chemicals in it to do something, make it 'live' or gave it colour even?'

'Wow, cool!' *Ace* replied, even he was surprised. 'Hollow fibres eh? I'll hit some weed and have a think.' This was his usual answer and always laughed at the look on his colleague's faces when he'd utter those words.

'I think he's a friend of 'Lucy in the Sky',' Bob said jokingly to Julie.

'Help me Josh' - Some thoughts and a plan…

'Josh! I'd like you to do something for me please.'

He came bounding down the stairs with his usual enthusiasm.

'In this folder are some press clippings and articles. I'd like you to cast your perceptive and amazing mind over them…see what stands out and place them in order, in your view, of naughtiness and 'deserving of retribution'…how 'dastardly' the deed was…in some sort of order and category. You'll find few saints amongst this lot son, but I'd appreciate your thoughts in any case, and of course, any news of whereabouts etc.'

'Why, what are you doing dad?'

'Something I have to do Josh,' he said touching the side of his nose. Josh instinctively assessed the matter as being 'secret'.

'Okay dad.' Not even the Gestapo would get anything out of Josh on this.

Robert Shape was using his son as a filter while at the same time building a picture on each of the villains that had stepped outside the law…and were getting away with it.

He had read through the contents of the envelope, the numerous incidents of frustration with getting justice, and of a downright lassitude of will by the proper authorities to pursue the 'righting of wrongs' when all the evidence was there, the way justice was easily deflected from the logical, normal path, quite often by vested interests. And in many cases it appeared to be sheer, naked greed…or incompetence.

As his thoughts began to coalesce, he thought of all the aspects and approaches on what he could do and toyed with dropping the elements into place, in some sort of order of difficulty, geography and plain nastiness to see how it compared to his son's thoughts, to work out how some kind of justice, *any* kind of justice could be both achieved *and* witnessed, seen and reported, to restore faith in the system. It became a speculative day-dream in much of his free time but as he continued to indulge his thoughts in his quest of justice, and the more he thought about it, he realised that he'd be 'on his own' and outside the law - but on the inside of 'right'...in his view. It became the driving purpose. The authorities have given up, 'But I'm not,' he declared to himself. And Dave's words floated back to him...

'Don't get caught,' he had said.

However, Bob 'looked in the books' and reflected; as far as he was concerned he was beginning to think, given one chance, perhaps even two that a wrongdoer should pay a price equivalent to the harm he has done...with added interest, in Bob's view - retribution, not to be confused with revenge, which he thought was guided by a different motive. In retribution the spur is the virtue of indignation, which answers injury with injury for public good...

'Yep, like that.'

But he would always give someone a second chance. Some retribution in his view, was the primary purpose of just punishment as such. He thought of the reasons for it but the main one for him was that without just punishment evil could not be dealt with effectively, could not be fully requited. Rehabilitation, protection, and deterrence were secondary.

***

But don't get caught. Hmm, how not to he wondered?

However reader, our Mr Shape was already thinking...not one to hang about with his reading material and his own ingenuity, he had looked at mad schemes from the past that came to naught. One of them was based on an idea from World War 2 - and a chap called Pyke...*And that leg of lamb.*

Already an idea was forming; what with Mr. Pyke's idea...and those fibres too...hmm.

Whatever his plan, he must execute it sensibly.

And he would leave that 'problem family' for later.

***

That evening, Robert Shape retired to his workshop. Mr Pyke and the pillow has provided the impetus for his next step…

The Crossbow

Several days later, Bob shape looked at his latest creations gathered on the workshop table...he particularly liked the crossbow, a crossbow with a difference; he had added an augmentation to it, an almost invisible but subtle addition.

There were so many crossbows out there available for sale, usually on the market for those of the hunting fraternity; he looked at the *Ravins*, Barnett Jackals *SAS Troys, Centrepoint Snipers* and the like...all wonderful machines but...also wonderfully complicated in his opinion, just by looking at them. There were cocking wheels, pulleys, compensating devices, sliding rails and of course, sights. Bolt speeds tended to be in the region of 250 - 450 fps (feet per second)...fast, but not fast or powerful enough for Bob. A one hundred pound pull would typically get you 450 fps; that's about 300 mph between you and me reader. As a comparison the speed of a pistol 9mm bullet (typically slow in gun terms) is roughly 1200 fps. Other bullets are usually twice as fast...about 1700 mph, but hey, I digress...

Bob wanted more speed, more punch, with the silence so he obtained a fairly basic model and set about improving on it...to remove much of the over-complicated attachments; he wanted simplicity - augmented by technology. As long as it had the stock, string and barrel...this would do. Then he set about fashioning a mould for all the parts that would be made partly of fibre glass, except the string. However, the limb - that's the curved, bow part - was made of a metal alloy that exhibited shape memory properties...the whole thing coated with Bob's special fibre-glass element that *Ace* had worked on back in the real lab.

'What's it for? *Ace* had asked.

'For a good cause,' Bob replied touching his nose. 'Actually, it's part of an MoD interest in new materials; you've heard of Nitinol? *Ace* had nodded. 'And then there's our on-going dabble into new battery technology...'

'Ah, the torch with no batteries by any chance - no *normal* batteries?' *Ace* had responded previously with raised, questioning eyebrows.

***

Back in the workshop Bob cast his eye over his bow. 'Exquisite,' he declared. And it wasn't just the crossbow; his bolts, quarrels or arrows...take your pick, were different too. Not wood, not aluminium, not even carbon fibre...but something quite different. When he tested his bow it nearly knocked him backwards even though he was already expecting the strong reaction.

His 'augmented' crossbow...his 'smart' bow, had some elements not fitted in other bows - and these were literally elements in the electrical sense. After the bow was cocked in the traditional way, the action of tickling the two part trigger to first position let loose an electrical surge...transformed into heat to the limb - which was made of shape-memory alloy. This has the ability to undergo **deformation** at one temperature, stay in its deformed shape when the external force is removed, then recover its original, pre-deformed shape upon heating above its "transformation temperature". The curved limb, by memory on being heated, wants to straighten to its birth-shape but was restrained...because the bolt held it in position. Bob could feel the whole thing strain like it was going to explode when he then fired the trigger.

WHAM! The bolt, an aluminium bolt in this test case, went straight through his dart-board. It had quite a kick too...a kick that surprised him, even though he was expecting it. He took note.

From the playback of a camera he had rigged up for the test he estimated the bolt's speed to be well over 700 fps - and it was the string that provided the real challenge. Normal string snapped so Bob took a leaf out of the bridge-builder's manual and scaled it down to use steel cable. While he was at it, he adapted the flight groove and fore-grip to take a special kind of bullet.

For carriage and mobility, the bow limb collapsed in half, so that it would fit snug in his rucksack.

His weapon was powerful - and deadly. He would tell Josh about the projectiles, and what they were really made of, later.

...and he needed to try it out. For real.

The Smug, Smirk and Sneer

He would not forget the look on the 'Cocaine King's' face even after all the time that had passed since the man was sent down, when asked before he disappeared to his cell where had he stashed his ill-earned gains..? He had answered with a smirk. Or was it a sneer? No, Bob considered 'sneer' a word that implies unbelief, however, the word 'smug' found acceptance, fitted nicely. Yes, *smirk* and *smug*, a smirk wrapped up in smugness. He would not forget the man's face in a hurry.

'Yeah, I'll *smirk and smug him* - just you watch… one day. Just like that Eddie Sankey who held us up and who's still crowing.'

'A cocky bastard,' Dave had said.

And nor would he forget the faces of the problem family in a hurry - its involvement in the soccer match and the supermarket trolley incident…faces, expressions, associated with that word 'smirk' - or sneer. And with total disregard for anybody else.

Yes, he saw that look on the lad's face then the laughter, after Bob had been ambushed from behind when the soccer match was over, that same smirk, the same lad, just before he had stepped in front of the shopping trolley the lad had 'bullied away' from the old man.

What a great word - *smirk* - however, he also hated it; it gave the impression that whoever was delivering the smirk, accompanied with bad deeds…well reader, you just knew he was going to 'go down' sometime if Robert Shape had anything to do with it; this was one of the things that drove him. And amongst that pile of articles from the envelope that had dropped onto his door-mat there were numerous cases like *his* case: too many. However, it began to wet his appetite, to give him an additional thirst for righting wrongs, and for retribution if he could.

Could? He *would* – definitely!

And he would ask of himself when dealing with 'the righting of wrongs' if the perpetrator was a bad person such as a scammer, a burglar – or somebody who was violent or perverted.

Whatever he did it had to be thought through...identification was not a problem, these 'bad buggers' - well, their names were known, but where were they...and how could justice be administered without any connection or comeback to him? How could he hang all this together in a plan?

From his initial thoughts it gelled; it transgressed to solid purpose...a mission, but more detail and a little more time was required. And he needed more workshop time; whenever he spent time in it he was inspired because to make his plans work, he needed the tools. And Bob could make these tools, could he not? And with a little technology to back him up...

The Rebel

'This should be fun...' Ed Sankey called to his colleague who looked up.

'Here's you and me on a pleasant day sat here with a cool beer, planning mayhem in town while designing our 'call to arms' - our banners and leaflets, all done on this tablet.' Sankey waived the tablet in his friend's face. 'Like the design? On Monday chaos will reign - all hell will break lose in London when we have the demo, organised at home in my lovely, quiet garden. So cool; the whole place will be jammed up again, just like last time,' boasted Sankey once more, waving the gadget again at his colleague. 'Have a look...see what you think.'

His colleague chortled along with him as he looked; they gave each other high fives then did a little jig on the patio of Eddie's house.

'I forgot...you got the drones organised?' Eddie asked. 'Put a new dimension to it all.'

His colleague answered with a thumbs-up and a grin as he moved out of his chair to leave. 'Laters, keep in touch.'

Yes...drones. If he'd looked up and over towards the High Street, he might have seen what looked at first like a helicopter in the distance...but it wasn't.

Eddie didn't watch his mate go, his eyes dropping back to his tablet. There were some finishing touches to be planned for the coming demo that remained; there was acute anticipation, he relishing the power he had to cause problems. He couldn't really care less about the theme of the demo although the banners would proclaim all injustices they could dig up, which generally was against authority, anything he couldn't control. And against those with money. Ironic he thought smugly, as he sat in the garden of his parent's very nice house; every now and then he needed a bit of comfort away from some of the unpalatable aspects of his colleagues' ways of life and unwashed, mouthy habits.

His parents' pad was his 'blanket', his cushion...both physical and financial. And a smoke always helped. It multiplied the excitement and enhanced the anticipation. A few drags followed...now he was in pleasant contemplation for what was to come. And he'd make the Chief copper, the Commissioner, the one with loads of gold or silver braid on his hat and on his shoulders, eat his words.

"We will take back control of our streets for the law-abiding citizens of London," he had boasted on TV, while stood alongside The Mayor. Sankey smiled at this and reached for another drag. He was in his late 30s, fit, possessing a wayward charm that, with his looks, attracted both men and women alike to him. If he ever thought of the chaos caused, or thought of people like the Josh Shapes of the world, he really didn't care; they were just acceptable collateral damage to him.

Oh yes...the contemplation of it all, free to do what he liked, propped up by a huge following on social media to boot. Happy days, fun days...a sweet life. Exciting.

What was left of it...

***

He reached over for yet another drag. As he did so and looked up, perhaps he may have caught sight of, a glimpse perhaps, or quick flash of the approaching object...briefly, very briefly. Whether he did or not, there was nothing he could do about it; it was travelling in the region of 5-600 mph, slower than a bullet but fast enough - and entered his body just below his heart.

His mind, just for a split second, registered a searing pain as he was shocked off his canvas chair. He was able to emit only half a scream as he coughed and gurgled, then unable to catch his breath, his face came up against the concrete patio. While his heart still beat, the concrete began to stain a crimson red as he continued to try to scream...but couldn't. What had happened...what had gone wrong in that split second? Before he blacked out his mind was able to register this redness and also a shadow, cast by a man who was now leaning down to him, a man in blue, looking into his eyes while saying, 'Enjoy your last *ever* trip Eddie.' He may also have briefly registered the ear-piercing scream emanating from his mother who had come running, yelling and shouting at the stranger.

'Help me, help me...!' she wailed not realising he was the last person to offer help, as he casually strolled away, the same person who considered it a good day's work...as good as the despatch of the 'Cocaine King', reader, where you started reading...

***

The police were quick on the scene as Eddie Sankey was rushed to hospital. The first thing they noticed was that he'd been shot which had left a hole in the chair.

'Well, whatever it was must be around here somewhere people,' the SOCO called. 'Must find it,' he ordered. The search began as the news came through that Eddie Sankey was now deceased...didn't make it.

But the police never did find what they were looking for, no bullet in the deceased; they searched thoroughly, uprooting plants and clearing foliage for the murder weapon but no luck, so they carried yet another minute search, every blade of grass, every shrub, tree and bush. There was a description given of 'someone seen' - a young man, who walked with a slight limp and who as wearing blue, but the woman witness couldn't recall if it was a coat or a jacket; she could not be more specific than that.

The CCTV pictures; there were not many on that avenue, but plenty on the expensive homes in the area, only caught a few passers-by; the closest they were to the mother's description was of a middle-aged man, but on the pictures his coat was brown...and he walked normally; nor did he seem in any particular hurry.

And as far as Mr Shape was concerned, that was one down; but there was much more work to be done.

The press had a field day of course. Students went on the rampage blaming 'the authorities' but in reality, the media could not find a ready culprit on which to pin the blame once the story had died down. The police cast around for possible suspects or organisations who might be responsible...and failed. As expected, the police received thousands of messages, most on social media but many were also sent, or deposited by other means - letters, notes, including a message wrapped around a stone and thrown from a moped into a waiting police car.

It's possible that they may have picked up on one message and if they had, they weren't about to share it with the public...just yet. It came as a modulated telephone drop under the title :-

'Unintended consequences...jam up the City and you will pay. Who will be next?'

It was dismissed as a crank call.

Mallock the secret

Did Mallock have a conscience? He often wondered about this himself but in a general sense, no. He gave no thought, had no misgivings about selling his poison and misery because he had that dream that would become reality one day, offering some peace.

But...but - if there was indeed one niggle he had to admit to, that would trouble his mind and haunt him from time to time, something that had happened not too long ago but long enough that it would drop off his mind, a worry that occasionally crept back into any conscience he may have had...well, the last thing he wanted was his lad causing trouble that may attract unwelcome attention, which could lead onto other things if they were not careful, things that happened awhile back. He couldn't forget the incident...

**

When his son agitated to be able to drive 'Dad's' car, against his better judgement Mallock had relented, probably because his drug business was on the 'up', matters were generally going well; he'd felt in a good mood.

But it turned out to be a disaster. There was no licence, no insurance, at least not for *Penny,* who was under-age to boot.

'Should anything happen son, I'll say it was me driving, but nothing's going to happen.'

But second time out it did.

His lad, the wonderful *Penny,* bolstered by a successful first outing, became cocky, emboldened. He wanted to impress. He wanted to demonstrate to 'Dad' that he wasn't just an empty air-head, a thicko - that he had skills and daring.

He scanned around - it had looked clear, little traffic. Building up quite a speed while in a 30 mph zone, he lost control, mounted a pavement and hit two pedestrians, a man and a young girl. Both went flying, over the top of the car.

They screeched to a halt...but only for a couple of seconds. In that time Mallock had taken a quick scan in the rear-view mirror...to see if a number plate had come off. No, no debris, no incriminating evidence. Then callously he shouted:-

'Get going son - don't stop! Keep going!' he shouted even louder. On the move he had quickly assessed the scene and considered it devoid of witnesses...there was no-one else about as far as he could ascertain. 'Just keep going son! Head home, NOW!' he said with some desperation in his voice.

***

The terrible accident may not have been seen, but it was certainly heard. A scream, a thump...and then silence. Front doors and windows opened, the full horror manifestly evident - two apparently lifeless bodies on the side of the road. There was nothing anybody could do but in fact, although both pedestrians survived the initial impact, the young girl however, succumbed later in hospital.

***

Mallock and son had hid away, not wanting to know who exactly it was they'd hit...only knowing that they'd hit two pedestrians and that had to really stay out of sight. They laid low. If he remembered anything from the news, it was that the man was associated with the law in some way and the girl was his daughter. The car was spirited away until made presentable; then being a bold brash fellow, displayed his car in plain sight, not too clean but not too scruffy either.

The fairly undamaged vehicle, a broken wing-mirror and dented bonnet were hastily repaired. And the son? Yes, he received a beating he'd never, ever forget.

***

No matter how vigorously and widespread the investigation by the authorities, the vehicle was never traced. The man could remember nothing. The police had patiently sat beside the young girl's bed before she eventually passed away, only recording a few mumbled words the poor child uttered before she drew her last breath.

***

It was this secret – only involving the two – that would creep into his conscience to upset his frame of mind and to disturb his peace.

'That's why, you bloody idiot...' he had said to his son, '...I don't want you doing anything stupid that might bring attention our way, like that brainless football thing you got involved in, got it?' Being told off like usually resulted in a back-hander across his son's ear, sometimes both of them.

'Yes Dad,' was the meek reply...he'd just have to be more careful in future.

Karl the Mechanic

Karl heard the boss returning that day. If he drove straight into the workshop it usually meant trouble with the car. Mallock had brought the car back looking damaged. Not badly damaged but definitely in need of tidying up. He climbed out...Karl thought he looked quite pale and distracted; and where was the prodigal son? Mallock had deliberately jettisoned his son half a mile back before returning to the garage.

'What happened boss?' Karl asked tentatively, he knew his boss could 'erupt' from nothing but right now seemed strangely quiet. Mallock had wanted to tell him to mind his own business but though better of it.

'You won't believe it but I actually I got stuck in a bloody herd of cows some farmer was moving down the road; what a bloody mess!' he said with mock-sincerity. 'I don't like my car looking tatty...sort it out for me Karl and make it a priority will you. Bloody farmers!' Karl knew that it was an order.

'Okay boss.'

As the boss left, Karl looked across at Molly, his lovely Collie who lay against the garage wall, one eye open, peering at her master.

'Looks serious Molly, doesn't it?' Karl always nattered to his pet as he set about his work, talking about 'this & that'. 'Aaahhh...the poor man's bent his car.' Molly drifted back to sleep.

***

He looked at the motor; a wing-mirror hanging on wires, front bumper looked fractured, but how on earth could the left wing get bent like that by cows he wondered? The head-light was smashed too. When he first watched the car come in and had a glimpse at the damage he immediately thought his boss had had a run-in with one of his 'Billie-no-Mates' - the boss could quickly turn any mild altercation into a serious argument; no, he didn't buy the 'herd of cows' routine. However, Karl took his new task as a challenge. While the prodigal son *Penny* looked after the heavy engine work, with tuning and suspension matters at the garage, Karl had found his niche in fixing and dealing with bodywork issues.

In this he was kept quite busy...most of the work was around minor scrapes, shunts and 'biffs' as he called them. He would straighten them all up plus a good polish....good as new. Many of his punters had a certain pride in their vehicle's appearance so Karl was always busy.

***

Later, Mallock had called in to see progress...the wing mirror took his attention...

'That mirror looks intact – the glass is okay; just needs snapping back into place; bit of glue here and there where it's split apart...not spending a load of dosh on a bloody new wing-mirror Karl.'

'No boss.'

Karl wondered why he just didn't claim all the damage on the car or garage insurance, but reckoned that something might be going on here...best not to inquire too much but orders were orders. Although he didn't like the boss or his son - both he considered a little too confrontational and not very appreciative of his work, he did like the work...for now, and they

allowed him to bring Molly to work; but if ever a chance
came up...

A Pleasant Odour and a trial run

'Mal?' Bob was on the phone to his farmer friend.

'Yes, speaking...'

'You know when you hitch up and do your muck-spreading...?'

'Yeah, why, fancy having a go?' he answered, chuckling.

'No thanks, but do you have a small version of that kit for small plots, something I could use that's hand-held?' Yes, he did...for smaller garden areas. Bob arranged to borrow it.

'Thanks Mal. I'll tell you about it later.'

***

It hadn't taken long to discover the whereabouts of 'the five' and the type of car they used. In fact two of them were brothers who owned the vehicle, a red Astra...according to the police.

Bob prepared his kit which included a wheeled trolley and a walking stick, picked up his 'face' which he was giving a trial run then set out. As soon as he was seated he donned the 'identity'. The journey to the estate where they lived did not take long; he was on the lookout for the red Astra and knew, courtesy of 'quantum computer mind' – Josh, where it would be. He drove past it when he saw the car outside the address, parked his own car three streets away and walked back via an empty bus-stop; the old man who emerged from the bus stop shuffled along the pavement towards the Astra leaning heavily on his trolley, then turned back to the bus stop and waited. It was not long before three lads came by, probably in their 20s, 30s, headed to the address with the Astra. It looked like showtime was coming.

When the elderly looking man saw signs of activity at the house, he got up and slowly made his way towards the vehicle...very slowly, shuffling, pushing his walking aid along with walking stick tucked into one of its pockets, then speeding up slightly when he saw the front door open of the house. It opened fully to disgorge five young men. He did a quick double-check with the photos he had.

Yes...it was them, Vince's 'crash scammers'...all sporting base-ball caps. And all the wrong way round – naturally.

As they came out they looked excited and were obviously relishing the prospect of snaring yet another unsuspecting victim in their nasty, lucrative scam...a scam the coppers were well aware of...there had been several incidents reported.

Vince's wife had not been the only victim.

The lads climbed in as the old man, whose name so happened to be 'Bob', closed in with a gait and appearance suggesting 'harmless old geezer' - or one may be inclined to refer to him as a 'doddering old git' - someone who seemed to rely heavily on his walking aids, slow, ponderous. His long stained coat appeared bulky nevertheless, the occupants of the Astra seemed transfixed as the obvious senile old man meandered across the street in front of the car. The driver had not yet started his motor.

'What the hell...what's 's he doing?' one of them muttered. 'Oi - get out the way,' he shouted winding his window down...which suited the old man just fine. He moved round to the side of the car slowly pulling out some object he had in his deep pocket. It was a hammer. Before they realised anything untoward was about to happen the other side window had been smashed in - followed by two party-poppers - poppers with a difference; these had expanding gecko tape and pepper that filled the car like the remnants of a discarded audio cassette tape you'd see on road-sides years ago, before CDs came along. They all shouted and swore, realising that they seemed constrained - entangled. Each struggled and fought like demented Egyptian mummies, desperately trying to escape their bonds of the Gecko streamers..

Bob then calmly opened his coat and and withdrew his spray-gun then proceeded to douse the whole inside of the car, and occupants, with mashed up, semi-liquid, wonderful contents of what Bob had managed to scrape off from many pavements, courtesy of dog-walkers. The shrieks, cries and gagging sounds told Bob it was all working well. Then for good measure, he laid about with his stick and the heavy end of his shit-gun, resulting in some black eyes and bloody noses.

Finally, he grabbed the by-now-very-smelly-driver by the collar and said to his face, 'We know your game; if we hear of any more scams like you are pulling, or if you proceed to hound innocent drivers, it won't be a bad smell and a black eye you'll end up with, it'll be a lead bullet...okay!? We know where you live and we'll spray your houses too. And by all means, please *do* inform the police.'

He shuffled off back towards the the bus shelter where Bob had left a large plastic bag in which he put the whiffy gun and his gloves. Thirty seconds later a *young* man left the shelter and disappeared.

Later, the furious 'scammers' asked

around...after of course, taking a shower and burning all their clothes.

The incident was witnessed but details were scant...and conflicting.

'It was an elderly man dressed scruffily - a grey coat,' said one.

'Yes, saw an old fellow, old khaki coat - didn't see anybody else around though,' said another. The only other details they were told was of a young man wearing a mustard jacket, walking briskly, not like an old gent at all. And it was made sure that the police were informed...however, more than one copper was heard to mutter 'Just desserts in my view'.

Bob came away with a sweet smell in his heart and a spring in his step...and thought that in the future he would look upon red Astras with fondness. He also felt satisfied and thought his new turn of activity - a new hobby perhaps - felt satisfying. Now he was looking forward to other things; he had bigger fish to fry. He had treated the incident as a trial run and was both happy and satisfied with the result. He might even venture to say he got a thrill out of it. He would build on this as part of the plan.

His life was changing.

***

A couple of days later...

'Anything happening with your missus and her car Vince?' Vince's face immediately broke into a smile and gave a thumbs-up. Indeed, the police had phoned to say that the 'scammers' were not pressing any charges - they had suddenly dropped them, which had put a big smile on Vince's face.

And Bob's too, who thought he'd tell him one day...it was then he noticed that Julie had heard their exchange and was now looking at him questioningly, perhaps realising there may be more to this exchange between Vince and her boss. Bob answered her look with a smile while touching the side of his nose. She understood.

'Excellent news. Anyway Vince...I'm going to have to take some days off and leave you in charge for now. I'll keep in touch with Julie and you of course, but things are coming to a head with respect to Josh, medical stuff, the police, and a few other things, okay?' Vince understood.

As each day brought yet more tales of the failure of justice, looking in the mirror that morning, once again, he wondered what he might be turning into. His previous, calmer nature was being replaced by a level of cynicism, his easy fluid manner becoming hidden, often replaced with dark thoughts - and revenge.

Before he was about to take up his self-imposed sabbatical, Julie had turned up at work once again sporting dark glasses. Bob knew what it was - and what it *wasn't*. It wasn't anything to do with headaches or migraines that was for sure, and he very nearly blurted out his thoughts on the matter.

'Julie...as you know I'm away for a few days. I shall be in contact and if there's anything you need - anything to talk about...please ring me.' Bob actually wanted to broach that certain topic but did not feel up to it just then..he suspected that Julie was feeling the back-hand of her husband but was too proud and private to say so.

He wondered why she stayed...

Eleanor and Julie

Those of both sexes that knew her, would describe Eleanor as an attractive, flighty woman. Here was one who possessed the full share of feminine guile. She was also a divorcee.

Newly employed with *Shape*, she quickly cast her eyes about - and homed in on Bob Shape. Eleanor Shaw her name, and as she settled in and found her way around she always managed to find time to divert her journeys towards the boss's area, usually falling into a false discussion with Julie as a reason to go that way. Julie was not at all fooled and it was evident that where Bob was concerned, recognised that the woman had a roving, beckoning eye. You see, reader, Eleanor's only goal in her shallow existence was the attention of the opposite sex - one who lived to break hearts as a child breaks toys.

Bob remembered the first time he had seen her when, into his office area swept a woman - quite unlike Julie and, it has to be said, perhaps past her youth but who radiated an exuberant vitality, who stood tall on long limbs. Bob reckoned her to be a strong-willed, high-spirited girl who knew what she wanted. Of generous breast she possessed a fresh-complexioned face with bold dark eyes and full sensuous lips, overall a figure of a pronounced attractiveness. Even Julie had looked up. However, two minutes later - and this was the first time either had seen Eleanor, he was already forgetting her obvious attributes after listening to her talk, the way she spoke; there seemed to be an insecurity, a wanting to please...to please too much for Bob's liking.

***

Bob had looked closely at Eleanor, observing her poise and grace but then subsequently cast his mind back to Julie as a comparison.She was a flirt.

'Seemed pleasant enough Julie; not seen her before. Is she one of the new lab-rats?' Bob could see the look on his secretary's face that said...'trouble'. She chipped in.

'I think she started last week, in HR,' Julie replied in answer to his questioning look. '...and she has a eye for you, even I could see that boss.' Julie actually blushed as she spoke.

'Well, what's not to like Julie?' he chuckled, 'I mean - just look at me,' he answered with a grin which then descended into a laugh.

This was an aspect of her boss's personality that Julie quietly adored...his self-mocking, his light humour and never taking himself too seriously...while she was stuck with her 'dearly beloved!

***

In Bob's eyes, women could represent dangers to a man's ambitions, distractions from the main aims in life - he recalling memories from his past, resulting in burnt fingers before he married.

One is not to suppose, reader, that Julie was unattractive although your eye would not be drawn to her first among a crowd with other women; however, she possessed elegance and confidence, the unblinking, soft gaze and the captivating but intriguing reserve...these were the quiet, almost hidden attributes she had in an understated way.

91

While the woman who had just called upon them, Eleanor, provided an immediate and pleasing appearance when your eyes arrested upon her, Julie was without any insistence of excessive or blatant femininity, but nevertheless was feminine to the core. She had a quiet gentleness combined with a certain nobility in the way she moved and spoke and although a little fuller around the waist and with a fullness of her breast, one would understand and realise that there was an overall attraction that worked by slow seduction of a man's senses, rendering her as not at all unpleasant, very different from the ready prettiness of the younger Eleanor.

As a secretary, and generally in social conversation, Julie was never over-voluble...unlike the talkative Eleanor who, in the space of two minutes, had conveyed the strong chatterbox impression. And Bob knew Julie for a listener, her interested and inquiring look when people spoke to her invited them to pour out their stories.

Nonetheless, with regard to Julie overall, he was of the impression that there was a sadness in her life. In any case, the lady was forbidden fruit. Married.

On occasion Bob and Vince would go out for a lunch at a local pub, yes, that same one where he would meet Dave on occasion, a favourite haunt for several businesses and it did not take long for the new staff member, Eleanor, along with a few other newly made friends, to home into the same watering hole, and somehow insert herself into any conversation that was taking place...as long as Bob was there. Julie, on the other hand usually stayed away, taking her lunch on her own either in the office or just taking a walk.

Bob remembered that hint of a fishing exercise from Eleanor...

'Who is your secretary boss - she seems a nice lady?' Eleanor asked one lunchtime. 'Has she been with you for long?'

Yes...a fishing exercise, Eleanor weighing up the potential competition.

'Indeed she is...very nice,' he replied, without wanting the 'fishing' exercise to continue.

Non-violent

From Dave, a phone call...a discreet enquiry; he asked Bob if he knew of any work going on at all on non-violent restraint systems? Dave had said frequently in their discussions that he did not like using tasers as the stock answer to restrain difficult or violent people. Often he'd had to use it more than once on the same person to affect a result and feared the consequences if, or should, someone suffer an adverse reaction...like a heart-attack.

'No, not that I know of Dave...and by the way, game of Squash next week?' This conversational swerve with the squash reference was a simple code which Bob used and which Dave knew, meant 'Yes, I do...and we can talk later on the matter.' And Bob did want to tell him about the Gecko tape...and successful trial!

So later...

'You know what a Gecko is Dave?'

Dave nodded, 'Yeah - a little lizard?' he inquired with raised eye-brows.

'Well, you may be interested to know...' said Bob as he expanded, hinting of a material that had been developed and that showed promise...based upon one of God's creatures, the Gecko...and another on the Hagfish.

'And the Hagfish Dave? Just look at this,' he indicated as he moved his tablet over for Dave to see. Dave was astounded looking at a video...'I'll have some of that!' he said. 'Impressive. How does it do it?'

'I bet you would; well, we may, or may not be, carrying out some research on these, in answer to your call about non-violent restraint. Stay in touch.'

Dave smiled. He too was quite astounded when he's first looked into this amazing fish - and how it dealt with its predators...which for *Shape Materials,* had sowed the seeds of yet another idea.

'Well, apart from using tasers, before all that I did spend some time as dog-handler...amazing creatures. Put the fear of God into any hardened thug...and me too – and I'm the handler!'

The Hag-Fish

Although not part of his, or the company's thoughts for non-violent restraining systems, of which the Gecko was prominent, Bob Shape was intrigued by a creature that he'd stumbled across while looking up 'novel defences'...the Hag Fish...for purely selfish reasons.

What a fascinating creature it was, he thought as he read up on it.

When attacked, the fish issues as a defence mechanism, a slime that expands fantastically, choking its assailant who, to avoid choking to death itself as it tries to bite or swallow the intended victim, has to spit it out.

'Now this is *really* interesting; I must look into this,' he said to himself...

***

The slime in question "has a very strange sensation of not quite being there," said one journal. It consists of two main components - mucus and protein threads. The threads spread out and entangle one another, creating a fast-expanding net that traps both mucus and water. Astonishingly, to create a litre of slime, a Hagfish has to release only forty milligrams of mucus and protein - 1,000 times less dry material than human saliva contains. That's why the slime, though strong and elastic enough to coat a hand, feels so incorporeal. Indeed, it's one of the softest materials ever measured.

'Wow...this is really cool,' he muttered. He read more.Apparently, Jell-O is between 10,000 and 100,000 times stiffer than Hagfish slime and that when you see it in a bucket, it almost still looks like water. Only when you stick your hand in and pick it up do you find that it's a coherent substance.

'Weird. Love it.' He showed Josh. 'Naturally, we can't completely mimic what the Hag-fish does Josh but we can sure as hell try...and is what I shall attempt to do,' said Bob Shape. Was Josh impressed? You bet he was! So was *Ace* - who was going to do the actual lab work *under* the heading of 'speculative materials'.

***

More bad news

When he looked at the papers that evening...

'Oh my God - here we go again!' Some drug bloke was coming out of jail soon...to enjoy all the trappings and proceeds...the proceeds from his drug dealings over the years. 'A nice house, from all that misery he caused, and no doubt he'll have a Bentley, Jaguar or Merc stashed away somewhere.'

The photo showed a smiling, healthy-looking man in his 50s, known previously as the *Cocaine King*. Then Bob thought of all those empty, hollowed-out, vacant-eyed hulks and wasted lives of the man's victims that he had fed with his dealings. 'This man is 'going down',' he announced to himself, 'Oh yes, no two ways about it.'

reader...this is where you came in...right at the beginning; he was the man who smirked, remember? And who is now history.

Keeping Score…

The assessments Bob Shape made after Josh had gone through them first, he had tabulated. He'd asked Josh to do so because his mind seemed able, God knows how, to pick up on 'invisible' detail. Bob was just fascinated by these 'powers' his lad possessed and checked that his special faculties remained in top form...

'May 2nd, 1801?'

'Saturday,' he answered.

'And 19 February 1872 ?'

'Monday.'

***

As we already know, nobody *knew* how he did it, it was almost freakish but Bob wasn't to let anything stop him tapping into this human quantum computer, to help him get justice for his family...and others too. Two weeks passed...time spent each evening in his 'shop' or researching various magazines and the net, occasionally fashioning various objects and trying to solidify his original thoughts and ideas into practical, useable tools and artefacts. He returned to Dave's articles to re-assess...oh yes, he knew that they'd come from him. Eventually, and along with an input from Josh with his thoughts from 'The Dark Side', he put together a list and because it was quite a long list he thought he'd pick out a few 'goodies' for closer attention and possibly his first actions.

However, there still remained too many, including killers - some who'd killed twice; violent people, greedy people, sexual predators...all needed sorting out but he couldn't do them all; he would bide his time and be more selective. He took another last look at his written list of cases and ambled across to his 'hut'...all fired up. He looked at his list again; there was work to be done.

Cases

Somalian rapist - struck twice more after being allowed to stay here in the UK.

Sex attacker...released early. Attacks another girl...the poor girl eventually commits suicide.

Thug who stole car - and killed owner who tried to stop him. Accomplices refused to identify him.

Thug who randomly punched OAP who ended up in hospital – gets just a few weeks in jail

Refugee blames war 'back home' for 6 sex attacks

Police woman crushed by crack-cocaine addict woman and her male partner

Travellers invade farmer's field - blackmailed locals to get it back.

A hit-and-run driver...who had 47 previous convictions for other crimes.

And of course, there was *that* family. The Mallock brood, he was informed. He wouldn't ever forget that nightmare by the railway track with Josh thrown onto it - almost in a casual manner. And each time he spoke with Dave there was always some news or event that involved links, direct or indirect to them...a suspected burglary or two, some violence in a shopping mall or cars vandalised. The latest tale was of some lout firing a catapult at cats and dogs...somebody with ginger hair.

'Sounds like our knucklehead,' said Bob.

Kind thoughts

At the watering hole…

Dave was waiting for Bob and told him of reports of youths acting in an intimidating fashion and annoying old folk; the reports came from a phone call.

'Let me guess…by any chance our 'friendly louts' from our favourite family…?'

'You got it.'

'Thanks for letting me know.'

***

Bob thought what should be done about these people making lives miserable for others…what would be driving them to do what they did. From both Dave and Julie during their chats, an idea had been briefly mentioned upon which he decided to follow-up…something new, and confided in Julie about it. Julie was of a quite religious bent and Bob asked her if there were any 'support' groups related to the church…or anywhere else for that manner, even Youth Clubs, the police, that might help out and provide support for wayward souls and to keep them on 'the straight and narrow' or to keep them meaningfully occupied. It was a difficult step for him to take; he was reminded of this every time he saw Josh's face; he felt that he would be letting him down somehow by going down this road. Josh's face was healing, although very slowly, its shape slightly altered without affecting his kindly, benevolent and striking countenance too much.

He said to Julie about Josh's altered features:- 'He'll have no trouble attracting the ladies,' to which she responded, rhetorically:-

'Indeed...isn't he the lucky one,' and then blushed while saying it. 'Yes, he looks terrific...he always was good-looking.' Bob smiled - he was used to Julie being not quite so forthcoming on matters such as these.

Have to try *something* he thought...forgiveness and all that. With these gangs and other thugs, who knows, there might even be nice lads underneath it all.

'Well, I'm excluding that nasty bunch from any considerations of kindness,' he told Julie; that would be a step too far as far as he was concerned. 'I just want to punch the sod Julie...and the rest of his family.' But he was having nagging doubts and second thoughts generally, about settling scores and getting even, except for those he thought were beyond the pale. It was mainly Julie who was responsible for a different approach.

'Everybody...everybody has some good in them,' she said after hearing him cursing under his breath.

'Not sure if I could swallow my pride or hide my anger with some of these people...and I'd probably lose it if I saw *them* again – the Mallocks.'

'Well, I could come with you if you like if we go to one of these group meetings to see how we can help, perhaps get some useful activities going,' she answered. 'Your policeman friend could help; he would or should know about these initiatives.'

Good point thought Bob.

It was settled...they would attend a session associated with Council, public members and the police concerning vandalism, general bad behaviour and rowdyism. Bob noticed that some youngsters, along with their parents or guardians, were quite amenable to attending activities in order to keep trouble off the streets. But there was a hard-core, always a hard-core - who were off the scale when it came to violence and terrorising the local community; this often included those who were supposed to be looking after them...yes, the guardians. Amongst this group were just three or four families who caused most of the misery. Bob quietly made note of this.

'Okay Julie, how are these 'untouchables' going to be sorted? The police seem powerless and the council don't really want to know...only wanting to deal with the easy ones?' Bob thought he'd might look a bit more closely at one of the gang hangers-on, a lost soul who perhaps needed taking in hand and who might flourish under strong guidance. Julie smiled...

'Could you trust him working in your company, what sort of job would you give him?'

'In the workshop initially. I'd get him to make something, anything, not just making the tea or sweeping the floor...and I'd be solely responsible for him.'

'Now that would be good,' she said. 'I hope it works...if you need any help..?' His appraising eyes looked over to her appreciatively...perhaps for too long because she caught his observation and turned deep red. He quickly changed the subject...

'And there's always the farm,' he suddenly mentioned. 'Not sure if Mal would be open to the idea, if at all, but I'll ask him.'

Lady - Judge Kitson

Robert Shape watched the TV with mounting disbelief. It had been announced that a judge had declined to deport a rapist who originally hailed from some foreign land because the treatment he might expect there would not be up to acceptable standards compared to the UK.

He had raped a 13 year old girl, his second such crime in 2 years. As had happened before in sad cases like this one, one of the girls had subsequently committed suicide.

The TV cut to sobbing parents...

Bob was shocked. 'With judges like that, a case like this...a woman as well! And what was this rapist doing out anyway? These people are putting the public's lives at risk,' he practically shouted to himself.

He made a note. He also began to think about the Rebel...the laughing idiot who had jammed up London and had delayed their desperate journey to the hospital.

***

'Josh, I have a name and a picture...need you to find out the address; can you do that? In fact two names Josh. When you've done that there's these names & their photos...I want to put a nice smile on their faces; there's five of them altogether,' he said as he handed them to Josh.

The first two both lived in North London.

'Hmm, so they are in fact not too far from each other; that's handy,' he muttered to himself. Onto the list they went...and because they were not too far away...

***

Within one month, both the judge and the rapist had met justice.

He was dead, she was in hospital, recovering...wondering what had happened to her.

A Slap - Julie's Black Time

Another slapping...over nothing really, and he had almost broke her glasses. Julie sat at her kitchen table pondering her situation. Her husband - *for better or for worse remember?* - was turning into an unpredictable monster. There were no fists at first - just barbed words then a hard push now and then, but more often these days, a back-hand slap across the face. These incidents usually followed a session with his favourite tipple, whisky. Now her life with him had become an existence of terror-laden anticipation where she had to think hard before she spoke...just in case she chose the wrong words.

And in the bedroom...? Well, he was brutal - even she knew this, although he was the only man she had ever known in the Biblical sense, it just wasn't right; it was akin to rape with pain and roughness all part the act, never any gentleness, never any kind words...or soft, gentle whispers. But what could she do? Now she hated it, but she had been brought up in a very religious family, and if that was the man you wed, well, that was it - *'until death do us part'*.

But were all men like him? Surely not.

That's when her mind wandered as it often did, to work, which she loved; it was an escape and her boss Robert Shape who, if truth be known, she so admired. What a cruel world she thought. There he was, a man she thought the world of and a widower to boot. Yes, he was younger than her, in fact he often made light-hearted but pleasant jokes about 'helping an old lady cross the road' if they ever ventured out for a lunch together, which they did occasionally - she was never offended by his light touch about her age, often laughing along with him.

She had never been a 'forward' woman with respect to the other sex, it wasn't the done thing. This had been drilled into her

'Does he ever think of me?' she wondered often but surely, these were wicked thoughts were they not - she must try and stop them...without success. *And* he has two adorable children, a ready-made family while she was lonely, childless, dejected, brutalised, with nobody to turn to. Her mind in turmoil and despair, she began to weep.

She simply could not put up with the way things were...

There was only one answer...she would have to move out - to find somewhere else to live but to do it successfully before her husband discovered her intentions, to do it over a period of time. She'd have to slowly and gradually move her essentials and other belongings and effects away from her house. And then one day she would be gone. But there was an abiding fear that if he discovered her intentions - if he ever found out - her husband might turn extremely violent should he find her new abode. Yet she knew her boss would help her if she was to ask, but was too embarrassed even at the thought of asking him for advice...she was simply too proud.

The Extensive Workshop - Bob & Josh talk

Bob took Josh into the workshop...he had serious things to discuss with him. 'Okay Josh, I've had a look at that list, the one I gave you recently and have compiled my own from it. I want to start with details of ..this lot; as you can see, we have the names of most of them already, now I need to know where they are living - or staying, or if they're already banged-up...'

'Banged-up?'

'Sorry Josh - I mean if they're already in jail...then just find out release dates if you can. Hack into the system if you have to.' Bob had to remember that although bright he might be in some respects, Josh was not street-wise with all the slang. 'You've already given me the judge just recently - and Eddie Sankey...?'

'Okay dad, well, we already know about Mr Sankey but I'm ready for the rest.' He relished doing this 'investigative' work for his dad.

Together they ran down the list.

'Every one on this list is going to get proper justice Josh, according to *my* rule-book.' The list was on paper...no computers.

'But what happens if they catch you dad?'

'I'll probably get a medal,' he replied humorously, knowing that would be the last thing he'd get. 'But they won't. And I'll tell you why not....come into my parlour as they say, and I'll show you.'

***

Bob's shed was quite extensive, quite long. The whole structure had originally been two sheds once upon a time, now joined together and the old brick building at one end had formed part of a garage many years ago, which also had what used to be an old outside toilet. But what had really attracted Bob was that the old garage had a pit...a proper vehicle pit that was at two levels. The whole thing was wide enough and big enough in which to walk around, however, he had extended it. The enlarged pit was now entirely and properly covered over, and anybody coming into Bob's 'shed' would never suspect that under his workshop, under the floor, was practically another room. Initially, even Josh had no idea...and Bob wasn't going to tell him about it...just yet. More time was needed.

Tools & Toys

Josh cast his eyes over the crossbow for the first time.

'There you go Josh...you like it?' It was Josh's turn to be in awe when he looked closely.

'Wow dad...Wow!' He was even more awe-struck when he had a go and fired it. After some talk on some of the finer points which Bob shared with his son, Josh asked, 'What else have you done dad?'

Bob proceeded to spill the beans on the work he'd been doing during late nights and weekends. He began with the torch...'Wanna see my torch...?'

The Torch...

It looked like a pistol-grip torch - like a garden water hose, but in fact it *was* a torch; however, it was also something else. Yes, it shone a light but had no batteries. In place of these was a high powered cartridge...*very* high-powered. The glass face was a cluster of LEDs - but the centre one was in fact a short barrel...but you wouldn't notice.

'How does it work?' Josh.

'You squeeze the trigger and the light comes on, silly.' They laughed. 'But seriously...if you twist this part...' and Bob went on to explain the serious part. 'See; innocent torch...but deadly.'

...and it could also double up, with a few changes as a Taser Strike-light.

The Walker

'Now take a look at this Josh...you see them everyday with old ladies hanging onto them like grim death with their shopping bags attached. Well, not this baby. You can push it, sit on it...dance with it if you like, and those triggers you see are for the brakes...aren't they? Well normally yes, but they also operate something else...just look at those metal tubes on it; quite innocent eh? But they are barrels that you can adjust and point, and that oxygen cylinder tucked away under the crossbar isn't really for oxygen - it's a high pressure cylinder that supplies....' and he went on to describe how a simple walker became a versatile, light-weight crime-fighting weapon...if need be.

'And before you ask...that innocent walking stick or brolly that sits in that pocket like old folk do - a Hurry-cane I believe - is also not as innocent as it looks.'

Josh had a huge grin on his face by now.

***

Then There was the Wheelchair...

'My God dad, what have you done to the wheelchair? It...it looks different...'

'Yeah...0-60 in 3 seconds...' He laughed. 'But seriously, it *is* different, not too obvious I hope; work in progress son, I'm still fiddling with it; not finished yet but when it is, *old* James Bond when he gets to 85 will love it! But now, take a look at these....'

Party Poppers / crackers

'You know those little party-poppers you pull to make them go bang with streamers going all over the place? Well, I've made a version you load into one of those paint-guns...or my special torch, only these crackers are modified. You know the car sensors that 'beep', the ones in the bumpers? Well, you put one of those sensors which I've really miniaturised, in my gun and fire it and when it gets to within three feet of the target, it explodes like the party-popper.'

'Then what dad, or have you put something different in the banger other than paper?' Josh had an excited and expectant look on his face. He knew his Dad...

'Yes, a compacted version of a Gecko tape...a new invention of ours, no glue required. In each banger there's about ten million miles of ultra-thin sticky tape, without the 'sticky'...well, not quite ten million, but a lot. When it goes bang the poor sod finishes up, hopefully, looking like an Egyptian mummy, all taped or trussed up for a while; quite helpless really. I've already used a version of it recently Josh; it still needs a bit of work. You can also put pepper in them. But I have to make sure that they open up and explode just before they hit the target otherwise it just becomes a useless, boring plastic bullet.'

***

A by-product from research emanating from inquiries from the medical profession for the treatment of wounds, cuts and burns and perhaps on a subject close to the heart of Bob's friend Dave, was the 'Gecko Gun' as described to Josh, using the Gecko-type tape, 'How to restrain a violent person without inflicting an injury upon them?'

The Gecko Gun seemed to be one answer. Yes, the extremely thin tape was indeed high tech, no glue, no sticky chemicals. But that was the beauty of it. Dave would love this.

***

Bob and his son spent all evening going over the toys - Josh's evident enthusiasm and excitement kept them going beyond midnight.

'I'm not going to sleep tonight dad...I'm too hooked and fired up.' It was rubbing off onto Bob too, if he was honest with himself.

'Well, we might as well look at the last two items while we're at it...' Bob said.

'What, there's more?' The grin returned to his son's face. 'What are they?'

'Okay...we have two more novel ideas, one of them based on nature....' He went on to describe his altered '*Hag*' sweets, his electric handshake and from where the ideas originated. 'I use them together Josh; first I can knock them out with the handshake then when they're out cold, I give them a Hag sweetie; well, that's the plan.' Josh had never heard about anything like his dad's *Hag* sweets but he knew about the police Tasers. Bob explained about the Hag fish.

'My electric glove is a bit different from a Taser son...as you'll see when I show you...one day. And you have to be careful with it...how it's used; you don't want to be electrocuting yourself do you? You need proper footwear and other kit.'

A Sound Sleep

At first, when Bob had thought about showing his gadgets to his son and of his intentions, he was worried how he might react. He needn't have, and Bob slept soundly because Josh had absolute faith in his dad. Absolute. Often, Bob thought about the absence of a 'mother' and in some respects, Lynda played a vital part in being a guiding, female influence, a light anchor...even at her young tender age; they worshipped each other. Bob was thankful how they had both turned out so far...and how horrified he had been with Josh's close brush with death.

These thoughts brought Bob back to his next move...who would be next? Mr Sankey, the idiot, irresponsible Eco-warrior, who, Bob thought, actually had had blood on his hands...he was already ticked off the list but there were many, many more.

Eleanor Interferes

'She's a bit obvious isn't she,' Bob had remarked to Vince during a lunch in the local. Bob realised you could not avoid Eleanor who, anybody would tell you, was quite attractive...perhaps dangerously so when coupled with the way she used her feminine wiles. She was always chatty and invariably good company at lunchtime sessions. However, both Bob and Julie knew her game but could not figure out why Eleanor was homing in on him. Okay, he might be the boss but Bob always thought that when God made him, God had been a bit stingy in the looks department. There were others out there even within his company who would not disgrace a male catwalk.

'It's not always about *looks* though is it?' Julie had offered.

'Well I'm sunk then aren't I Julie...got nothing else to offer have I? I'm completely stupid at times and can't fathom what women really want in any case...don't know my way around the fair sex at all.' He suddenly realised what he'd just said; Julie had turned beetroot red. 'Sorry Julie - you know what I mean...?'

Oh My God! If only he'd ask me! I'd tell him, she thought, still flushing. Stop it, she told herself. It was those wicked thoughts again. Then she realised that in reality, she too wouldn't have a clue...she simply wasn't like that but always discarded any notions as far as *he* was concerned, thinking that she was too old for him in any case, by nearly ten years, besides, he appeared to show no interest, how could he - why would he? She was married. And trapped.

The 'Old Biddy' Episode

Eleanor did not appear to be the slightest bit embarrassed when in the presence of either of them, Bob or Julie - being quite adept at dropping hints and innuendo in an off-hand way. Quite brazen actually. But from one lunch occasion, word had come back to him that Eleanor did possess both a potty mouth - and *nasty* with it; she had made comments about others who were not present at that gathering. However, she had skilfully camouflaged her remarks, a damning with faint praise, uttered with smiles and laughter. One of those maligned in this way was Julie, so Bob was told.

It was now common knowledge that Eleanor could insinuate and swear like the best of them; she could certainly brighten any gathering or conversation but Bob thought he'd check out her lunchtime performance for himself...because of Julie. Yes, he did indeed have feelings for his secretary.

Three of them, lab-rat Keith Woods, Vince and Bob walked into the pub and were greeted by others already there which inevitably included Eleanor and her companion Terry (Theresa). There was a buzz in the pub...the talk flowed, but inevitably, a voice was heard above others - Eleanor's. She looked over towards them and typical Eleanor, engaged mouth but not brain.

'Have you left your secretary behind, you know - Julie, the useless old biddy?' Silence suddenly descended upon the group - and then an awkward pause. Eleanor suddenly realised that this had been perhaps a ribald too far, even if not meant seriously. Not funny at all, as most of those present knew Julie.

'Oh, that's cruel, Julie's lovely,' one of the girls answered. More comments followed all indicating support for Julie. This had the effect of bringing momentarily, acute embarrassment to, and silencing Eleanor. Briefly.

Bob knew that if someone described an old woman as an 'old biddy', they were saying in an unkind way that she was silly or unpleasant, although Bob knew it was also a harmless expression often used to describe any old lady. However, and considering Eleanor's frequent visits to the office over the weeks, he had thought her so-called innocent jibe was perhaps the result of, and driven by, an element of jealousy towards his secretary. Bob also knew that increasingly, Julie had had more 'dark glass' episodes but knew would never say anything to him about her very private life. And yet he so wanted to help her, always feeling her sadness but was too afraid to inquire. It was forbidden territory, and Julie had to be defended.

After a further pause, Bob chimed in wagging his finger,

'Eleanor... "useless"? If Julie is a useless old 'biddy' secretary then she's a *very good* useless old 'biddy' secretary, and I couldn't do without her.' Some clapped or cheered Bob's words. Even Eleanor smiled as she mouthed 'sorry' in an attempt to recover the situation, but Vince said to Bob shortly afterwards...

'I think you made an enemy there boss; you should have seen her face back then, although she soon recovered, laughing along with the rest of the crowd. Watch her - and watch out.' The event didn't linger in Bob's mind; it was soon forgotten.

But not in Eleanor's.

The Message

Julie opened up her phone...a message - a video clip;-

"Julie is a useless old biddy" -

...and it was her boss's voice speaking those very words as she could see. Nor was he laughing when he uttered them; he had a serious expression on his face. She was stunned.

'What!?...' Julie nearly collapsed...staring at her phone. It was as if she'd been struck. A sob broke from her as she slowly made her way to her armchair and sat down, almost feeling her way. She watched it again. And again, still not quite believing it...

'No, surely not...he's not like that. It can't be true, there must be a mistake,' she cried, momentarily outraged. But there it was - in colour - those words. And who sent this anyway? Her emotions went from her previous admiration of Bob to suspicion, to rage, to hate and then back again. 'Is this what he really thinks of me...some old bag or biddy he's hired, probably out of pity!? No this cannot be...*he's just not like that!*' And what with events at home, an attempt at some reconciliation with her husband...all the pressure; she burst into tears.

Her mind went over past conversations or incidents trying to find any clue - *any* he may have dropped, any hints about her age; well yes, but only in fun, surely? She couldn't believe that he would be one these smarmy, two-faced people who said one thing to your face...then another, as soon as your back was turned, to somebody else.

Feeling upset, she *so* urgently wanted to see him, to speak to him and to find out why he had said it and what was going on. But it was a long weekend and it would not be until Tuesday before she saw him again...a whole weekend to fester. Bob was her friend...surely, as well as her boss, but could she really face him right now...if that's how he felt. And if true, it would be a total humiliation for her, a complete embarrassment, having harboured such admirable thoughts about her boss and their friendship at work, something she looked forward to each day.

But 'hold on a minute,' she thought...and her common-sense began to re-assert itself. 'Don't get paranoid about it' - it has to be some mistake, some joke. Not being *that* experienced in romance matters however, she just knew, or hoped, that he was not like that...to be that shallow. She would wait until she was back at work and tackle him then. And she would wait just a little while before sending him the clip..........

Now it was Bob's turn to stare...at his phone. And alongside the clip Julie had asked, 'Have you seen this Bob - do you know anything about it?' He was shocked, baffled, and worried for her sake. Baffled because he knew he had actually used those words --- but not like that...or had he? He thought back to recall the occasion, suspicion slowly settling upon Eleanor. But why? And how?

A Correction

At home...

'This video clip...' Bob ran it for Josh to look at. 'I know what I said on the day and indeed I did utter those words being said but not as they're presented on this clip son; this has been doctored, yes? Am I right or am I right?'

On matters like this - IT - Josh was a whizz, he just knew his way around transference and interruption algorithms whether it was in a audio or visual context, but his real skill lay in his ability to detect something amiss - what a detective would call a 'hunch' - in what he was viewing or listening to.

'Methinks this, these words dad, is just a string of words taken from a longer script, so yes, it's definitely been messed around with, and you can probably see looking at their faces in the background - look, her face and his...with their expressions, they are responding to your words like it was out of sync.'

Bob was relieved. 'But hang on a mo son...let's just check your magic brain once more; Jan 10th 1858...?'

'Sunday.'

'So we're still on form.' He felt better already.

***

Eleanor came into the office, as she normally did a couple of times a week and quite brazenly asked, 'Where's your secretary - Julie?'

Bob fixed her with a knowing look. 'She's off...not well, and by the way Eleanor, something for you...perhaps you can help me; should you know of anyone who may have recorded or reconstructed a phone video from last week in the pub that lunchtime and 'shared' it...you know what I mean, then I'd like to see the complete and original version sent to me please. Asap. No further action will be taken; get my meaning? I don't want to know who did it - I just need the complete transcript.' He then nodded to the door...in dismissal. But she had to say something...

'But phones are private stuff aren't they...?' A mischievous perversity - probably quite normal in her eyes he thought.

'Indeed they are, however, that person wasn't the only one recording just then. Reputations can be trashed both ways Eleanor. You understand.'

Later when talking to Vince... 'Think she got the message,' he had said later to him. 'See what happens.'

***

Julie hadn't turned up on the Tuesday. This worried Bob but was relieved when she showed up the next day. They looked at each other for several seconds before Bob broke the ice.

'This has to be a joke Julie...it has to be. You know I wouldn't say anything like that; somebody's messing us about.' He looked straight into her eyes when he said it.

Julie was relieved; there was no hesitation, no waffle in his response - and he looked just as hurt. Then he moved to close his door while asking if she believed him.

'Well, it was quite a shock when I first saw it, I was hurt.'

'I asked Josh to check out the whole thing; he thinks it was made up. Here look at the real thing...' He moved his own phone so that they could both watch. 'See? The important word 'if' is missed. You know I wouldn't want to do anything to hurt you Julie.'

Both became aware of how close they were to each other and she was taken completely by surprise when, with both hands, he pulled her face to his for a kiss - a kiss that lasted several seconds, before she sprang back, embarrassed, hot and bothered, as she realised what had just happened.

'Oh Bob!' she gasped out loud, startled, then slapped him hard as she broke free. 'Why did you do that? That was wrong - you shouldn't have. I'm not that kind of woman.' Flushed, she was trying to recover, to get over her embarrassment. He had taken a liberty...it was a violation.

Bob was shocked at being slapped by the very woman he quietly adored. Before she could say anything else he said:-

'Sorry Julie, I deserved that. Please forgive me but that's how I feel about you. I've been wanting to do that for a while. Oh God, I'm really sorry, digging deeper aren't I? Dreadfully sorry that I may have hurt your feelings but I just couldn't help myself. I know I shouldn't have done it. So sorry.' Then he noticed tears in her eyes.

There was a shade of bitterness, as if of reproach, mingling with the regret in his voice.

Julie did not know where to put herself...was she outraged? Yes, at first, but her anger subsided a little during a pause...now she was just flustered, not so much because he had kissed her...it was the actual kiss that was responsible for her turmoil. And what a kiss it was. She just could not put it out of her mind. It had been a few seconds of both shock...and pleasure. It was why she now felt both flushed and out-of-sorts - with some guilt attached to it; she was married...didn't she belong to someone else?

Bob broke into her thoughts. 'Julie, Julie, I won't breath a word of this, it won't happen again I promise. If you want to move to somewhere else...oh, God; I'm sorry Julie, I really am, I've ruined everything haven't I?'

'It came as a complete shock...I'm not that kind of woman; let's pretend it didn't happen.' But her heart was torn. Was it conscience, guilt, fear of her husband? 'I'm upset...perhaps I should leave.'

But neither could pretend it hadn't happened: he couldn't...and truth be known, nor could she. There was that very small part of her that enjoyed the experience and was glad he had kissed her, was flattered, but her conscience was in control, battling her heart and feelings, her honest feelings. Then in her mind...

The Angel that sat on her shoulder intervened...

"Stop Julie! Stop and think! Surely..*now* is the time to strike...romantically, to admit how you feel. Tell him. Tell him *now!* Fall into his arms an apologise for the slap, a slap that preserved your femininity and modesty. It's what you've been dreaming of. He's sure to accept you. DO IT!"

'No!' Said the Devil's voice on her other shoulder...

'He doesn't want you - he would have taken you a long time ago if he really wanted you. Forget him!'

Her mind continued in turmoil; she sensed that the invisible link between them was breaking, that he was sliding away, that a barrier had descended. It was now or never - she needed her courage; the situation if acted upon immediately was still retrievable, and to her advantage, the Angel voice said.

She hesitated...she so desperately wanted to turn the clock back thirty seconds, a minute. There was more in that hesitation than either of them could have come near to imagining. Indeed, her whole destiny was in it. Upon such things do human fates depend, that had she taken the plunge, to retract those words, to admit her transient anger and outburst, given her true feelings towards him, then both their lives would have been different from the moment onwards.

But her courage and pride failed her.

***

She said nothing and awkwardly they moved away from each other, the hidden barrier now more defined and entrenched. And of course Bob had said those lovely things about her following the slap but she had made matters worse and destroyed everything now, because of her pride. The seconds drifted by as the situation became uncomfortable for both of them.

She cursed her own timidity - and cursed again...remembering his kiss and his warm strength.

***

And Robert Shape cursed his own timidity – and cursed again...he too remembering that kiss, and her fragrant softness.

He tried to lighten the atmosphere; he made an attempt...

'That was a good slap, I can still feel it - and I deserved it; I'd hate to be on your wrong side when you're really angry,' he said with a weak smile.

'*Oh Julie – even now the situation it is recoverable,*' that voice said. '*Come on Julie.*'

But Julie's emotions were paralysed. She just put up her hands and shook her head then said she'd like to take the morning off, as she quietly gathered her coat before leaving.

***

'That went well; what an idiot I am,' he muttered to himself. Nor was he sure if she was ever going to be back but heaved a huge sigh of relief when she turned up after lunch - with few words. He just wondered how long this awkwardness might remain. As he brushed past her in the office, savouring her perfume he whispered, 'Are we okay Julie?'

She quickly nodded, then said, 'I believe we have a busy afternoon Bob.' The professional Julie was back, all was good it seemed although Bob wasn't so sure.

'*Is this still the same woman called Julie?*' *he asked himself.*

***

Julie was on the horns of a dilemma. At that time, she and her husband had attempted to retrieve their marriage as they both had realised they shared a misery which could not go on, so had sought counsel, the result being that they should try resolve their differences and give the marriage another chance. He would attempt to control his temper and be more considerate towards his wife. For her part, she would do her best, on his insistence, to reflect the fact that she was married to him and not her job, and that perhaps she should find work elsewhere. This was the part of the arrangement that worried her.

Therefore as this opportunity presented itself, she made the decision that quite soon she would terminate her position as Bob Shape's secretary and leave *Shape Materials*.

Bob was devastated but nevertheless accepted the decision, he too wishing he could turn the clock back, only further.

It did not take long before Julie realised she had made a huge mistake; her husband's promise and sweet-talk was a sham, he reverting to form fairly quickly while Julie was now away from the job she had loved - and away from Bob Shape. However, and on the plus side, it did not take long before she found other employment, helping out in a supermarket, although she would continue to look around for something more challenging.

Now she had to find somewhere to live...then to leave her husband. The last thing she wanted was for him to know either where she now worked or where she might live.

Lady Who Went Ga Ga with Law & Order

Judge Judy Kitson stepped out from her *Evoke* and crunched across the gravel towards the front door of her home. It had been a busy day for the judge and dusk was settling...she had spent most of the day still dealing with the fall-out from her controversial decision on deportation.

During the recent interview with the press she said that of course, she regretted the death of one of the victims who had been raped by Naresh Segu, the man she refused to deport, but that she must look at the bigger picture - that he too was a victim and to deport him would inevitably result in him probably facing a death sentence for crimes previously committed from where he originated.

Many thought – 'So, what's wrong with that? Two rapes in this country - with a suicide - and sexual violence in his home country; why wouldn't you want to to get rid of him?' thought a certain man, including a sizeable proportion of the population from a straw poll conducted on the matter.

***

Perhaps her mind was still occupied by this as she moved towards her front door, oblivious to her surrounds because amongst the gentle rustle from a slight breeze, was another sound. She may have heard it, a rustle perhaps, just as the 'drug baron' may have heard something; we shall not know. Either way it made no difference as she felt a sudden prick in her neck...but paid not too much attention to it, apart from thinking, 'Must trim back these thorns…' as she rubbed her neck.

She loved her garden that, it has to be admitted, resembled a veritable jungle in places which was just as she liked it; this was deliberate - her gardener had followed her specific instructions because these days, she simply had no spare time to tend to it herself.

But suddenly, her mind asked a question…why was she now kneeling in the bushes as her clothes snagged on the foilage? Now she was laid out flat on her side, not able to control her body; that's all she remembered. Darkness had followed.

She woke up cold, wet and staring up at the night sky realising she had little strength, but eventually managed to crawl into her house. It was only when she was inside and sat on the floor, dirty and exhausted, she noticed the envelope stuck to her sleeve.

***

The envelope had contained a message…

Your family is not young but at least they are still alive…unlike the rape victim of your rapist.
Being a Rape victim is a life sentence.
A warning to you and your policy.
We know where you all live.

Quickly on the scene, the police went through the procedures and looked at all the possibilities; a deliberate targeting – with a warning. Nothing in the house had been disturbed. Considering her role and position it was put down to a warning about her political decision on deportation.

The garden and grounds were thoroughly searched...and searched again; nothing was found to be missing even though she had a fair amount of cash on her, but in the absence of any kind of weapon, they were stymied.

CCTV was scrutinised. From adjacent street cameras a grand total of of 22 people were recorded as having passed near the vicinity of Lady Kitson's home, including six dog-walkers and an assortment of couples pushing prams and shopping buggies, including a gaggle of elderly ladies headed towards the bus-stop who were accompanied by two older gentlemen, one with a shopping walker.

The perpetrator - or perpetrators - had covered their tracks well.

Because of her position, considerable pressure was brought to bare on the case, but suspects remained sparse.

However, the DCI on the case had an opinion... 'Somebody has sent a message...' he confided to a colleague. '...about her comments, I'm pretty sure of it.' This was his private view, although his colleague nodded in agreement.

***

Two hours earlier, and not far from Lady Kitson's home, Naresh Segu, who was wandering back to his digs, still surprised, indeed very happily surprised at the recent cancellation of his deportation back to his home country, was offered congratulations by a man who seemed to know him and who appeared out of nowhere...

'Well done mate - I bet you're glad eh?' the stranger said with a welcoming smile, offering his hand to shake. By instinct, Segu responded in an automatic way, taking the proffered hand. The next thing he knew when he came round was he was helpless on his back, having been quickly dragged by his feet into a narrow alleyway and behind a waste-disposable bin - which the man who was pulling the unfortunate Segu, thought quite appropriate.

The taser-glove had worked well.

As he gasped, trying to revive his senses, a soft capsule was pushed into his mouth while a gloved-hand kept it shut as he attempted to spit it out whatever it was, forcing him to begin to swallow. Then the hand was removed; Segu was vaguely aware of the man moving off. As soon as he tried to spit it out once more, he found he couldn't. Whatever it was in his mouth just seemed to be getting bigger...and bigger, and going the wrong way. When he attempted to stand, he staggered and gasped as a glutinous mass crept sluggishly down his throat. Now he was choking. No matter what he tried, he was being internally and slowly consumed with no room for breath, until he collapsed...death following shortly.

It was determined that the Somalian had choked to death...probably on his own vomit.

'Could have been drinking...heavily, and passed out?' was suggested by the investigators. That was quickly ruled out...bloods were normal.

'Could have been ill,' someone else ventured.

A local search for any witnesses provided little information but two people came forward to report of a medium size man seen walking close by, a man with a limp...slim build.

'A limp you say? That could be useful,' the detective noted, and one of the witnesses, the elder of the two said he thought that the man he saw actually looked quite familiar, like someone famous...in films or on TV.

'Really...who, what like a TV of film star you mean; any idea?' The officer cast a glance towards his colleague. 'Interesting; anybody we know?'

'He was in that film *Some Like it Hot*. It was on last week; that's it, he looked just like the actor in it.'

'Yep, know who you mean; well, it's obviously not him. He's dead...sometime ago,' he said rolling his eyes. 'But thanks anyway.'

'I've heard of the film...but who was the actor in it?' asked the copper of his accomplice.

'There were two main actors actually,' replied the other, 'Tony Curtis and Jack Lemon, but it was before your time sunshine.'

***

The man who may, or may not, have looked like an actor from an old black-and-white film...the man with the 'electric' hand-shake - which had worked perfectly, Segau had gone down immediately - had picked his location well. It was quiet and close to appropriate suitable features of foilage with an electric junction box close by...and some bins, all out of immediate sight.

The man who had worn the special glove - who nearly always travelled on public transport for these events and now on a bus - scanned his tablet assessing the next job, but if truth be known, he had wondered about Judge Lady Kitson...and the kind of retribution he was thinking of – for her. In the end he decided that in this case it had to have a sense of proportion. Even thought he'd liked to have rubbed her out...permanently.

2nd Conversation

Another lunchtime, on *that* bench...a shadow fell across the magazine on his lap...

'Hello, I thought you might be here.' Out of the blue the young girl from before had suddenly appeared and as before, seemingly from nowhere. He had been otherwise completely absorbed in an article on Quantum physics. She then sat down beside him.

Surprised and he had to admit, also pleased, he shuffled closer while taking in her presence in more detail. And as before, it was she who began and moved along the conversation in just the same excited, bubbly manner she had done before. When she spoke he noticed that now she was in fact of a more mature figure in her dress. He wondered; perhaps no longer at school now, no blazer, no pigtails - and fuller in both breasts and hips. Her face, her whole appearance, had also taken on an almost ethereal look. He leaned in a little to interrupt her flow...

'But you must allow me to ask you...your name young lady - and what do you do? Where are you from? How did you know I would be here because I don't come everyday and it's awhile since I saw you last.'

'My name is *Stella* and I am a nurse...in training. I like to look after people,' she replied in her unique, animated way. 'This is my mission. And I know you have your own mission don't you? We must all have our purpose in life must we not?'

The revelation, the presumption that he might have a mission shocked him because she was right. Who is this girl...no, this *woman*? And how would she know in any case?

Then she went into the problems she had sewing buttons on her clothes and her concentration. 'My hips hurt when I sit sown for any length of time as do my hands...I had an accident a long time ago. But I must go now...I have much to do. They and my Dad will be ready for me. Bye bye,' and rose to leave.

Just like that! And *ready for her*... Who was? What was all that about?

Once again, Bob was astonished...why would she tell him this - about buttons, sewing, having an accident, and about 'being ready'? There was no fluidity in her conversation, no natural flow; she just chopped and changed. When she had spoken he could only sit, fascinated - and listen.

As he watched her move down the street he could not help but wonder if she was a troubled child in some way; did she not have any friends? He endeavoured to watch her carefully to see which way she went - and to follow. As he stood up to go his magazine fell the floor, which he quickly recovered, but when he looked up to pursue Stella, from a suitable distance of course, she was nowhere to be seen.

'Bloody hell, where's she gone?' he mouthed. There were few people about but he was intrigued by her ability to become lost from view. 'Oh well, next time...' If there was to be a next time; and he was sure there would be, then he would not let her out of his sight. He was a little perplexed by the unusualness of the encounter and felt an awareness of something extraordinary about her.

As before, he could not shake off their encounter. Should he be worried about her he wondered?

Side Bar - A Shock for Karl and suspicions

There was no excuse this time...it's has to be a new mirror. Mallock had come back fuming as he drove straight in...

'Some bastard hit my mirror...look at it, the same one you fixed awhile ago...remember? And this was in the bloody car park. Look at it Karl - a bloody mess. Bloody typical!'

One of his favourite words – 'bloody', reader.

Yes, Karl remembered; that was some time ago now...what, a couple of years at least? His previous temporary job had held up well.

As before, the mirror hung limp against the door...and definitely not repairable as far as Karl could make out. 'You know what to do…'

'Yes boss.'

Another order, only this time he'd have to pull it apart, *really* pull it apart, probably rewire it and then cement it all back together. But then he suddenly realised that a new wreck that had arrived last week, now at the rear round the back, was the same model. He hurried outside to see. Yes, sure enough it was and the wing mirror was intact, but of the wrong colour. No problem, he'd soon paint that up after all, he was the bodywork guy was he not?

***

He soon set about the task, carefully removing the mirror from the write-off. He would paint it to a match and while it dried, dismantle the broken original from the boss's car.

It was while doing this task as he admired his previous quick repair work, he spotted a light-coloured object, a piece of paper perhaps, enmeshed within the guts of the swivel assembly.

'How did that get in there?' He hadn't noticed this before but he had to admit that his previous repair was a hurried, more-or-less superficial job but on closer inspection he realised that it was what looked like a plastic name-tag, but broken. As he eventually pulled off the shattered mirror, he detached the white name-tag for a closer look.

Indeed, it was...or used to be, a name-tag, faded, the safety-pin still on the back but the tag was damaged or broken, The name on the tag was '*David Carr...*' - if that *was* the full name...he couldn't tell if it was just part of a name, with the rest missing.

Just for one second he thought about asking his boss if he knew about this...the tag and the name but thought better of it, after all, why bother his boss? He was only interested in it being fixed.

But it bothered Karl.

The reason it bothered him was because the first time when he had to fix the car, even then he hadn't really bought 'the herd of cows' explanation, and he'd also spotted blood on the bonnet back then too. However, as the car was maroon in colour, he wasn't that sure...then, thinking it might just be the result of a cow's passing injury - were they not susceptible to occasional fence injuries?

But on top of the bonnet..?

And who might David Carr be - if that was indeed the real name?

Revelation - David Carr

Karl hit the net. There were few '*David Carr*s' listed and none with any connection to his boss, the garage or the car. He went further, and he couldn't tell you why he did this, a hunch, an off-chance perhaps, so he followed up with a look for 'cows and vehicle collisions', 'hit & run animals' etc. just to find out about insurance and who was usually responsible but still without success. However, the 'hit & run' words brought up several press releases from both local and national news outlets, of real 'hit & run' incidents when people had died or had been seriously injured. It was amongst these that he spotted from the past and quite local, a press article - the police were looking for help in tracing a vehicle involved in a 'hit and run' in which a man and a young girl had been seriously injured.

The date, if Karl could recall now, fitted in with the 'cows' incident. He'd check in the garage register.

Now Karl knew that his boss, and in fact the whole family probably, had fingers in many pies and was involved in murky dealings...knew that Mr Mallock was a bad-ass. But this...? Surely not, not *that* kind of bad-ass? Nonetheless, he decided he'd tread carefully on matters about car damage and cows from now on, especially when he found a follow-up article reporting the girl subsequently dying of her injuries.

So, one dead, one seriously injured.

This episode now played on his mind; who could he tell, or share with, this disturbing news or of the suspicion he had? Who could he trust?

Police Matters - Lady Kitson Fall-Out

Some sort of Crime 'Street Cleaner'....?

The press had been pushing for answers...was there a connection between two of the murders? It hadn't taken long for some sharp-eyed news outlet to deduce, and link, the judge with the unfortunate Naresh Segu.

Addressing his executives following the death of a the judge...

'Please tell me again,' asked the clearly irritated Chief Superintendent. 'One dead, One seriously injured on the same day and not far from each other, one of them a judge. We all knew her. The Assistant Chief and no doubt the Minister will be demanding answers.'

It was flak-jacket time...the 'proverbial' was about to hit the fan. But now a political dimension crept into the equation - that the two assaults might be politically connected?' He'd been previously briefed, but this was going from bad to worse.

'With these crimes we can only make the assumption that it's likely.' He had been shown the newspaper article again and the outcry at the time. 'Yes, of course I remember it well.....' he trailed off to a pause...then, 'Two high-profile victims on the same day – linked by the same circumstances. 'It cannot be tolerated,' he told those gathered.

'Are we that surprised Sir? There have been several high profile cases recently where the media thinks the public has been short-changed with respect to justice? There have been 'rumblings' at both local and national level. We're not sure yet if it's a concerted effort by a gang, group or cell, wanting to put pressure on the ministers for a toughening up on crime; there's an election next year. Or it could be some maverick operating alone. Then there's Mr Sankey; might his sudden and unexpected demise be part of all this...a pattern?'

'Indeed, so I'd like a concerted effort on the Intelligence aspects...and push our 'plants' and informers. Don't forget we have a good links with GCHQ so leave no stone unturned on this.'

The Thug

The thug, one Mr Dorat, was due out and having been a 'good boy' while inside, he was coming out early, too early for the relatives of the man he had killed, the father who had told off Dorat for fiddling about with his car parked outside his own home, and who, having taken umbrage at this verbal lashing in front of his mates, punched the father without any warning, then kicked him while the victim was down on the pavement. His wife had come rushing out screaming, frantic to intervene and save her husband from further assault from what seemed to be a young man who suddenly stopped and walked off with two mates in tow. Nor had he shown any remorse as he walked off...or when he was sentenced.

This was the history.

Now he was being considered for release after only eleven years inside which meant that he had, when released, a whole chunk of life ahead of him; he'd been in his late teens when jailed. The victim's wife was distraught as were her daughters...the parole board had, in response to enquiries about the felon's release, said decisions were solely based on whether a prisoner presents a risk to the public...etc. etc.

'Oh really?' thought Bob. 'What happened about punishment, doesn't that count any more? Husband killed, daughters left with no dad...and yet this unfeeling, vicious thug will have a whole life to enjoy.'

'But not if I can help it...' he said out loud.

***

The thug, that's what we shall call him reader, was stepping out of a newsagent arm-in-arm with a young woman. It looked as if there was not a care in the world for this pair judging from the happy countenance written on their faces, even when they momentarily dodged around a doddering old man who hogged the whole pavement and who was practically leaning on his walker trolley for support as he nudged it forward at a snail's pace. The old man recognised the other man's face although his hair was now different from the photos he'd seen. Twenty yards further on, 'walker man' stopped, turned around and called out a name...

Both the woman and her male companion also stopped and turned to face the caller, the younger man caught out on hearing his name because he was advised while 'inside' to always play ignorant, but he replied anyway, 'Who wants to know...? Bugger off old man,' he said when he realised it was just what looked like a harmless old dosser and therefore no threat, as he moved a tentative step towards the elderly gentleman.

The woman could not recall exactly what happened next, only that her companion who was then between herself and the old chap, fell gasping to the ground clutching his throat. She may have been vaguely aware of a sound, a swish followed by a fleeting moving object that flashed towards them - as if someone had thrown something, but then noisy traffic was passing so she wasn't sure. When she rushed screaming to her companion, calling on the old man to help, not realising that he was the reason her man had fallen, there was blood everywhere on her companion. He managed to gurgle... '...S Sh Shot, I've be...' before passing out.

Within thirty seconds people began to emerge from an adjacent laundrette and the paper shop. A car pulled up to the kerb too...many were helping, phoning...but it was all to no avail. The thug was soon dead; and the walker-geezer was long gone.

The area was cordoned off and became a hive of activity within the barriers; all local premises were scrutinised, households questioned and CCTV film examined. When it was determined that he'd been shot the police diligently examined the area and surrounds minutely - twice, every square inch of them and for a brief moment thought they'd struck lucky when they found the signs of a fresh ricochet on a wall nearby. It was clear that something had hit the wall with force and left a trace of blood, which was determined to be the victim's, but no matter how much more they searched, they never did find any bullet.

Groomers and 'Gardening Man'

'These girls - how old?' Bob asked.

'About the same age as your daughter,' said Dave.

'And they were being fed booze and drugs by this lot you say?' Dave nodded.

'And where has all this happened...?'

'Manchester – Manchester area.'

A group of Asians, well-known in town for hosting 'grooming and sex' parties involving very young girls, mostly white, who were plied with drink, smokes and drugs, had escaped the attention of the police and authorities - some say 'who deliberately turned a bind eye' and who had been deflected from apprehending these criminal gangs for the sake of racial harmony. Riots had ensued last time two brothers had been arrested and yet the law-abiding Asian community knew this was happening and that it was against their creed and culture. Even Imams knew but the group responsible considered themselves a law unto themselves...and untouchable.

One girl had died. The young girl in question had been brusquely forced out of a car on a cold freezing night following a seizure during one of these parties. She was still bleeding when found, from allegedly having been raped.

'Why don't they arrest them?' Bob.

'Evidence. They all...the whole gang, always deny it all completely and clam up; one of the principal culprits, the one who seems to be the leader according to the coppers on the case, did a runner back to his home country. Some say he's back, his name's Mahmud and usually has two others with him - Mo Bashir and Disal Sheikh. It's these three mostly responsible - they commit nearly all the crimes and yet they, apparently, continue to lure young girls, often stoned out of their poor minds to these 'booze and pizza parties', because *Everyone loves a pizza, don't they...?* and yes, some are in Care and the bloody authorities know what's going on!'

'Booze and pizzas eh? So who is supposed to be in charge of these 'Care' facilities Dave? *Who* is not doing their job, this obvious dereliction of duty?'

'They just keep passing the buck from one layer of management to another but the overall boss is a Ms Bishop - and she definitely does not like us.'

'Us...what the police?'

'Yep. It's probably why nothing gets done. The word 'racism' is often bandied about.'

'Any addresses, any info I can have Dave?'

'Have some faces...photos.'

'They'll do...including Ms Bishop's too, please, but bloody hell...Manchester - quite a way away.'

He looked up this Miss Bishop, listened to her on video from various news clippings and what she had to say about the grooming; she always avoided, or failed to condemn these grooming gangs directly - always giving the impression that it was the girl's fault, all who were white.

'She's totally failed these girls, and now we have one dead,' he mumbled to himself. The buck has to stop somewhere...and she's it. Meanwhile, certain sections of society, the press and social media were telling anybody who would listen all about 'White Privilege'.

'Oh really? I'm sure these white girls feel really privileged being raped,' he had said to Dave later. As for the distance, well, he knew he could always rely on an old mate of his who lived in Chorley, just along the road from Manchester.

***

'Josh...can you do your magic on these pictures?' Josh soon got to work on them and he was helped by other information Dave had supplied. And each time Bob gave him a 'task' he noticed that Lynda began to take an interest too. 'Just putting the world to rights darling,' he would answer. She was certainly not fazed at all and seemed only too keen to be part of the process; how could she forget Josh's beating after the soccer match, frighteningly close to the railway track? She would shudder each time she thought about it...so close to death.

Josh worked his magic – he now had several screens up and running in his room; he scanned them all. They all indeed lived in the areas around Manchester. Bob thought about this although not for long; it just meant another busy weekend...soon. He would scrounge a bed for the night or two from his old Chorley friend...do a little surveying, lay of the land etc., however, he needed a method of dispatch for this job; something different.

The torch or garden water-spray idea might do. And the face...he would use a coloured one but only slightly tinted. Then there was the issue of gaining entrance once he'd found out what kind of abode was involved; he needed a tactic that would be adaptable.

***

A few days later, somewhere, a long way from London at the door of an apartment…and as a result of a blunt, cheap offer that had been pushed through the letter-box a day or two earlier…

'Ah…the pizzas are here!' said the man who opened the door tentatively while looking over his shoulder to his mates in the room, then turned his attention back to the pizza man…and paused. 'But hey pal, how come you dressed like that?'

'What, you mean like *Gardening Man*? Well, my day job is this - Pizza delivery Sir - but straight after your delivery, I'm off to a fancy dress party, that's how…as *Gardening Man*. Got all the kit as you can see.' He handed over the large box of pizzas then proudly took a step forward in dramatic fashion while showing off his gear - gloves, a garden spray gun in one loose holster, a bug-gun in another, a pair of proper gardening boots, stylish knee-pads and what looked like a up-market green visor on his forehead, not to mention his fancy, long green cape embroidered in large italics - *Gardening Man*.

'Ta-raah!' he announced exaggeratedly. The inhabitants were agog.

The smell of the room had hit him straight away…a mixture of smoke, booze and no doubt other substances. He quickly scanned the place…beer-cans and Vodka bottles lay on most surfaces, including 'packets of three', quite visible. And the leader whom he recognised, was sat down. A computer was on in the corner. Seeing their inquisitive stares at his unusual head-gear and visor,

'Just for show…how I identify my plants - from an app…can't keep looking at books while we're gardening can we? The pages get all messy,' the man said as his eyes looked upwards indicating his visor which had also flashed to his retina, photos of the men.

Yes, it was definitely them.

'Cool,' one of the occupants said. 'Does *Superman* hire you?' Laughter, including *Gardening Man* who went along with it, then asked:-

'Not yet, but I'm sure he will when word gets around but first, do you mind if I use your loo please...I haven't stopped for hours and I'm bursting,' he asked, nudging forward with a smile.

'Sure, even *Gardening Man* has to go sometime, innit.' They all laughed some more, pointing the way.

Their last laughs. Ever.

***

That's how he got in...

After the man took the pizzas from him he moved in. Hidden underneath his cape on his back were a couple of very, *very* high pressure cylinders, with tubes that fed his garden hose down through his sleeves to his hands in which he held his instruments of retribution, and you wouldn't be able to tell at a glance the difference between a Hoze-Lok, a tyre gun or even a shower spray.

He moved in the indicated direction but stopped next to the ring-leader while lifting his spray gun...which wasn't just a spray gun. Pointed directly at the leader, a loud **Sphat!** rang out which toppled Mahmud backwards over the settee on which he was perched, blood gushing from his neck that he now clutched. He gurgled and coughed, or tried to, as he crashed onto the thread-bare carpet. *Gardening Man* then quickly turned on the others who were momentarily frozen, transfixed, and fired twice more from another 'innocent' garden gun from the other side, straight into the heart of one, and into the head of the other, but only after making sure they heard his words...'No more grooming for you lads...*innit.*'

When he left a few minutes later, the three were dead.

And the pizzas? Such a waste he thought. They had to be real of course - that enticing aroma to wet their appetites when he entered as part of the distraction. Moving over to the computer, *Gardening Man* tapped out a message...

"We know who the other groomers are...they have a choice - leave the UK...or go the same way as these perverts."

He added these names to the message then hit 'print'. He wasn't bothered where, or even if, it was connected to a printer...the police would eventually find 'something' when they came.

***

On his way back, now divested of his kit, he considered...three down, three 'crete bolts expended - which, wherever they ended up, would shortly dissolve so the law would never find such things as 'bullets'; there weren't any to be found. And he hadn't needed his Hag sweets.

The next day, the three deaths did not make the front pages in any of the main papers but were prominent inside some of the front covers, with various mini-headings such as local turf-wars amongst Asian groups, some hinting even at the attacks being racist, although no one would venture as to who might be responsible.

***

He scanned his map and headed in the direction of a Ms Bishop...the authority figure ultimately responsible for allowing the grooming to continue right under her nose and who had turned a blind eye to the exploitation, drugging and rape of young girls...nearly all white girls some who were supposed to be 'in care' courtesy of Ms Bishop's department. *Her* care. Why she would allow these criminal and sordid activities to continue without official hindrance was anybody's guess...although Dave told Bob of his opinion.

'For racial harmony reasons; mustn't rock the boat.'

'Oh yeah...whose harmony? Certainly not the dead girl's or her mother's harmony.'

***

It was quite late in the day when a man stood outside the house of the leader of the Council Child-Care Services; he'd already switched on his face, a touch darker than when he had started off on this mission. Now he had watched her return just as he had with Judge Kitson only this time he waited until she was unlocking her front door: -

'Aha - I'm glad I've caught you...it's Ms Bishop, yes?' said the man who came through the gate after her, dressed in Post Office garb plus the typical Hi-viz jacket. 'I have this for you to sign - for this package,' which he held out while holding the inevitable tablet for her to take and sign. The lady was at first startled by his sudden appearance. In answer to her evident surprise, 'I've been up and down the street delivering and someone told me that you usually came home at about this time so I'm in luck eh? Saves me, and you, having to go back to the main Post Office.'

She nodded but didn't say anything. She was about to take the package when the 'postman' suddenly reached out and took her hand in his...the hand wearing the 'glove'. She jerked, then with his hand still holding hers, he let her sink to the floor, half-swooned and disorientated, then pulled her inside and out of sight. When she opened her mouth in an attempt speak or cry out, he popped a *Hag* sweet into her mouth, followed with an ample squirt from a water bottle. She coughed and spluttered, and the more she swallowed and tried to breath, the worse it became, until breathing became impossible but before her breathing ceased...

'That's for doing nothing about the grooming gangs, you useless piece of...'

Then he walked away, leaving her to choke. Around the corner his appearance changed as he upped the voltage to his face and with the pocket-switch, changed the colour of his clothes - including the Hi-viz gear that were made up with his special fibres. He disposed of his special shoe-soles later.

This transformation was repeated several times...a politician, a TV star and a sports personality. Even himself.

As you can see, with due precaution the man who'd been wearing Post Office garb had effected his departure - unseen.

'Council Exec Found Dead' the local paper announced. It went on... 'Mystery surrounds the death of Child Care Services Chief Bishop.....' etc.,etc.

And it took no time at all before the killing of three 'groomers' and the death of Ms Bishop were linked...it was obvious. The local authorities had been previously criticised in the past...repeatedly for its lamentable stance on the issue of grooming; all this left the police wondering how, and who, had the necessary 'inside' intelligence and ability to be able to deal with the perpetrators in such a clinical way.

When two more...two more who were on *that* list, were found separately, floating - one in the docks in Manchester, the other in a pond near Rochdale, it became apparent to the remaining groomers that somebody meant business. Four left for foreign lands. However, when the 'elder' of this nasty bunch, one who should have known better, was found dead in a ditch and another found slumped right outside his house, propped up against his front door, that was enough...travel to a certain country with one-way tickets suddenly picked up.

All those found deceased were over-dosed, one found with a slip of paper seemingly from another member of the gang saying, 'Ta mo – good stuff...need more. Wen.'

$$***$$

While these events were causing the police problems, a certain thug, yes, another thug reader, named Yilmaz who originally hailed from somewhere near Turkey, was counting himself very lucky...he too had escaped deportation. You'll meet him later reader...

Shock for Bob...

It was at this time Dave gave Bob his news, and it was bad...

'You know I've been seeing a specialist with my 'problems', visits to the hospital and all that?' He then told Bob that what he had was cancer and that it was stage 4...terminal, barring any miracles, a cancer that had spread.'

Bob was shocked - and choked...which then affected Dave. They both broke down.

'When Dave...how long?' They weren't exactly sure but it was not long Dave said. Robert Shape looked at him...this unassuming man who always shared the laughter of any situation where humour could be found. And yet, when Bob thought about him, he realised that in fact, as before, he actually knew quite little about him; he was the man from the police station, or Police HQ, or somewhere, a place he'd never visited himself as they always seemed to meet up at only one place...their favourite watering hole. But the news plunged Bob into depression for several days.

'You never know Bob, something might turn up, don't look so glum.' said Dave, the 'half-full' kind of guy but it also made Bob more determined to right more wrongs.

'What a cruel world,' thought Robert Shape.

Police Matters

The meeting in the large conference room had been in progress awhile now, a meeting called because of some sharp-eyed journalist who had began to make a link in a number of seemingly random killings for which no-one had yet been apprehended. Many ranking officers were present.

'Everybody, your attention please,' called the Chief. Silence descended upon the assembly. 'I must admit that apart from Judge Kitson and Mr Naresh where there was an obvious connection, we have not been able to link the other recent murders apart from the fact that all the victims were all felons recently released from custody, all having served their time...or were on bail. The journalists are hinting at a complete failure of natural justice in these particular cases and that somebody 'out there' might be attempting to restore - in his, her, or their view, some retribution and justice.

'I have already had a call from the Police Commissioner about Lady Kitson. Do we have the models, algorithms and databases on our system that could be used to work out a pattern, to anticipate a next strike...the next target, if this is indeed what's happening? If so I'd like the Intelligence personnel on this please? So far we have the two victims we've already mentioned but we also now know about our 'Drug Baron' - one Mr Hutchins, cut down in his drive and of course the recently released Mr. Dorat who had served 11 years, only being released last month. As for Mr Sankey, well, we can't find any connection at all with previous activities; it may be simply a disagreement on tactics from another anarchic group wrestling for headlines, people like the 'open borders' crowd or the movement for 'free drugs', but I wouldn't have thought even they would descend to murder quite frankly.' He paused and took a sip of water before continuing...

'Just recently...and we've all heard of the 'grooming' scandal involving Asian gangs and young girls, three suspected perpetrators were - and I can only use the word 'executed' - because that's what it was, an execution that took place in their apartment. A message was left indicating this might continue unless the law gets it finger out, to use a colloquial expression...or the other gang members will also finish up in the same way. Indeed, this is precisely what has happened, as you know.'

This piece of news resulted in outbreaks of huddled talk and murmurs within the audience. 'So someone - or perhaps another gang is settling scores. To 'take out' three would indicate more than one person was involved....

'While we're gathering information and evidence - and other Chief Constables are doing exactly the same, I shall be preparing my own a report, as will they, for the Prosecution Service to digest with hopefully highlighted aspects of perceived injustices, poor evidence preparation, sentencing leniency, witness intimidation and other factors that have lead to victims or the general population believing they're getting a raw deal and which has lead to the prominent media headlines.'

One executive asked if a list should be drawn up of those who might possibly be next in the firing line but decided that would consume a disproportionate amount of resources, away from normal policing.

Another piped up, 'Besides, where would you start...the justice system hasn't really helped us in this regard has it? We'd be second guessing poor outcomes, poor outcomes such as, in our view, lenient sentences or acquittal on technicalities, plain obfuscation - and even as a result of political pressures, which have contributed. There's certainly cases that went the wrong way for us as we know, which attracted adverse publicity. We simply could not spend our time having to babysit every felon who comes out of jail.'

Nothing concrete came from the meeting except a bland statement of an initiative to engage and monitor 'intelligence' more closely...be more diligent. However, amongst the many messages received by the police which was kept away from the journalists at the time...

'THE DEATH OF DORAT WAS THE
EXECUTION OF A ROGUE – TO ACHIEVE
JUSTICE'

The news eventually filtered down reaching, via sub-committees and numerous other smaller meetings, to the likes of the man on the frontline - policemen such as Bob Shape's friend, Dave.

The Thug from the Med

'So what's the story here Dave about this Turkish fellow?' Bob asked. They'd been having a very quiet and sombre discussion about Dave's on-going medical issues which they often did, when they moved on to the latest let-down in Law & Order.

'Ah yes, Yilmaz. He's not British, he's Turkish and he's here illegally, doing now what he did back home when he was a gang member there, street robbery, violence, even against women - and of course, drugs. The usual stuff.' He continued...that apparently Yilmaz was going to go straight, get in with other legit Turkish food outlets when he arrived, but found 'proper work' and long hours too hard as a way to earn the money; it was easier simply to rob people. 'He also has an unproven rape and sexual assault charge on his ticket here in the UK, 'a person of interest'; the usual story...and he's also spent some time in other holiday hot-spots in the Med. The police in both Cyprus and Malta wouldn't mind a word with this guy.'

'Nice bloke. Right, so why is he still here; why isn't he back home in Turkey?'

'They tried, and you won't like to hear this Bob but the judge ruled that it would be in breach of his Human Rights....because he was 'embedded' here in the UK - part of a UK gang, would you believe!'

'A gang? Seriously, really?!'

"Fraid so. Another enlightened judge!'

'In that case, I'll have to see if I can get him a one-way ticket out of here,' Bob said touching his lips as he was wont to do.

I'll deport him...permanently, thought Bob. 'Just tell me where he can be found Dave.'

**

As part of the 'intelligence' feed, Dave had also passed on information about a couple of 'pushers' operating quite blatantly on a busy street near Preston Road in the city...which was not a million miles from where Yilmaz operated with his gang of thugs.

'It's over in the Wembley area - as in football, that way.' Dave said.

**

Bob had no qualms. So...three likely targets; he picked up his foldaway bike, rucksack, his 'face', his voice-modulator, his cool pencil-box and headed for the tube realising it might take more than one trip.

And so it turned out...no sightings on his first excursion but the next day when he repeated the journey...even he was surprised at the almost brazen attitude a dealer struck as he 'moved' his drugs, plying his trade openly on the street. And surprisingly, there appeared to be another team nearby from what he could see...two teams operating and obviously aware of each other - he could see them both from his vantage point.

Occasionally, a moped - or in some instances, an E-scooter - would appear from nowhere and hardly stopping, hand on something small. These couriers went back and forth throughout the morning passing an old man lying on a bench with his bottle, seemingly oblivious to what was taking place right by him...an old man who had commandeered the whole bench to stretch out with his brown paper bag and an old copy of *The Racing Times,* dressed up as yesterday's loser.

And Bingo! There he was:- Yilmaz, just like his photo, walking past the bum on the bench towards one of the dealers. Bob Shape had been reading up on what he called 'dispatch' drugs and chemicals as he had seen the wild-life programmes on TV many times, how various animals were brought down with darts to fit tracking devices etc.; but what was in the darts? Or what do vets use on pets? A few names cropped up such as Ketamine and midazolam; actually, there were quite a few.

He looked again at Yilmaz.

'Hmm, about 90-100kg and stocky - his mates looked of similar build, maybe less. No matter,' the observer estimated. He remembered on reading about Ketamine...3 ml for each 100kg and quite effective even after a cold stress. Perfect. But he'd adjust the dosage...to make sure. The darts were already in the cold-box, one that looked suspiciously like a pencil box, '...where I keep my sandwiches guv,' should anyone ask.

***

This 'observer' - this bum - well, he stirred, taking a swig from his bottle; picking up his rucksack and gathering his coat about him in slow fashion, swaying slightly - he staggered to the end of the bench using the back to steady himself.

He spent a few seconds rummaging in his large coat pockets, smiled to himself then moved off, tottering along carefully, gingerly - the pavement was both uneven and very busy; he had to keep up appearances.

Twenty yards from the first dealer he levelled his little torch and fired. The dart, containing rather more than the proper amount of ketamine, went nicely, cleanly, into the man's thigh. Instinctively, the dealer looked down, swatting away what he thought was an insect such as a wasp at first, while trying to keep tabs on his customers. It must have stung more...he had to rub it, but harder this time, then for some reason found he couldn't control either his leg, then his arm. He reached out to his colleague to steady himself realising his vision and balance was going; it was probably the last thing he ever realised. Ever.

'What's up man?' one of his colleagues asked as he noticed his colleague begin to sag. His other minder moved away with a worried look on his face, none of them noticing an old man moving in the opposite direction, headed towards the other pusher. A minute later, the 'oldie' was close to the second group with Yilmaz amongst them. It was at this moment that they were noticing the commotion further along the street - a man was lying on the pavement which made them all pause from their immediate business. Which suited the old bum just fine, a well-timed and fortunate distraction, time for a quick reload, one for the high-pressure torch, another for the dart gun - one in each pocket.

As Yilmaz and the rest in that small group were becoming aware and worried about the increasing crowd forming down the road, the bum with his torch who was moving closer, had let loose. Yilmaz collapsed to the floor immediately, clutching his chest. There had been no sound that you could hear above the street noise.

While people had paused, seeing a man falling to the pavement, a second discharge took care of the dealer, who, like the first, thought he'd been stung. His plight was at first ignored until he too eventually succumbed. Within 20 seconds, all the druggies and hangers-on had vanished, except the dying Yilmaz and two pushers lying on the pavement. The bum then moved calmly to the nearest prostrate pusher and announced in a loud, gruff voice to anyone listening in the gathered crowd,

'Hey look, a drug pusher - looks like an overdose here, and over there too,' and walked in the direction of the other crowd as phones were being put to use.

But he never reached the other group; the old bum had slipped into an adjoining alleyway to wards a parallel street where he picked up his chained bike and rode away. He was satisfied.

Later, the local police received a message; how someone had hacked into their system they would never know.

"If you want more druggies, thugs and perverts removed from your streets - like today, we'd be only too happy to oblige."

Fall Out - Police Matters

"CARNAGE ON THE HIGH STREET"

In the local press, these were the headlines the next day with additional reporting on three deaths of alleged drug users / dealers. Some Nationals also recorded the deaths.

The police were heavily criticised for doing little to curb drug crime - and violence in general, with the usual calls for more police presence, more 'beat cops'. The usual excuses were trotted out by both the local council, the Area Super and others in authority. However, it was a single press comment that really riled the authorities, the police especially...that stated that those responsible for the three killings was more in tune with the public's sentiment,

'Whoever carried this out - give them a medal!' was one cry.

'He's keeping our streets clean',' was another. This title stuck...*the Street Cleaner.*

Another subtitle... *'Oh, the irony!'* When it was revealed that one of them was a failed 'deportee' the article went on, 'Not only doing the police's work, this assassin is now doing the Home Office's work too...Yilmaz permanently departed/deported, *sic*!'

***

The police knew it was a man, even had several cell-phone pictures of him from the public plus some CCTV shots, an unkempt individual who seemed to sneak about unseen, but in plain sight. And then disappear. A scan of CCTVs for the whole area provided no continuity, there appeared to be no matching links for the man's description, clothing and colours. Or even an age for him.

'Perhaps there's more than one of them...working as a group,' it was suggested.

They froze all the pictures they could muster...there were more than one hundred people all told in the time frame pictures but no solid leads.

***

The very next day, two more pushers - well-known to the Law - and who obviously hadn't got the message from the recent news were found over-dosed, tied together around a lamppost. Naturally, they were found by a dog-walker late in the evening...who else?

'Lamp-posts have their uses,' some wit had remarked in the local rag.

They were put down as the victims of a turf war.

***

With the deaths mounting the police seriously began to wonder if it was indeed and inside job; someone appeared to have information from the 'inside track'. Amongst the executives, and with the intelligence they had so far, discussions took place in closed meetings initially to thrash out 'who' could be behind the killings...the 'who' ranging from an organised gang, a political group or just a dedicated individual.

'A dedicated individual has to get his knowledge from somewhere...can't do it on his own,' they said. This was acknowledged although the political aspect was not entirely discarded.

Further down the ranks the individual coppers had their own opinions and theories…

***

'Ever heard of *Serpico* - Frank Serpico?' Dave asked Bob Shape.

'Name rings a bell."

'He was a New York copper back in the seventies who single-handedly fought endemic police corruption. He had few friends as you can imagine. Well, our Lords and Masters are wondering if there's a version of him who may, or may not, be acting in similar fashion with the intelligence to take on the villains, not police villains, just normal villains...the ones we read about everyday in the papers who seem to be able to escape proper justice. If you've seen *The Equalizer* …? Similar – more modern though...a tough, ex-military black fellow righting wrongs...'

'Like the sound of him; I wonder who our current *Serpico* could be?' Bob asked, smiling. Dave smiled with him.

***

'Josh...any of your 'psychic' connections on Julie's whereabouts?' He'd been in the habit of asking Josh but for some reason...

'She's a blank Dad, nothing. Sorry.

Bob realised he'd lost something when they had parted and was increasingly worried that she may have left the area, and not just locally. but he would keep trying.

***

It was after the Yilmaz episode that Bob decided to alter his approach, literally, for his eliminations and that was to use a mode of transport usually favoured by mostly the young pushers...a moped or a scrambler. He already owned a Triumph one which he'd had for years. but decided that an upgrade was in order, besides, he'd needed to tailor any new machine for the job.

'Time for a change,' he told Josh. He picked himself a Triumph Street Cup, second hand. This bike would set him apart from the younger criminal fraternity who preferred the smaller bikes, including mopeds. The *Street Cup* was powerful enough, quite capable of off-roading and very comfortable. He would adapt it.

As soon as he received it he set about implementing a couple of changes...a Velcro strip to go over the *Triumph* logo on the tank - and a swivel, detachable mounting over the handlebars, one that wouldn't get in the way. And of course, to go with it, his jacket and helmet, both of which were colour-changeable...not by removing them of course but by a colour-change, controlled by a little toggle on the lapel.

He was ready to go...

Cards on the Table

Dave knew there was something going on with his long-time friend...that on some level he was becoming perhaps directly involved in certain 'events' that had recently occurred; and of course he read the papers. However, not for one moment did he suspect that his friend might be a killer...and that there was probably somebody else involved on the scene.

There was the car scam that suddenly 'went away', that Bob had seemed interested in. The frequent requests for information such as locations and names, well, he didn't mind too much at first...always glad to help but now that his personal situation had changed dramatically, he actually felt a freedom to do more, to really help, without having to worry about any 'comeback'. He knew he would be in no fit state to care by the time any so-called 'comeback' happened; he wouldn't care by then. That's if there was any 'comeback'...

He knew how passionately Bob felt about justice, meaning 'injustice' the way things were today and guessed that their friendship relied on a mutual goal and trust, but something was holding Bob back. And he wanted to know what it was...he had his suspicions. Dave had come to the conclusion that with his poor medical prospects and the fact that he shared much of Bob's disgust with the way it was these days with crime and what little punishment went with it, he was unafraid to approach his friend to find out what was going on, wanting to play an active part in what he suspected Bob was doing. And if he was caught, so what? He wouldn't care.

Over a heart-to-heart he informed Bob of his suspicions and that he had nothing to fear about Dave spilling the beans to his colleagues and superiors. In fact, he was going to help him in any way he could.

Bob Shape felt almost honoured - and grateful when Dave told him of his own suspicions - what he suspected might be going on. In truth Bob, after the initial shock of Dave's medical prognosis and prospects, he thought it a convenient time to come completely clean.

'Okay Dave, it's cards on the table time...after what you've told me, it's only fair I share what I'm doing, my goals and such-like,' then proceeded to outline his plans. 'But I need you to come to my place; I'll bring Josh along too who, as you probably know, plays a part in all this, without knowing everything. Between the two of you...well, you're my 'intelligence' - my spies.' Later, he told Dave he felt quite honoured that Dave had that trust in him...and understood Dave's reasoning.

***

When they eventually got together in the 'workshop' which by the way, had mightily impressed Dave, Bob began to reveal a few things...

'Right, and first of all, you've obviously heard in the media of the deaths of quite a few 'baddies' as I call them, but let me now show you why, for instance, the coppers never find any bullets...'

He went on to explain about some information and and an invention by some scientist he'd stumbled upon from World War 2...now entirely forgotten, but which he'd put to good use in his quest for justice and keeping one step ahead of the law.

'Remember that nice leg of lamb Josh?' He went to a freezer and brought back what looked like an old-fashioned school-kid's pencil box they use to make decades ago, except this one was modified. He placed it on the table and slid off the lid. Both Dave and Josh peered into it expectantly - to be presented with four arrow-bolts that seemed to be 'smoking'...made of ice, or what looked like ice, as the white mist formed around it.

Their jaws dropped.

'These crossbow bolts, sometimes called *quarrels*, I call them 'crete-bolts, are made of a mixture of water and sawdust then frozen in the moulds, and kept frozen in my nice little and very well insulated pencil ice-box. And at the end, that little compartment is for my 'crete' bullets for my extremely high-pressure gas gun. Proper bullets and guns make too much noise as well as leaving explosive or chemical traces, not to mention smell.'

I played around with the ice-sawdust mixture and settled on a certain ratio and by heck, this mixture is hard, very hard...as hard as steel almost. You could even use Weetabix in the mix...but you get my drift.'

Both Josh and Dave were mesmerised, Dave gingerly removing an arrow, having a closer look.

'Careful...it might stick to your fingers.' Bob.

' 'Don't they melt?' Dave.

'Of course they do...*eventually* but definitely not as fast as plain ice does as they found out in WW2. And out in the open on a nice day...or of course *inside a nice warm body, they'll melt – just like the leg of lamb.*' That made them both look up. 'Don't you remember how they packed ice in the past? Usually with sawdust. When mixed with sawdust it has certain thermal qualities that allows it to resist melting, but eventually it will melt but nowhere as fast as plain ice.'

Dave began to smile, slowly nodding. 'So the evidence just melts away leaving no trace or very little trace, no matter where it ends up. Amazing Bob, amazing,' he repeated.

'That's right - and the shaft - even the point and yes, even the quill is made of my 'crete, fired from my augmented crossbow,' which he went on to show them and reveal the augmentation. 'They never know what hit them! I can even make ice-darts; I've used them already.'

Josh then joined in, 'Now I know what you mean about that leg of lamb and these...so cool!'

They laughed at the pun.

'Yep, literally - and no fingerprints, no noise and no bore-signatures. Those investigating might find traces of woodchip, perhaps some wool of even paper, but unlikely to make any connections,' Bob added.

***

The induction continued long into the evening with both Dave and Josh completely absorbed, in particular about the shape of heads...human heads.

'In order to make the gossamer masks as comfortable as possible *and* with the shape-memory filaments practically invisible, not all heads are the same, right? Well, when a voltage is applied to alter the shape slightly, which will move the skin - shape-memory remember - long heads, wide ones, round ones, like Churchill's etc., I've basically put them in five different groups and looked at the possibilities of some famous people's faces, with corresponding ages too that can be added. I might add a couple more categories...haven't decided yet.

I take full-front and side views of a head, make the mould...then make the gossamer face. It's so microscopically thin, I reckon it's thinner than make-up! Switch on the power and 'bingo'...Elvis turns into Cliff – groovy or what?! Or old man into young man without the need for any ridiculous paper masks or stockings. Just the flick of a switch...he'll feel the movement of the skin, but there's no electric shocks...the power is miniscule.'

'Where is this power source - what is it?' Dave.

'Aha. Some of it in my hollow-fibre clothing. And my belts, some belts thicker than others; you'd be surprised what you can pack into a bog-standard waist belt or an innocent looking crash helmet. Miles of fibres, all rechargeable of course. The hollow fibres also provide the means by which I can change colour of some of my clothes; I have very small hard-plastic tubes...or should I say very narrow bottles which are in fact, mini-reservoirs containing different coloured fluids – all connected up. Throw a switch and BINGO! - in goes the new colour. You'd be amazed that it only takes a few fibres to fill up to really alter the colour change of a garment.'

They listened, open-mouthed. 'But what would you say to the coppers if one day you were ever stopped and searched Dad, with all that gear on you...and wires?'

'Simple; I'll just tell them it's a medical treatment for both my neuralgia and migraines I have, the device interrupts the pain. And I'll produce a medical note to prove it. But I have to keep you shielded because it's me who's actually doing all this; my neck. You must understand that this is serious stuff. I just need you two to provide the feed when I need it - and so far you have. In addition Josh, I'd like you to break into the police system and monitor them so I know what you lot...' he said looking at Dave now, '...might know and might be planning.'

'My God - you have it all figured out...obviously dead serious about the whole thing. I suppose I don't blame you...I can see why. I only wish I could take a more active part,' Dave said while Josh was simply too excited about it all...and almost dumb-struck.

Bob came away from it feeling better, having now shared his 'other' life, his passion and intentions, with Dave.

***

'Josh...any psychic connections on Julie's whereabouts?' he asked – yet again.

'She's still a blank Dad, nothing. Sorry. I think she's carrying a lump of Kryptonite around with her. '

'Okay...and how's it down on the farm?' Bob always asked how his son was doing.

'Fine thanks Dad.'

***

As with football, Josh's face lit up as he proceeded to tell his Dad the of all the 'goings-on' with Mal and his animals. Bob Shape could not get enough of the young man's smile...like a beacon.

'Well, I have an idea...tell you more later.' Mal had fed back to Bob Shape that he could do with more like Josh..total absorption, always keen, motivated and always accompanied with a smile. Tireless where helping animals was concerned.

'If you know anybody else like him and who could help look after some of my kit, some of it languishing around the farm? Mechanical stuff mostly...and dirty.'

'There's a guy at work who has a young lad looking for some action; I'll ask - let you know.' But it was not to be, the young fellow had taken up a part-time job in IT...as many do.

However - and Robert Shape hadn't forgotten about 'the good in everyone' talk with Julie, hence his idea.

A Mechanic and his dog Molly

He had noticed him and remembered him, an accomplice of the idiot...yes, the idiot with a face like a smacked bum...trying to steal away the old man's supermarket trolley, the lout who had thrown Josh onto the railway track and whose 'dad' had attacked Bob when he tried to intervene.

He was younger in appearance and seemed to be, Bob guessed, of those easily lead, perhaps of a timid temperament, one who looked up to a 'leader', good or bad. However, and although he was alone this time, the lad was walking a dog, a Collie perhaps - a sweet looking creature...the dog, that is. Bob also suspected that this young fellow was probably an unwilling, reluctant accomplice in the activities of the so-called leader from the time before; it was his restraining manner Bob had noticed in the times their paths had crossed...and recognised that perhaps he had unfortunately mixed in with the wrong company.

'Lovely dog,' Bob had said, in an attempt to reach out to the lad. In a beckoning manner, Bob crouched down, inviting the dog towards him. Before the lad could say anything, as the dog wagged furiously, Bob asked, 'Yours...you like animals?' The lovely creature was called *Molly*. 'Nice name,' said Bob Shape.

The lad nodded...and his initial suspicious, if not frosty demeanour that Bob had detected as he had approached, melted away as the young man began earnestly to tell Bob all about his pride and joy - a surprise for Bob as he had wondered if the lad would reciprocate in conversation after what had occurred in the past. He was also remembering what Julie had said about opportunities and idle hands, so he was taking a punt.

The lad's name was Karl who told Bob that he worked as a garage mechanic. This Bob already knew about and also knew that he worked alongside the nasty individual who we also already know of, do we not reader? Twenty minutes of amiable chat followed until eventually, Bob had asked him if he would like to spend some time on a farm...with sheepdogs, not unlike his own - and perhaps other animals? Karl's face had lit up...just like Josh.

'Let me have your number Karl and leave it with me...you'll have more fun on the farm but I warn you it will be both enjoyable and hard work; however, if you like animals as I see that you do, you'll settle in, no problems. You'll love it. You never know Karl, there could even be a few things to fix on the farm to top up your engineering skills; I happen to know that the farmer needs some help in that department.'

Bob Shape had to chuckle when the young lad had told him who his supermarket trolley accomplice was clled - *Penny*, and also interesting to find out that the family ran the garage he worked in.

When Bob phoned, Mal was quite enthusiastic, having had the thought planted by Bob some weeks before and was keen on the idea.

'If it keeps him on the straight and narrow and enjoys it into the bargain, I'm all for it, besides I cam always use another pair of hands...but I'll keep him busy.'

'If you like, I could put Josh alongside him for the first few days when the holidays start?'

Mal had nodded. 'Even better – *two* pairs of hands.'

***

The whole idea of prising the young lad away from the family of thugs had come to Bob from the first encounter with the supermarket trolley episode. Bob could tell that the young Karl didn't really want the be there and be taking part.

With both Julie's and Dave's suggestions about getting idle hands busy and to be doing something different, something useful, well the idea had remained stuck the head of Robert Shape. And in truth, anything associated with Julie gave him reasons for optimism, apart perhaps, of the gulf that had opened up between them following what he thought was a simple misunderstanding, his mind often drifting back and recalling the event as well as her hidden, silent charms.

'Thanks Julie,' he mouthed, looking upwards. 'Oh Julie...where *are* you? I miss you.' Her beacon shone ever so brightly. Wherever she was.

The Drunk

He sensed it. Walking into town mid-afternoon; a copper having a few words with a man who was obviously inebriated...the policeman attempting to escort the drunk off the road. Traffic was being held up.

Two young men several yards away were observing, enjoying the spectacle it seemed but not getting involved. Josh, who was some distance away sensed a looming incident in the making...he couldn't tell you why he sensed this, that the two observers who stood next to a bus stop, were perhaps taking a greater interest than would be normal...a problem in the making.

The copper duly shuffled his man over to the pavement. It was only then that the drunk, as drunks are wont to do, began to resist and warble with a raised voice, but still on his feet. For some reason the copper was unaware that one of the observers had made a move towards him, who then paused adjacent to a rubbish bin, briefly searched within it and extracted an half-empty can of drink - and was about to throw it at him.

'Watch out!' shouted Josh to the copper who turned and looked over and saw Josh pointing. The copper was just in time to see something being thrown in his direction and ducked, forcing the drunk to do the same. The half-empty can of drink narrowly missed its target and clattered noisily against a fence spraying drink over it. The two observers turned and ran off - the can-thrower yelling, amongst laughter, obscenities which may have included such words as 'pig' or 'scum'.

The copper moved the drunk along the street, looked over to Josh and said 'Thanks', with a thumbs-up, then came over to him, thanking him again. Pleasantries were exchanged and Josh being Josh, told him he just knew the man was going to do something and offered his name.

'I'm PC Proctor...William Proctor,' he said in response and pointing at his tag, 'And I'll attend to those two later...I think I know who they are. Here's my number should you need it lad.'

***

On hearing of this encounter, Bob Shape was proud of his son. 'You're officially part of the fightback Josh! Well done.' And when Dave heard about it, he said, 'PC Proctor? Top man - a good bloke from what I know of him,' when Bob mentioned the incident with Josh.

Following this incident, Josh and the policeman had maintained contact via emails as Josh had expressed a desire at the time to know more about police cars - and all the kit they carried in general.

Changing Rooms

'Please tell me more...it sounds just up my street. I vaguely remember something about this on the news or in the papers,' Bob said. 'I remember that feminists and the trans lot had verbals about it all.'

Dave outlined the story...an individual, some bloke known to be a bit of a loner who could apparently not get on with, nor strike up any relationship with the opposite sex, visited his doctor, enquiring about the possibility of changing or wanting to change his sex - all on an official footing of course but it was all part of a plan...he strung along the medical profession quite easily.

When later they visited his apartment they found it was all a sham, he hadn't taken any of his prescribed medications that would begin his transformation, while he continued to visit female toilets and changing rooms in gyms and Health Spas. If anybody asked, 'he was 'identifying' as a woman' - and receiving much support from the half-way house fraternity...the myriad of 'hotch-potch-don't-fit-in-with-blokes-and-girls' brigade. At the same time, females, real females, had began to get both suspicious then alarmed at this new trend.

'Just another way to being a pervert - putting some sort of bogus legality to it all,' some of the gentler sex had proclaimed.

This man had form. Since beginning his transformation he was often spotted in or around female 'safe places' and, as far as Dave was concerned - and many others too - was milking his medical situation, using it as a Trojan Horse. He became quite bold in his quest for access once he had began and fallen into his voyeurism routine. But basically, he *was* a pervert - a failed 'voyeur' trying to get his kicks from weaselling his way into what used to be sacrosanct female territory, to glimpse girls and women in various stages of undress.

Anybody who dared criticise his attempts on changing sex were pilloried on social media as well as in some parts of the press, by the 'Trans and inclusivity' lobby...another Trojan Horse expression and excuse, as far as Dave was concerned.

On further reading Bob's thoughts immediately went to his Lynda, and imagining the shock she'd have if she ever encountered this situation.

***

'So what happened to privacy? Have you ever had a woman 'identifying as a man' come into your changing room eh?'

'No such luck Bob!' Dave replied laughing. 'As you know, it's always the other way round and the real women are up in arms about it all.'

'I can imagine. So what happened - what's the hoo-haa all about?'

'Well, a Mrs Simpson and her daughter went to their Health Centre for their weekly session. After they'd finished...' Dave went on to relate that 'mum' was ready first and leaving the changing room said to her daughter that she'd head upstairs to the cafe and order lunch. 'See you up there,' she had said.

Her daughter being 15 was doing what 15 year-olds do as they 'get themselves presentable'. She was aware that somebody else was in the changing room, in a cubicle, because she could hear the movement but thought nothing of it...another girl obviously. However she was not aware that it was a young man - a young man who was covertly watching her through the curtain.

The girl was semi-dressed making adjustments in front of the large mirror. It was then the man came out out of his cubicle to apparently comb his hair - just as she was doing; the only trouble was he was only wearing underpants...and she could instantly see that it was a man.

She had screamed, then dashed back into her cubicle for refuge...but he had followed her, telling her to be quiet. It was in the cubicle where the assault took place, molesting her before carrying out a finger-rape.

'Bloody hell,' said Bob. He thought of Lynda. Then of Julie; both would be destroyed.

'She and her family were absolutely distraught; the girl was suicidal. The police were involved of course and you'd think it was a 'slam-dunk' case eh? Not so; the gym had a policy of inclusivity not widely known to the punters. Besides, he said in his own words that they'd had become mutually aroused when seeing each other in states of undress and started to pet etc., then she had panicked.

It became her word against his...and here's the rub Bob...you are not allowed to say 'his' word...it's her word against 'her' word.

'Eh, really?'

'There was some mouthy bitch on the box spouting out about his/her rights and the rights of non-binary people transitioning from one sex to another. The upshot of it all Bob...a destroyed family and a year lost from school by the young lady who is now mentally scarred. And this bloke will keep doing it under the protection of 'Gender inclusivity'.

'But who allowed this...who made the policy - got a name?'

'Got two...one male, one female - some chap who's 'halfway' and that mouthy woman we saw on the box - Denise Crump. And here's where they hang out, their addresses; I knew you'd ask.'

'*Crump*! Is that for real? Christ, with a name like that I wouldn't be changing my sex, I'd be changing my bloody name! And don't tell me...she'll change into a 'Dennis'. And the gym policy, who made, who has accepted this policy for the Gym?'

'The Area Manager, a Gary Hudson. He was put under pressure by the usual loudest voices to do so, it has to be said.'

'Thanks. Okay then, so the poor girl and her family have not had any...justice?'

Dave shook his head, 'Looks that way...so far...' then added, 'Looks like the authorities including the police, are in thrall to the 'Queer' lobby.

***

It did not take long to track down the 'changing room perv', as Bob liked to call him now. If an address was to be found, Josh would find it and additionally, because there was a picture available, the address just came into his head...as with the rebel-rouser.

'And Josh, can you also find out where this perv's supporters hang out...the ones prominent in the papers, especially that mouthy bitch, Ms Crump?'

***

The man in question, the changing room pervert...he was found soon after - on a child's swing in the park early one morning.

Quite dead.

***

Initial thoughts by the detectives; it looked as if he'd been shot, shot in the thigh, then while incapacitated, placed on the swing with the swing chain wrapped around his neck, his own weight providing the strangling force. They were not quite sure what actually killed him. Did he bleed out, or was it strangulation; what came first? The bleeding, with the swing apparently also playing its part in the death, all complicated matters in determining the cause of death. A certain person wasn't bothered by this...the 'perv' was now history.

***

As he related to Dave later...and how the chains of the swing may have complicated matters...

'It reminds of a nasty accident I nearly had involving being throttled way back when I was kid; let me explain about your neck.

'Compression of the jugular vein will increase pressure in the head to an unbearable extent - that's what turns some victims blue Dave – as you know. And pressure, here -' he said pointing, '...on these arteries, carotid I think they're called, means the victim can rapidly lose consciousness, lack of blood to the brain and all that.

'Then there's Strangling. This can also put pressure on the nerves in the neck which can affect vital functions. One of the main nerves in this system is the vagal nerve-'

'The what?' interrupted Dave.

'The Vagal nerve...and you can die instantly from neck pressure - it carries a load of signals; it can instruct the heart to simply stop beating.' Bob paused. 'Amen..' and smiled.

'Wow...' Dave responded, 'Got it all figured out, eh?'

'Well, as I said, I used to be a kid on the swings and I remember nearly throttling myself on one 'cos we used to sit on the swing and then get someone to twist us round and round, wind us up - and then let go. We'd spin like crazy! I'd lose all my precious marbles out of my pockets. Ropes were better than chains though, anyway, I nearly became a cropper when my neck got caught up in it the rope. So it gave me the idea.'

***

'*Bizarre death in kiddies play-park!*' was a local headline. The trouble for the police was the absence of any murder weapon or of any bullets, even after completely shutting down the whole park and carrying out a minute search for clues. Someone did come forward saying they'd been returning home late in the evening, went through the park and did see what he thought was a man on a swing - not moving - just sat there.

'No way was I going to strike up a conversation,' he had said, not realising that the man was probably already dead when he passed by.

***

There were of course across the country, always reports of 'dogging' in parks but not normally in this one, the police having considered initially that this was some sad-masochistic ritual gone wrong. Or perhaps a jealous rival, until the dots were connected up by the police looking at his record, including a message in the form of a tune, sent to the police, based on a Sixties song... 'He *ain't heavy, he's my brother*' ....except the words had been changed to 'He ain't heavy, he's my *sister*,' - poking fun at the perversion.

The coppers of course didn't release *this* message; but somebody made sure it came into the public domain, and reader, we know who, do we not?

***

The 'Trans Brigade' went ballistic, accusing the police of hiding the truth and naturally Denise Crump was the most vocal amongst those who supported the dead man on the swing, as the young girl's parents looked on in disbelief.

'And what about my daughter?' they asked. 'Who is looking out for her and the other victims?'

It became ugly. 'She must have egged him on...must have flaunted herself,' was the response from supporters of the pervert. 'He had the right to be in that changing room,' they cried. 'He's just as much a victim of the establishment just because he doesn't want to conform!' A 'he' or 'she' the papers asked. Oh, the irony of it all. The young girl's parents were horrified.

Someone duly made note of this development...and who was spouting the warped views.

But there were other comments made too...as other messages rolled in, feeding the media frenzy, usually along the lines of...'He got what he deserved,' etc. Some said, 'They need help'...

'Yes, they do need help - and we help these nasty weirdos in our own way,' came a brutal response.

'But they were born this way, poor sods...'

'Well, after a rape, they can die that way.' Another response.

***

In their pub later, Dave said to Bob, 'Well, indeed there are those who we all know who live 'the other way' and provide a significant contribution to our society; just look at those who know what, or who, they are and who provide us all with wonderful entertainment without ramming it down our throats.

Then there's the malign element, the nutters, who cannot accept that many people believe, or think, that some ways of life are not quite normal, even if they only think that...and yet these militant twerps actually *want* you to like it, or accept it's quite normal and that you're not allowed to call it weird or a perversion, abnormal, and that you *will* or *must* accept it's mainstream. Or else!'

'Careful Dave...or you'll have me reaching for my pencil-box! But there's always a range of opinions. However, when it strays into assault or sexual violence under the cover of inclusivity - or anti-discrimination, then they are fair game.'

'So how did you do it?'

'Two 'crete bullets, one top of the thigh, the other where it hurts. Obliging of him to have sat on the swing. Made things easy for me. I had noticed that he'd spend time casually sitting on the swing - always the same one, during his walks; and yes, I watched him several times. I also made sure it was on one of his evening walks - dark. Also realised his walk usually took him in the direction of the Health Centre.'

They briefly lapsed into silence as they watched some pigeons and Sparrows plaguing the families a few tables away as the children just made matters worse by offering and throwing chips and crisps...as Mum and Dad cursed. Their pet dog, sat under the table also benefited, eventually stirring itself to take advantage of the families' largesse in snacks.

'Feeling peckish Dave? I'll get some more crisps - watching those families over there tucking in has made me feel hungry....just hope the birds don't do a Hitchcock on us!'

They didn't. In fact to their amusement - and a touch of smugness as they tucked into their own crisps and peanuts which were spread out over their table, not a bird came close, they were left entirely unmolested.

'Strange that, we must have the mark of Satan hanging over us - I wonder why,' Dave said rhetorically and rather morosely. 'We must be doing something wrong - long may it continue!'

Although they talked some more about the usual law and order blunders and failings, Bob Shape detected that Dave's heart was simply not in the conversation so much. This left Bob feeling worried.

***

Returning home after work, Mr Gary Hudson, the Health Centre Manager, having settled in with a coffee to catch up on the TV...well, he was sure he'd locked his windows before going to work and yet the blinds were moving...a breeze coming from somewhere so when he stood up to investigate he was horrified to find a neat, round hole in the front window. His initial thought was 'a bullet" - someone had shot at his house. Then his thoughts made him look at the opposite wall where he noticed one of his pictures lying on the floor, smashed and a corresponding mark in the wall from whence it came.

Now he was worried and reached for his phone. It was while he was on the phone to 999 he spotted a small note on the floor amongst the broken glass and being house-proud and not wanting to convey the impression to the police that he was an untidy character, he picked it up and was about to dispose of it when he realised it was a very small, typed note. He squinted hard, so small was the font. It said...

'Your inclusivity policy sux - needs changing - to exclude weirdos. Remember, we know where you live.'

Mr Hudson's front room and garden was duly turned into a Crime Scene. The coppers couldn't figure out how the message made it into the house; nor could they find 'any bullet'. Apart from a mark in the wall and a stain on the carpet, they found little else.

The usual questions followed...

'Any enemies, anybody with a grudge...?' At that time, none that he could think of. But a connection was made...

He now realised that the changing room business, following the attack on the young girl, was a policy with which he was not entirely comfortable initially; it was a step too far in his view but which had a strident vocal following in some quarters...a minority group it has to be said - and with some trendy political pressure had been applied, had lead to this inevitable result.

Thinking of the message and the hole in the window, he decided he would put forward a change in policy, a policy which had always lurked in the back of his managerial mind on the subject and which should satisfy all parties. He would propose that...

There would be three lots of changing facilities and toilets. Male, female and Trans, with no cross-fertilisation between facilities.

When together next, and as he put it to Bob: -

'Male...those with 'tackle'; female...those without 'tackle' - and Trans, those who can't make up their minds or who are undergoing change. And then when the physical change is completed they can then take their rightful place in the right bog...sorry, changing room.'

'Sounds good me,' was Bob's answer.

***

But that was not how Denise Crump thought about it, in fact she raged against any idea that Trans people should have their own 'safe area'; they were entitled to unfettered access to whichever 'gender WC facility' they liked - in her view. She said the proposition was 'outrageous' and would fight it 'tooth & non-painted nail'.

However, Hudson had support from the feminists who inevitably wanted 'female' places to be exactly that...'female' places, and not be part of some hybrid, experimental equality driven mission just to satisfy a minute, a very minute, percentage of the population.

'It's like they want to ram it down your throats, as we said before,' Dave had remarked to Bob.

'Where does she live exactly?' Bob asked.

She usually takes the tube from King's Cross St Pancras; here's a picture.'

'Perfect. I'm going to be a nasty bastard Dave, I'm afraid.'

'I'll watch the news...' he replied.

***

He set himself up...a coat, on the big side; hat, 'face', his small-dog-in-a-basket prop', false arm, then set out.

***

The Underground platform was crowded...'push-and-shove' crowded. Perfect.

It was the push; who pushed who? No one would ever be able to tell. The extended false arm placed our man too far from the target - too far to be obvious.

On the Underground, Denise Crump disappeared under the wheels of an incoming train having stumbled apparently. Or was she 'accidentally' nudged?

The station was shut down, CCTV was analysed but it proved too difficult. Too many people clumped together, too confusing to evaluate properly.

There were no leads. Indeed, perhaps it was just an accident. They didn't have a clue.

But one man did.

***

Then eventually another message arrived for the police re the unfortunate demise of Denise Crump.

'We can cancel too'
'Hmm, another weirdo 'gone'...and there are many more out there. Busy!'

This message immediately changed the nature of the investigation but again it proved difficult and too much time had passed, however the police persevered, trying to make out who was who amongst the hundreds of travellers in and around that particular Underground station. And someone carrying a pet in a basket who appeared to have been, just like everybody else on the platform, caught up in the crowded hustle.

'God knows what the poor creature must have thought,' a copper remarked during the more detailed analysis, on viewing all the CCTV play-backs. 'What was the silly man thinking taking it on the Tube?'

***

'You do realise that she'll be quickly replaced - plenty of volunteers,' said Dave.

'Oh, I know, not bothered, just one less on the streets. And look who's going to be busy?'

Bob answered. 'When a few more are found tied up on swings or elsewhere, you never know, the penny might drop. Someone might get the message.'

Police Matters

'We have someone out there...settling scores and tweaking the noses of the 'Woke' brigade and the Trans people,' This - the view of the Police Forces.

The usual suspects – the groups who formed part of the 'too much time on their hands' twerps who screamed that there was a hidden Fascist group operating 'out there' trying to silence 'us free-thinkers' as they described themselves, were in full-flow.

'Fascists?' said Bob. 'Me?..but I don't wear a uniform,' he answered his reflection in the mirror.

'Any news re Julie?' Bob asked yet again...with the same answer; no luck.

Poor Ned

'You might want to read about poor Mr. Ned Spalding, Bob,' said Dave, handing him a slip of paper. It was a copy of a news article.

'In a nutshell; from small beginnings...woman, all by herself sets up her own company working all hours of the day marketing knick-knacks and some clothing that she actually makes herself. She becomes successful, employs three others...life is looking good for her.

Her name was Rebecca Spalding.'

'*Was..?* Go on...' invited Bob, his heart beginning to sink.

'Well, amongst the clothing she marketed was a quirky 'his & hers' range for adolescents - quite popular and quite innocent.' Bob's heart sank further – he knew what was coming.

'Please don't tell me...somebody who wasn't a 'his' or a 'her' objected?' Dave nodded.

'So, the PC brigade or Woke warriors, whatever they're called these days - joined in the fight, couldn't accept the defined 'only two sexes'. Long story short, she - and her business - were targeted, hounded to extinction...she was harassed where ever she went. And then one day, her father found her dead when he went round one morning. An overdose...she had also left a note; here's a photocopy. Bob, I wept when I looked into this...but you're probably better placed to take it up - I just don't seem to have the energy these days. Needless to say, her father, Ned Spalding, is heart-broken. And now in a rage. But what can he do?'

Bob Shape was already boiling, furious inside. 'Who are these people...these self-righteous cowards?'

'That's the problem Bob; they hide themselves behind woke-tags but many are quite brazen, open and proud of what they do even when they know it's affecting people's lively-hood. However, I have a friendly journalist - police do have such contacts - who did some quite deep investigative work on this case and some others too; here's a list of names who crop up frequently, given me by this journalist, this *person*,' he said with a smile while touching his nose, '...of the principal people involved in the 'cancellation' and the hounding of Rebecca Spalding. There are at least seven of them involved in this particular case so far as we know. Many others of course jump on the bandwagon as a result of Social Media. One good thing...they all live in London or thereabouts. Quite handy for you. Your starter for ten...?'

Bob took the list.

'The journalist said that two on that list are brother and sister and that out of the seven on it, four of them often meet up regularly, no doubt to plan a 'cancellation' or two in this cafe, adding that none of them actually lived there and that they all came from the City area.'

'Ta mutchly Dave. Makes your blood boil doesn't it...well, it does me.'

Bob noticed the address, that the cafe - *The Sesame Seed* - where they met was not a million miles from where his colleague Vince lived. Somewhere near *Finchley*. 'But I think I might have a cure for these idiots...' There was that twinkle in his eye as he said it.

'Whatever you do Bob, please let me know about it, after all, the poor bloke has lost his daughter, the apple of his eye...I wouldn't be disposed to show them any mercy when you find 'who did what. Go get 'em Bob.'

'Absolutely...will do.' Robert Shape wondered what he'd do if anything happened to his lovely Lynda in these circumstances; he would be destroyed – at first, then he'd move heaven and earth to deal with those responsible.

And Dave's words and tone had surprised Bob. Not normally one to express an opinion, Dave was usually quite happy just to pass on the information and the valuable intelligence. Nor did he ever give a hint of being at all interested in the 'how it went down'; he appeared sufficiently happy just to know that it did – that scum was removed from the streets. Could be the father-daughter relationship, especially after seeing Mr Ned Spalding weeping on TV.

But Bob was thinking that Dave's appearance had deteriorated - not looking well at all.

***

With Vince...

Looking into it, Robert Shape found that even though the clothes Rebecca Spalding were 'his & hers', they were available in all colours, not just your typical type-cast blues and pinks and as we know reader, adolescents were always difficult to please when it came to clothes.

'So what's the beef then?' he said when he was with Vince. 'What's the matter with these people? These people are worse than your car-scammers in some ways Vince.'

Every now and then Robert Shape and and his working colleague Vince would get together to talk business matters away from the company surrounds, usually followed by a meal. And together they would 'spout' - just as Bob did with his mate Dave...solving the world's problems.

'There must be something lacking in their lives. That cafe that's mentioned...*The Sesame Seed,* it's not your traditional Greasy Spoon, more of a trendy boutique bar - some artisan joint, almost round the corner from where I live,' Vince said.

Vince, having been on the receiving end of the evil intentions with the car scammers, was still shocked about the woman...and how her father must be feeling. Like Bob, the father was a widower.

'An unusual name for these days...*Ned* - quite old fashioned, almost like a throwback to Charles Dickens. But poor bloke...I know how I and the missus felt with the car and that shower of shits and all the nastiness that went with it. As for the police...fat lot of use they were! God only knows what this poor *Ned* must be feeling. Somebody needs to sort out these...these...'

'*Scum* is too nice a word, right?' said Bob. Vince just shook his head...then nodded.

'Way too nice. And do you know what I would do...'

***

They usually had these meetings about once a month - and as before and as Bob knew he would, Vince, who would have embarrassed Genghis Khan and Attila The

Hun for being too left wing, launched into this tirade, but always with a twinkle in his eye.

And Vince had no idea about his boss…

The Sesame Seed

The tall woman tottered through the door of *The Sesame Seed* unsteady on her feet, perhaps unsure of herself while carefully negotiating the small step, and the battered wooden glass-panelled front door. The opening door rang a bell, which appeared to make her jump, however, pleasant odours of coffee beans and cinnamon assaulted her senses as she looked around, searching for faces she'd memorised from a list in the press copy. Aha...there they were, deep in conversation. She moved in their direction then picked out a table close by, having ordered a pot of tea.

On closer inspection, an observer may have noticed that the tall lady sported an unusual pair of spectacles...spectacles that also magnified sound, a sound that would be piped straight into her hearing device. She stirred her pot while listening...it was not long before confirmation that this group was indeed part of the list, was forthcoming. The tall lady was satisfied.

After about ten minutes, she made an obvious but awkward move, intending to approach the 'group' sat nearby. It was to be a stilted introduction, she appeared to be upset, in tears.

'Please pardon me but I just could not keep it inside of me any longer after overhearing parts of your conversation for which I do apologise profusely,' she said. 'Your words I heard rang true in my ears and in my heart...and as you can probably guess, I am a *Trans* - and having a truly awful time of it.' A sob escaped her.

The three sat nearby were initially shocked into silence, agog but on closer inspection - and by the tone of the voice this stranger possessed, made them react as if they'd just discovered some long-lost uncle.

The stranger continued, 'I used to be *Sandy*, a male; now I'm *Sandy*, a woman, going through hell trying to put up with all the hassle, buying new clothes, the name-calling, sneers, queer looks. I'm at my wit's end. It's awful, it really is.' Tears appeared on her powdered cheeks.

The tall woman was obviously in distress, which prompted an immediate and sympathetic response, one of the women moving closer while putting an arm about her shoulders. Soft words were uttered along with much 'tutting' and head-shaking, 'You poor thing,' and 'Oh, it's terrible, we know, don't we *Scags*,' The man nodded. the others vigorously joining in.

'You can talk to us,' one of them said while standing up. There was more nodding. 'I'm *Leggy - Scaggs* is my brother but we're 'its' really. And this is *Wheatgerm*,' she said turning and indicating the third member, a woman, as far as the tall lady could make out.

'You are so kind,' said the lofty woman. She observed that *Leggy* was of middle height, slim, while her brother was of soft countenance, pudgy...and quiet.

***

It did not take long before the sympathy began to be replaced by oblique, minor rants against certain groups as they opened up to this imposing and clearly oppressed 'person'.

A few minutes later they were joined by a fourth member, a woman, quite a shapeless individual. From this moment on, she took over the conversation for the group as the tall, upset lady sat back and listened while occasionally answering the odd question about her experiences. The new arrival was not only verbose but 'potty-mouthed' with it. As she settled down, the tall lady piped up...

'I knew from my very early days when young that I was not really drawn to tanks, aeroplanes, cowboys and soldiers for my toys and even today I still have my fluffy teddy bears at home which I adore,' she added almost in embarrassment.

'Ahhh, Teddy Bears,' one of them said. Smiles and nods all round. They all sat down.

Sandy continued. 'I also wondered what to do about my voice, a real giveaway...what do you do - how can you make it more...*female*? Imagine having a voice like George Clooney?!'

***

The tall lady listened intently to the responses and on-going conversation, occasionally hearing of the various minority groups who, in all fairness, should be 'dictating the rules and setting the new laws for society' in the their view, potty-mouth with the loudest voice.

'We seriously need to shut these people down,' she said in reference to those trying to maintain the *there are only two sexes* status quo. And indeed, a few choice swearwords were thrown in for good measure. The tall lady smiled and nodded, realising that this group were a bit too strong for her tastes on the matter...and said so.

This led to a loud diatribe from potty-mouth on how the Trans community should take the battle to the cosy mainstream...regardless of the consequences.

The tall one continued... 'All I want is to be left in peace - to be able to go about without feeling guilty.

But what about that poor woman last month who committed suicide...what was her name...that was bad. I can't remember now? That was too much...'

This was a leading question from the tall lady, who was inwardly horrified to hear the so-called justifications for the actions taken against Rebecca Spalding and her enterprise; there was absolutely no remorse shown by this group now sat with her, of the girl's suicide. Oh yes, they'd descended upon her like a pack of wolves without a thought of the consequences? Indeed, the siblings boasted that they had protested outside her house...seemed proud about it.

These people were on a mission. The tall lady had heard enough.

'Well, I must thank you all for your welcome support but I must leave now. Perhaps we can meet up again...you've been such a comfort.'

They all nodded with smiles while one of them did a mini-clap.

Contacts were exchanged. As she had tottered in, the tall lady tottered out...her mind made up.

Sesame Feedback

Dave seemed improved since the last time they had met

'Are you sitting comfortably Dave? Right, the Woke Warriors - let me fill you in...' and proceeded with the feedback as promised, what had happened in *The Sesame Seed* and of the notes he'd made while being *Sandy*.

'Dave...I think they were completely taken in yet I must have looked like *Mrs Doubtfire*! As for the voice...?! Anyway, managed to squirrel away a couple of contacts - even an address. And God help anybody who uses the wrong form a of pronoun address from what I can gather. Utter bonkers they are Dave. And they always have an eye out for any good deed that can be turned into an excuse for Woke action, something they can deliberately misconstrue...for a 'punishment' to be dished out. They have a range of contacts, advisors and help-lines on such things as...

Romany heritage, Gypsies, Fat phobia, Advisors on non-binary identity, 'people of colour' – that's coloured people to me and you. *Advice on the rural queer experience* - whatever that means...and I don't want to know either! And they certainly told me what sexes there actually were. *Female, Male, Intersex, Trans, Non-Conforming, Personal, and Eunuch.'*

'Eunuch!? That's an old one...' Dave.

Bob took a sip of his beer...

'Maybe they shouldn't drink out of plastic bottles, I reckon it's affecting the chemical make-up of their silly minds. Did you find out who was responsible for the hounding of Rebecca Spalding, who was behind it all principally?' asked Dave.

'Think so, a potty-mouth creature who goes by the name of *Edgy* is certainly one of them. She...I think 'she' actually *is* a 'she', and I will be meeting up again soon, another session in Sesame Street.' Dave smiled.

'So...if I got up and started singing *Walk Like A Man,* (that would be by *The Four Seasons*, reader) I'd be in trouble? Or maybe not, you never know.'

'That's about the size of it...'

'What about your...*Mrs. Doubtfire's* voice,' he asked grinning.

'Well, I did ask them how you could modify your voice if you had a 'too obvious a male tone' as a Trans, like George Clooney's voice...'

'Or like Lee Marvin, John Wayne?'

'How about HAL 9000 or Mrs Brown?'

'HAL 9000...who's that?' Quizzical look from Dave.

'The smoothest voice in the world. From '*2001 A Space Odyssey.*'

'Oh yes...' They laughed together...but there was serious business to be taken care of.

'Let's hope they don't take up the 'slavery' thing,' said Dave as he chuckled, adding, 'Because I think a very, very distant relative of mine owned some of the slaves that built the pyramids, so I'd better watch out!'

***

Bob laughed out loud but Dave was on his soap-box now...

'What po-faced gits these people are with these loony ideas they have, ideas which always find response among the useless people with too much time on their hands, for they are ideas which gave these worthless twats the opportunities from which, in a well-ordered society, their stale, lame, infantile and bonkers idiocies would exclude them.' He wasn't quite finished yet…

'And, and…don't they realise that it's only a bad case that needs to be urged intemperately.'

'Wow Dave…anything else? You're on a roll.' These had been yet more words from Dave that surprised Bob…again. He even seemed angry. Not like the usual 'Dave' at all, blowing both hot and cold at the same.

Bob knew that Dave was up against it with respect to his medical situation and was 'getting things off his chest and deserves to be cut some slack,' thought Bob.

Swimming Lessons – More Sesame Seeds

They were sat around the same table again - there were two more this time; pleasantries had been exchanged with a few Anglo-Saxon words thrown in by the potty-mouthed *Edgy* and although mindful of her verbosity, and overbearing presence, the tall lady considered that of the group, the two siblings were the real determined characters, both who were able, from a warm greeting and innocent smiles, could instantly transform their expressions to a cold, hard glance. Like a warning.

This was confirmed by the conversations that followed their arrival - they didn't say much but their few words and accompanying tone signalled a complete lack of sympathy or of concern towards their victims, just coldness...as if the poor family deserved it. And expressing it all in what the tall lady could only describe as glee, when recounting some of their exploits. The tall lady smiled...but in her mind she was planning...

'Now all this gives me warm feelings; makes me want to really cuddle up to my lovely teddy bears...wonderful.' Behind the smiles of the siblings she was sure she detected a hidden sense of horror from behind a glass-like stare from *Leggy*.

An hour later, Lofty Lady stood up, 'I have to leave now...you've been so kind, so inspirational listening to you so thank you all. By the way, I did find a very good *Trans* outfitters that really caters for the likes of *us...me*. It's not like those shops we used to see on Wardour street in London back in the 60s. Call me if you're interested. However, I'd be careful folks, just in case there's push-back...there are some real nutters out there,' the tall woman said addressing them all in a sweeping glance.

She paused - was about to tell them if they hadn't asked, her whole name, but her with the Potty-Mouth beat the Tall Lady to it.

'It's Nelson,' she answered. 'And by the way, I'm hoping to organise a *Swimathon* for people like us, you know how things are these days or how they can be when it comes to swimming, showering, changing and the like; anybody interested?'

Looks of both surprise and perhaps concern registered on their faces.

After a moments silence, she followed up with, 'I take it you can all swim...? I hope you can,' while moving off without waiting for any responses...smiling as she tottered out once again.

It wouldn't <u>male</u> any difference whether they could swim or not...

***

'What was that all about?' they muttered in unison after tall lady, *Sandy*, had left. 'Swimming? Really? She's an odd one,' said *Edgy*. Weird.

'Is she for real...I don't trust her,' said sister, her brother nodding along in agreement. 'I have no sympathy at all for that woman who topped herself, who was trying to ram down our throats the predictable mantra of 'His & Hers'.

But they were fascinated nonetheless. Especially in the shop the tall Lady had mentioned. Later, they phoned her.

The Lessons

'Hello girls and boys,' said the stranger to the two youngsters, brother and sister who went by the names of *Leggy* and *Scaggs,* and who were sat at a table sipping a beverage. They looked up, a little surprised at this stranger, a man sat on a tricycle who had crept up upon them silently. He dismounted and came over.

The siblings were not quite sure what to do as the man came closer, but they did notice that he was wearing a jacket - a quite bulky jacket. And yet...was there not something familiar about him...his features?

'Remember me...?' he asked, smiling. He knew they wouldn't...and plainly they didn't, but they were suspicious. They had in fact been waiting for '*Sandy*' who was to take them to the non-binary shop.

'Who are you...? asked one of the siblings of this strange man who seemed to know them, a look of unease spreading across their faces.

'I'm to take you to a shop...' *Sandy*' has sent me and I believe you are *Scaggs* and *Leggy*...? Hop on, it's not far away...' said the tricycle man, '...and I think one of your friends is already there...*Edgy*?'

On hearing *that* name they relaxed – they all knew *Edgy* and tentatively moved towards the unusual contraption, a tricycle which was in fact a popular mode of transport not unlike the rickshaws of the East, a rider with two passengers sat behind. They slowly clambered on just like a couple of tourists. 'Cool,' muttered pudgy *Scaggs*, but *Leggy* looked apprehensive, worried.

'You can strap yourselves in if you want...up to you,' he said indicating the buckles.' ...has all the mod-cons...yep, even cup holders,' he said laughing.

They declined but were surprised when they realised it was partly battery-powered as it silently moved away and surprised again when it was not going quite in the direction of town as they had thought.

***

That same morning, Potty-mouth *Edgy* was listening to the radio, a programme called *Past Hits* or *Old Hits* or something...she liked music in the background while carrying out research:-

"And that was 'The Teddy Bears' with *To Know Him Is To Love Him.*" said the radio man. It was a tune that *Potty-mouth* had heard before and quite liked even though it was from way before her time. And Teddy Bears...she smiled, suddenly remembering that tall woman...that *big* woman...and *her* teddy bears.

'Teddy Bears?! Pooh! Definitely not for me!' she uttered dismissively.

"But...an interesting fact for you folks," continued the radio man, "...did you know that on that song, the drummer of *The Teddy Bears* was a chap called Sandy Nelson...yes, the famous drummer who had other hits with *Teen Beat, Let There Be Drums...*"blah, blah blah.

Potty-mouth *Edgy* paused. That name sounded familiar; where, no - *when* had she recently heard that name? Yes...the tall Trans woman, but then…

'OMG! And her bloody teddies!' she shouted at no one. 'A coincidence..? Nah, this must be a joke. Have we been taken for a ride? Bitch! Shit! Bastard!' she cried out again. But yes, the more she thought about it the more convinced she became.

They had been conned. She'd better tell the others, and quick.

'Where are we going? asked *Leggy*. The rider appeared to be going in the wrong direction.

'A short cut round this large pond then over that little bridge you can see then straight round to the back of the street - quicker,' said their rider.

Suddenly, he cried out, 'Ouch Ouch! Got cramp...ouch!' He stopped the bike, seemingly to rub his leg. 'Bloody cramp! Sorry about this,' he said dismounting, 'My bloody leg, here,' he said pointing at his calf as he then began rubbing it vigorously, the siblings looking on, fascinated for a moment or two. 'So sorry...'

When they glanced up from his leg, they found themselves looking at a photo he was holding up right before their eyes.

'What..' said the girl before she was cut off.

The man's face had changed - a deadly, menacing look had replaced the friendly countenance.

'Oh YES! Look closely at this picture...CLOSELY,' he said in that same menacing tone. It was a photo of a grown man in tears, weeping. 'This is Ned Spalding, father of the poor woman you and your stupid cohorts of idiots hounded to death. Look at him. LOOK AT HIM! He's broken!' They recoiled before his obvious wrath whilst trying to get off the bike which was now positioned close by the pond's edge. 'I wouldn't move if I were you otherwise...' he was now brandishing what looked like a walking stick.

'Let us go! Let us go you pervert, you weirdo,' shouted the female.

He chuckled. 'Me? A weirdo? Ha!' he announced as he switched off his facial augmentation device while slipping on a wig. Weirdo? The irony. 'I ask again, remember me…?' he said now with a forced smile. But he was glad he could now 'relax' his face - it was beginning to ache.

Their jaws dropped. Then, 'Oh, oh, it's you, Ms Pansy, Sandy. I knew it! I knew you were a fake,' said the young woman in a measured tone. 'C'mon *Scaggs*, lets ge…'

A quick prod from a stick he brandished stopped her dead.

'My cattle prod…just a few volts,' he said. Now they both looked fearful. 'I did ask last time we met if you could swim, remember?' he said as he repositioned the trike; he had their full attention now as they both sat motionless, thinking he was going to move off in another direction, the bike now pointing towards the small brdge. He moved little closer beside the machine and said…

'Please forgive me but I have to do this for Mr Ned Spalding…you ridiculous, callous, unfeeling pair of shitty bastards.' said the man who had called himself 'Sandy' quite recently.

He opened his bulky jacket, exposing two bright yellow spray guns. Transfixed by the appearance of the spray guns they curled up, turning away, perhaps waiting - expecting - to get soaked, but instead there were two '*sphats*' as the guns spat out two darts…into the legs of the siblings. Both yelled as the darts hit and sank into their thighs, *ice* darts of course. They squirmed and struggled in their seats trying to remove them. But then their actions becoming slower, more laboured.

Desperate pleading, worried, fearful looks were searching for his gaze, his help even.

None was forthcoming except him raising his arm to say-

'Bye, bye girls and boys; and now for the swimming lesson...are you ready? Hope you can swim.' he asked looking into their faces' He noticed that there was still a sign of recognition and consciousness - and also fear in their eyes; they knew...*knew* that their end was nigh.

The man reached to the side of his tricycle and yanked a lever, tipping them both seats backwards into the cold, murky waters of the pond. 'Enjoy,' he muttered, knowing if the drug didn't kill them, they would drown anyway.

They floundered meekly as they sank, the dying look of surprise and despair on their faces while attempting to mouth an utterance, but as the waters closed over them, they were no doubt already on the stairway to...no, not heaven reader, but to somewhere else.

The last he saw of them was just a collection of bubbles.

Dave Happy

Bob Shape was not in the habit of passing on the details of 'what went down' after Dave had given him information, he already knew Dave *knew* what he was up to, however, having seen him become so worked up, agitated and upset about Ned Spalding, Bob decided to tell him what had subsequently taken place...how he had dealt with it.

Dave listened in silence, saying nothing until Bob had finished. Then a smile developed slowly across his face as he put out his hand...for a handshake. 'Excellent...brilliant, Bob. Ned and his daughter are avenged. Thank you. How do you, no - how *did* you come up with that idea? Don't tell me, I'm just happy it's done. The streets are a little cleaner.

'Just a matter of consequences...if you destroy someone's lively-hood just because your warped brain can't accept other opinions then…expect push-back.'

Dave nodded.

***

However, Bob Shape did not mention that he might have been responsible for another body found floating in a river not too far away from from *Scaggs* and *Leggy* were eventually found and another unfortunate who had slipped and stumbled into the path of a passing truck. Wearing headphones, it was deemed he had been lost in his own silent world - not paying attention. However, all the deaths, all the victims were known 'wokers'. Not workers. *Wokers*.

There were few words in the press - "Body found in river..." etc. etc. ". "Lorry death..." etc. etc. All had traces of banned substances in their bodies, whether their demise was an accident or not.

3rd Conversation

'Hello..hello,' the voice cried out several times, getting louder as it approached. It was *that* voice. That plaintive voice...who else could it be but *Stella*? Even so, he was again taken by surprise to see her and by her sudden presence.

'Where on earth did you spring from...again? he responded, but pleased, nevertheless.

'From over there - didn't you see me...? You are troubled,' she said. 'Why are you troubled?' Her appearance had changed somewhat from last time as he struggled to recall how she had looked before.

'Well, look at you...you were different last time...and now you are different again.'

Indeed she was - and a forlornness in her countenance was also manifest. He also noticed she looked a tad untidy.

'Oh, but we can't talk of such things,' she readily answered, talking with her unique, almost child-like babble. Like before he was intrigued to study this...this woman, as there was little hint of the girl from their first encounter. She was a little more rounded, her hair grown longer, her clothes more sober but creased, quite a transformation...in such a short time. Indeed, he knew from his own family experience with his own wonderful Lynda, just how quickly the transformation from young adolescent, to young lady, or should he say *woman*, could take.

She repeated, 'You are troubled are you not? I am troubled too...I may have to change in order to look after people. You need to change too I think...I can tell.

214

And you are not really happy, are you.' It wasn't a question.

Bob Shape actually blushed despite himself; he knew a blush is not to be commanded; he actually felt as a young boy would feel, immature and perhaps even foolish...all because of her words.

'We all have our troubles *Stella*, may I ask what yours are?'

'I feel sad with you today. It is because I can't do what I want to do, what I must do...' and for the first time she had actually paused before continuing, '...but I will try - you must not worry about me - I am alright; I know you think about me but I'll manage and put up with my hips and my joints. I'll still come and see you...but you must settle and do something different...promise me. It's time for me to hurry again...you know I'm always busy...much to do. I can't talk to you any more now...must go, bye bye.'

'Hold it a minute...' he responded, as his phone suddenly vibrated in his pocket and a noisy group passed by. 'Blast it,' he muttered. '*Stella*, hang on a minute while I answer this,' but when he looked up a few seconds later she had vanished amongst the crowd. Now he was really perplexed, but he also had a feeling of sadness although he could not tell you why exactly.

This was the third encounter and yet...he felt that her presence was almost timeless; he needed answers if only to satisfy his extreme curiosity about this young lady, a complete stranger who fascinated him.

The Hack

Bob reminded Dave about any hacking incidents.

'Our man 'Ace' was hacked although not at work, but on his home computer...you must have something under investigation? As long as it's not too far away...'

True to his word, Dave gave him an email address. Bob then asked Josh to delve into it and the story behind it - a naked, blatant attempt at blackmail....after having plundered £10,000, an old lady's life savings. It was 20 miles away where the unfortunate lady lived and the police simply did not have the resources to look into it.

But someone with an unusual name did.

***

It was just another semi-detached house, like many in the area. 'What made you go for this one Josh?'

'The Google Map antenna in my mind, the feeling I had; just drawn to it...and it's a 'he' by the way Dad, in his twenties my mind tells me. Need to see his face though, to be sure, and here's the actual address.'

How the hell does he know this, wondered Bob? Simply amazing, but how long will he retain this gift, these special powers? Their doctor, along with his own research, indicated that his powers would probably diminish with age and maturity, depending on where in the spectrum of autism he sat.

Better get cracking then...

***

They stood on the street not far from the address then walked towards it. Both looked middle-aged, one taller than the other - and both sporting geek baseball caps and shades. The shorter one carried what looked like a control box hung around his neck and stayed back on the street as the taller one walked up to the door and knocked...then saw the doorbell plus camera on the wall, which he was expecting; he rang it, looked up at the camera and waved. While waiting he surveyed the immediate area, noticing the very nice motorbike stood in the drive to the side of the house. No doubt the occupant could afford it on the old lady's life savings...

About 30 seconds later he heard someone bounding down stairs inside, then a rattle of locks. The door cracked open.

'Sorry to trouble you Sir but my drone was hijacked I think, and maybe, just maybe, has finished up in your back garden somehow; could you please take a look?' said the caller. As he spoke he stepped back a couple of paces proudly showing a control console, like Josh's. The subtle move ensured that the occupant, with buds around his neck also moved into view as he took a closer look...obviously a gadget-man. The older man looked over his shoulder back towards the younger man standing on the pavement, who gave a 'thumbs-up'. Indeed, it was the man they wanted.

'If you do find it in your garden could you let us know please...here's my number,' and handed over an entirely fictitious contact...typed of course. The occupant wasn't very communicative - he just looked at the control box, took the note and then nodded, closing the door.

***

The older man was back two days later; the bike was still there. He rang the bell. Music was playing in the house so he knocked loudly. After a few seconds, once more the sound of stairs being used was evident and once more the door was opened. For several seconds they looked at each other...

'Ah, sorry, no, didn't find it,' said the occupant guardedly. Bob Shape knew he wouldn't because there wasn't one to be found. The caller thanked him knowing he probably hadn't bothered to look, then said:-

'Actually, love your bike...if you wouldn't mind - may I take a look? Just love these machines. I noticed it when I called the other day. I've got a bike myself, a *Triumph*.'

Well yes, he had a bike, but not like this obviously powerful example, however, it was something to talk about. This resulted in the occupant melting a little and engaging in minor chat with the caller.

'I have three bikes,' was the surprising admission. 'Got this one a few months ago. It depends on my mood which one I take out each day,' he said with a gleam in his eyes.

'Ah yes,I know the feeling; all the leathers...?'

'Absolutely - all the gear,' he said as they moved round the side towards a small lean-to garage. Inside, the older man appraised the scene which included the other bikes.

Then he said nodding, 'Wow, nice collection, quite a few quid here eh?' It was noticed that Motorbike man's pallor suddenly underwent a small change. The caller continued, 'If you don't mind me asking, what is it you actually do...apart from scamming old ladies out of their life-savings?'

It took 2 seconds of shocked silence...and the 'older' gent knew immediately that they had their man, whose face went deathly pale. Before the scammer could say anything, Bob continued:-

'Before you do anything, we know your 'handle' - we will *always* know your handle and location...we know everything about you, you squirmy little shit. You might think you're clever and covering all your tracks but we're cleverer...how do you think we found you here...? Now this is what you're going to do Mr Motorbike man...' The occupant was about to turn to leave his lean-to when he was suddenly paralysed by a shock, collapsing to the floor and then lying there prostrate, staring along the concrete floor, the taste of blood on his lips.

The caller moved closer then leaned down to him. 'As I said, this is what you're going to do, and I know you can hear me...' he said as pulled out a huge syringe, making sure that the prostrate motor-bike man could see it...

***

'So what happened?' asked Dave when they were next together.

'When he realised I could kill him, at any time, he took notice, especially with my syringe in evidence. He no longer has his bikes, he actually had four bikes, and I filmed his 'office' for insurance. Managed to get quite a few thousand for the bikes which will go to a certain old lady...it was my magic glove that did the trick...helped along with a nice large needle.'

'What you might call a result!' Dave responded.

'Ah, but that's not all. Just as I left I punched him on the nose...hard - a real gusher, and a few teeth too! I said, "You can of course go to the police, but somehow I don't think you will," I told him. I also said that if he had any spare cash left over, to get a dentist to fix his recently rearranged teeth, the ones I had rearranged!'

Dave laughed. Which 'face' did you have for this?'

'Middle-aged and quite ugly, in fact very ugly! Also had to have a face for Josh, just in case; fixed him up to look like *Alfred E Newman*; remember him?' Both laughed.

'Oh my God – that takes me back. You're quite *Mad* you know that!!' Dave responded.

***

'Any news re Julie?' Bob asked yet again...with the same answer - no luck, but he would keep asking, he was not going to give up on this lady.

'It's that lump of Kryptonite she carries around with her Dad.'

She was frequently on Bob's mind these days.

67 Burglaries

'There's a bloke coming out of jail soon. Don't know if you remember him, some low-life called Michael Fenwick who has been in and out of jail over the years for 'this and that', with over 67 burglaries to his name...and guess what?'

'What?' Bob looked up at him.

'You're gonna like this - believe it or not, one of his past victims was the old lady, the lady who was scammed, the one you've just helped out, the one whose hubby fought in the Korean War who passed away recently.'

'Ah, both robbed *and* scammed - suppose it's the same thing really. What are the chances of that? So the poor old bird lives her life, builds up her little nest-egg, looks forward to a retirement with the old man, maybe occasional holidays only for low-life scum, *two* low-life scums, to destroy her dreams. I take it he's not far from here then; give me the details of this Fenwick...definitely prepared to travel far to sort him...all the misery he's caused. His days are numbered.

Burglary really is awful, a stranger in your home rifling through your castle, through your personal effects; and from what you tell me – sixty seven houses; he'll just carry on, he won't stop, it's all he knows; a drain on society. I'm always prepared to give someone a second chance, maybe a third, but that many, sixty-seven! I'll sort out this bastard. It's not as if he's hungry and is stealing baked beans, is it.'

***

Fenwick's operating area was forty miles away. Bob would have to make more than one journey for him. Subsequent surveillance told Bob that his favourite watering hole was *The Red Lion,* a lively aspiring working-class meeting place that also attracted local employees and management, who would drop in after work for a glass or two before going home.

Bob went in to assess. Three separate bars and an eating area made up the establishment, and although it was generally quite well appointed, he could see that one area was likely to be the 'spit & sawdust' section. However, he was surprised to spot his man Fenwick deep in conversation with two well-heeled looking couples, judging from their dress. With a small glass of beer and a magazine he spent thirty minutes listening-in innocently, and soon realised that it was part of this man's modus operandi; he was doing a verbal shake-down of potential victims via pleasant banalities, no doubt to find out their worth...and where they might live.

Bob Shape noted that Fenwick was also quite well dressed and a smoker, of all-sorts, judging by the whiff he caught off the man as he passed by to take a drag outside. Not quite as tall as himself, he was of slim build...which made sense really considering what he did for a pass-time...no Billy Bunter here squeezing through cat-flaps!

***

He left having obtained the measure of his man, but waited outside in his car and when Fenwick emerged, followed him to a house which turned out not to be his...probably.

'Ah, he's shacked up with some lady, perhaps his alibi,' Bob said to himself. He took note of the address and sent a message back to Josh to find out who lived at this house. Indeed, Josh came back with 'Mattie Hogan'. So he's shacked up there with Mattie; but Bob wasn't bothered where exactly our prolific burglar lived...this address was as good as any. He hung around for a while to see where he actually called home, but it looked like Fenwick was staying put for the night, he'd have to come back another day, so departed.

***

It actually cost Bob Shape three round trips but for 'Mr All those burglaries' but it was going to be worth it. He did not bother to trace Fenwick to his own digs, let's face it, a nice warm bed, a woman...better than doss-down digs that he probably lived in, Shape surmised. No competition.

***

After the leaving the *Red Lion* he followed the prolific burglar part of the way back to his fancy piece's address and anticipating where he was going to finish up, arrived close to the house a couple of minutes earlier than him. It was now fairly dark.

The house was part of a terraced row with open-fronted gardens but with front door and open porch; hers was at the end. As Fenwick walked up to the front door, a dark figure stepped up behind him.

'Excuse me, if you're going in, this is addressed to the woman who lives here I believe; can you give it to her please,' said the dark figure.

Fenwick pulled up, obviously taken unawares - and surprised at the sudden presence seemingly from nowhere. In the gloom, he made out an outstretched arm that appeared to offer him a letter. As he paused and peered closely at what he was being given, he muttered, reluctantly, 'Okay mate...' and took the letter and continued towards the house while turning away.

Fatal.

The stranger who proffered the letter, and who was also sporting what appeared to be a walking stick, stepped closer and having assured Fenwick's identity, prodded him with the stick. Fenwick recoiled, staggered a little sideways, desperately fumbling around for support, and failing in this, sagged to the ground, his limbs jerking and quivering – as the stranger mumbled something along the lines of – 'Your burglary days are over sunshine.' Another shot followed from the walking stick...ketamine this time but Fenwick had already lost his faculties as he sank down.

His assailant moved to reposition him in a sitting position within the porch, practically out of sight. Quickly and deftly, Shape placed a few items in Fenwick's hands and then his clothing and one near his semi-conscience body...all paraphernalia that would make any investigation an immediate connection to a life associated with drugs. With prints of course.

The dose Shape had administered would normally take down a Zebra so slim-built, weedy Fenwick didn't stand a chance.

That's how his girl found him first thing in the morning as it was getting light. Her scream was heard all the way along the street.

***

As expected, the police surmised yet another tragic drug-related death. All the prints traced from the evidence at the scene belonged to Fenwick, and items of jewellery were found in his back-pack, no doubt some of the booty from the previous night's 'work'.

In some quarters, the police considered this to be a positive result, notwithstanding the amount of paperwork it generated, but looking at his record...

'No more burglaries for him - and for us of course,' said the Inspector.

Bob knew it wouldn't have taken long on the police grapevine for Dave to get the news. Dave nodded and smiled when they met up again, an acknowledgement of another 'wrong 'un' put away, before they began to chat and sip their drinks.

A Double Killing – She began to cry

Bob was now quite used to the way Dave passed his info, usually opening with the same words… '-you may want to look at this..' or ' seen this Bob? Or 'check this out.' And so it came to pass…

***

'Yes…another one Bob; you might want to look at this…big news right now,' said Dave, passing Bob Shape a scrap of paper with an address on it. 'It's the address of a link; you won't like it,' he added.

'Another scumbag, another terrible deed unpunished by any chance?' asked Bob. 'You always give me bad news…and work,' as he chuckled.

'Worse…' Dave had nodded.

***

It was at times like this when Bob wondered how much danger Dave might be exposing himself to with respect to his own job, his own security…the risks he must be taking to make available and furnish Bob with the snippets of intelligence; how does he get it - his 'info'? Does he have colleagues - or his own *Serpico* on the inside helping him? Feeling bold one day - he did not want to pry too much, he tackled Dave on the matter:-

'Bob, you don't have to worry about me at all…I promise you that,' he had responded. There the matter had rested.

When he returned home he fired up his lap-top and opened up the link from the scrap of paper Dave had passed to him. A name popped up with a big picture.

Charles Brentford. A double killer...of children.

Bob hadn't noticed; his daughter had quietly walked into the room towards him, coming from behind.

'Who's that Daddy?' Lynda asked looking at the screen.

He was taken unawares whilst browsing...black-and-white pictures of two kids on the screen which was accompanied by a sub-title, "*Families of murdered children shock*". He quickly shut his computer, momentarily surprised but also annoyed with himself for exposing her to the headline.

There was silence between them for several seconds. Should he, or should he not expose her further to the sad tale of two grieving mothers who had lost their kids to a vicious murderer. He decided on the former.

An infamous double killing decades ago...the murderer had accosted the two children, a young lad of eight and a pretty girl of fifteen - they lived on the same street - both on their way together to a choir rehearsal. The killer had punched the young lad unconscious then raped the girl before strangling them both.

A true monster. There was a picture of him...Charles Brentford his name.

Described as being a tall, a powerfully built man with a swart, cruel face that was nevertheless not ill-favoured. This was how he used to look over 30 years ago before he was caught.

Bob sat Lynda down and related the the whole sorry saga. However, when he told her that he was in fact being released soon, a middle-aged man now, Lynda cried out.

'Oh no Daddy...oh no, oh no, he can't! Why, how can he come out? He looks horrible daddy.' Tears were forming on her cheeks as she began to cry. Her reaction brought tears to his eyes too.

Dave's 'inside' information contained not only the man's probable new name and identity but also likely locations where he might end up living, all very sensitive information not even the normal police would know about - only the 'authorities'. And perhaps a young lad named Josh.

Bob comforted his daughter. 'Don't you worry your pretty little head my darling.' He too had wondered how this man could be released.

'"He's done his time...he's no longer a threat..."' were all mealy words spouted by the Parole Board, and others who should have known better.

Which meant the man's fate was sealed.

...and members of the Parole Board frightened...frightened because their cover was blown, their computers hacked as a result of one member of the Parole Board's name being revealed...by Dave.

***

Josh had gone to work on it; suffice to say it did not take long before all the names of the Parole Board became known to Robert Shape, including some contact addresses. He didn't need to know, or get into and amongst their database workings - just knowing their addresses and family details was sufficient.

'What does a Parole Board do Dad?' Josh.

'Well hopefully, you'd think they're there to keep real nasty people, killers, especially child-killers, in jail - forever, away from the likes of you and me.' He paused before continuing, 'It's there to protect the public from those who are about to leave prison...to see if they are still dangerous or not, whether they can safely be released into the community Lynda. It sits as a court and makes risk assessments which, we are informed, are rigorous, fair and timely, based on information supplied by the prisoner, the prison and probation service and other expert witnesses.

'Unfortunately, and as you can read almost daily, thugs and killers who have already killed once, have been released only to carry on their thuggery and killing. This particular one, him in the papers who is coming out, should have been strung-up a long time ago.' Bob also thought strongly that there should be consequences regarding decisions made...when more crimes are committed by those previously released...

Freedom

One can imagine his thoughts reader...as Charles Brentford stepped out into freedom after all the years inside. A sky - instead of a ceiling - with fluffy clouds floating, drifting slowly across the blue expanse. And a breeze across his face too. Fresh air at last.

However, not quite *totally* free...he was electronically tagged. He was also banned from going near relatives of his victims and faced restrictions on using the internet.

Accompanied by members of 'the authorities', none of them in uniform, they quickly made their way to the waiting vehicle that would whisk him away to a temporary address, a probation hostel, next to unsuspecting families who would have absolutely no idea who their new neighbour might be, before moving on once more to take up residence in his new accommodation, along with his new name, the name of Mr. Astley.

'Nobody will know your name will they.' It was a statement from his current controller. '...and that's how we want to keep it, eh?' Brentford nodded. He was thinning on top, wrinkled across his pale countenance and eyes that darted hither and thither, face wrinkled...considerably.

***

Bob Shape didn't have a recent picture but certainly had the new address so he familiarised himself with the immediate surroundings - the shops and general layout, especially both the local newsagent and Post Office, to which he would frequent for odds and ends, but never dressed as, or looking like 'Robert Shape' who had to take up temporary residence for a few days over a hundred miles away from his own home.

Soon, Bob began to see what the new-look Brentford...now Astley, looked like. The man had been inside for over thirty years. Indeed, the new hair-piece and tint Brentford now sported was quite becoming thought Shape, as he watched Brentford make his way along the street.

'Need a plan,' Bob said to himself.....

***

The woman approaching the pedestrian crossing had a considerable stoop and was barely able to shuffle along as she leant onto and clutched her trolley like grim death, her walking aid - one of those contraptions you could sit on if need be; so it had to be sturdy, it had to be stable...not too lightweight, the essential metal work substantial.

Such was her stoop, the poor dame was almost bent double and her choice of clothes didn't help the overall picture; a loosely hung brown coat which was probably too thick for the weather and an old beret; but one could imagine her in her youth, she must have been tall in her day when younger, standing straight, proud and upright, perhaps pretty, which would make her of similar height to perhaps other people we know of, or read about.

A strange sight and shape was she.

***

The pedestrians had gathered on both sides of the controlled zebra crossing waiting for the little green man, endless traffic moving past.

My, it was busy at the junction! Really crowded.

The lights changed and the crowds, which included the shuffling dame, surged across the road - well, some surged while others took their time - Mums and Dads holding children's hands while yapping orders, and of course, the more elderly.

After the exodus of most of the pedestrians from the crossing - and as the lights changed back to red once more - new crowds formed on the pavements...except that one amongst the first group had been rather slow in making it across, a man...a man who appeared to move aimlessly after having reached the other side, his staggering and erratic movements causing consternation amongst other pedestrians.

They tried to skirt round him. Words were exchanged. The man finally reached an entrance of sorts - he cared not of what kind - to some establishment adjacent to the crossing, slowly sagging down against the wall until he was sitting, knees slightly bent out in front, head lolling from side to side, his hair-piece now askew.

It was then that a member of the public realised that the man was in a poor way and called for help.

***

The person with the stoop and heavy coat eventually, after an appropriate interval and having moved away, became upright and uncoated after having collapsed and folded his walking 'companion' - a companion quite modified although you would hardly notice the difference reader, to dispense almost silently, a slow death...a small 'crete bolt fired at close range, tipped with a substance which was definitely not agreeable to the human body.

Did the man know he was going to die? Well no, not at first - not with thoughts of all that freedom ahead of him to enjoy rattling around in his mind; but he would have felt a prick, a sting on his thigh, maybe an insect? He felt it just as the green man had appeared as he was about to step out to cross the road, however, and within about five, maybe ten seconds, when his legs no longer seemed to obey his mind he would have began to worry.

A form of sanctuary beckoned - an entrance to a building which he made for while attempting, without success to scratch his leg but his arms would no longer move either as he wished them to move. He managed to reach the doorway. Just.

Alas, it was all too late for the man who now slumped in a doorway propped against the wall.

***

So ended the life of the man who used to be called Charles Brentford - the man who had ended the lives of two children decades ago - the man who had never uttered, or shown, any remorse.

Now he was really free...of life. And the world was free of him.

***

A nod of acknowledgement was forthcoming from Dave later.

'I don't know about Serpico Dave, but I probably looked more like Serpico's Mum in that role!'

***

Robert Shape thought how he would have loved to be a fly on the wall for the conversation between the Home secretary and the Chief Police Commissioner.

When the news broke it was headline story in most of the press. The police were furious…

'How did someone get to find out…?' etc., etc. 'Who leaked it?' 'Find the mole'.

Naturally, there were those who claimed 'just desserts' and 'justice properly served…in the end'. But there was also elements of the establishment - usually liberal - who thought it disgraceful and that no one currently serving in jail for murder right now, but who might be due out on the parole board's say-so would be safe if confidential information could be compromised, and not guaranteed to remain just that – confidential.

Excellent, thought Shape…therefore keep killers inside.

The Suspicions of a garage mechanic

At Mal's farm...

Karl was in a contemplative mood. Should he confide in Josh's dad of his suspicions about Mallock and how he might be using the garage as a front for his dealings with drugs - and perhaps *hiding a secret*...

***

'Josh, your Dad's a good egg isn't he.' It was a statement, but it took Josh a couple of seconds to separate out Karl's meaning as they'd just been feeding the chickens. Josh was like that.

'Oh yes...he's brill, a star,' he replied with a big smile.

'Any chance I could see him sometime? I have an idea for him, see what he thinks about it.'

The request was a camouflage. Even with Josh, Karl would not confide or seek advice on the matter forefront in his mind right now, even though he'd struck up quite a friendship with Josh and to a lesser extent his Dad, in who Karl recognised a sympathetic character - one who was likely to provide the best, almost 'elder' advice.

'Well, he picks me up later; is it about cars?' asked Josh in all innocence, knowing of Karl's garage job.

'Could be.'

When Bob Shape duly turned up Karl was able to sideline him for a moment or two. Bob realised that he was eager to talk - that this was a little bit more than just a friendly chat that Karl wanted...there was obviously something he wanted to get off his chest and knowing of his association with the Mallock family and his garage job, said:-

'If you want a quiet word, there's a park bench...' and proceeded to arrange a lunchtime chat with Karl on the same bench he used occasionally, that same bench where the strange young lady would appear and talk to him.

On that bench...

Karl related the background events along with his suspicions to Bob Shape...

'So you believe that it was Mallock's car that was the hit and run vehicle?' Bob said.

Karl nodded and went on to outline the events in more detail of his boss's return that day including, with his 'mechanical' intuition, about car damage and cows...augmented by his subsequent discovery of the name-tag in the wing-mirror and then, of course, his follow-up archive search of the news. Karl produced the faded name-tag.

'Well the name is almost a fit Karl...' *Carr'* – but it looks like the tag is incomplete.'

Karl went on to explain the events in greater detail and how the whole saga had sat in his brain, troubling his conscience...always there, pushing other thoughts away. He needed to tell somebody as a means of sharing the burden.

His own lone parent, his father, who had brought him up was definitely not of the sympathetic kind and over the months Karl had come to appreciate how open and welcoming Josh's family was; so it was to Bob Shape that Karl sough solace and advice.

They were in talk for at least half an hour when Karl suddenly took his attention elsewhere - something was distracting him, had made him look over Bob's shoulder.

'There's a lady over there waving at us,' he said to Bob Shape. 'Do you know her?'

Bob Shape followed his gaze. Across the green in the park was *that* lady....*Stella*. She was vigorously waving and smiling at them.

'*Stella*!' Bob Shape called out in surprise.

'Hello – I saw you there. I can't stop,' she called. 'Busy girl that I am,' and turned to go away saying, 'I'm off to join someone - someone special. Bye, bye. Bye bye,'

'Anybody I know *Stella*?' Bob responded, even as she continued on her way. Now why did he ask that he thought?

'Yes. Bye,' as her voice faded as she moved off.

Bob could not tell you why but he suddenly felt saddened; he wanted to talk to her but she was now headed away, mingling amongst others in the park. He stared awhile...another strange encounter with this oddball and mystifying woman who just now, looked so happy. He also felt that he would never see her again.

'Who was she?' Karl asked, who was also bemused by her appearance. 'Very pretty,' he added. 'She seems to know you.'

'That's the problem Karl, apart from her first name, I haven't a clue who she is.' He promised himself that one of these days 'I'm going to find out more about this *Stella*.'

***

The pair resumed their conversation. Bob said he'd come up with a plan. 'With respect to Mallock, leave it with me Karl.'

However, the *Stella* distraction that had intruded upon their conversation resulted in Bob completely forgetting about Dave, so intrigued was he with the encounter just as before, that he could not shake the event from his mind.

***

However, Karl's revelations provided Robert Shape with more ammunition - just what he needed - the motivation was already there, but first he had another matter on his hands right now - a problem with Travellers. He would deal with them first and save the best for last - Mallock & Co. He realised of course that each time he promised himself he would do this, something else cropped up to get in the way…and what else was it he was supposed to do…or ask, or find out?

'One day…one day,' he told himself.

Travellers

They sent the young ones into the shop first - the young ones who helped themselves to whatever was easily to hand - sweets, little brooches and other items of jewellery, an assortment of knick-knacks worth pennies, plus several bottles of perfume...some of which was definitely *not* worth just pennies.

The lady on the till had quickly spotted a looming threat and called for back-up, her husband, who duly arrived like the 7th Cavalry and asked, when he saw what the kids were up to, to 'please leave'.

And it was all on camera.

Thirty minutes later a crowd had formed outside the shop, some of them tinkering with the owner's car parked outside his shop. Then they, and this included the original young ones, went inside to further torment the shop-staff.

The 7th Cavalry came once more and tried to help and control the situation to stop the pilfering but in vain, as he tried to move them all out of the shop. Voices were raised, bottles of perfume emptied or smashed, or both, and eventually, the till rifled as the owners lost the battle to restore any order.

The police were called but fists flew before they arrived resulting in the 7th Cavalry falling to the ground, smacking his head on the edge of a hard unit on the way down.

Now an ambulance was needed. Quite rapidly the shop emptied...of both people...and goods, as soon as the sound of approaching sirens was heard but not before a bottle went through the shop-front window...and the tyres of the owner's car were slashed.

'Yes, they were 'Travellers' - that give the other Travellers a bad name, and who took over a park, and who brazenly accused the shop owner of molesting their kids and wanted to press charges,' said Dave.

'However, some CCTV evidence...not clear it has to be said, pointed the finger at the travellers. Anyway, certain members of the 'Travelling Community' have been arrested. The shop-owner is in hospital with a swelling of the brain. You can imagine what his poor lady is going through and all from nothing to extreme violence in less than twenty minutes.'

'Yes, I remember; and you told me that they, the two who have been accused, are getting oodles of Legal Aid... just to rub it in. Do you know who...' but before he'd finished, Dave was already passing over a note with the solicitor's names on it - *Hardy & Sons*.

'Thanks Dave...this is just not right. Just wanton vandalism and violence by a group who consider themselves outside the law...with no prospect of ever seeing the inside of a prison cell. Untouchable. Be most grateful if you could forward me the CCTV footage. It's time I put my drones to good use...'

Dave knew that something was going to happen, and looked forward to the 'how'.

***

The shop-owner – our Mr 7th Cavalry - eventually came out of hospital but was never going to be the same man, the same loving, hard-working husband, again...not with the brain damage sustained during the ructions when the travellers had practically ransacked the shop.

His wife and their daughter valiantly soldiered on, displaying an indomitable spirit in the face of outrageous provocation from the criminal element within the mobile, caravan community that saw themselves as a peace-loving minority, constantly under harassment by the authorities...in their view.

'So thieving's okay then? No, sorry, no excuse for bad manners, then wanton violence - but they'll find out that *my* bad manners will be *really* bad! Who's the leader...the top banana of this travelling bunch?'

'Somebody called Fred Goyshin.'

A Field

The 'Travellers – yes, the very same group that had caused chaos in the shop, moved into a field used for general grazing although at the time they moved into it, there were no farm animals there...just acres of open space. An easy target. Perfect.

Well-practised, they had quickly cut and removed the gate lock, letting it drop into the mud.

'That's how we found it M'lord,' should they ever be questioned, '...it wasn't locked'.

Within half an hour the field was awash with a variety of caravans hitched up to Land Rovers and a few other heavy-duty SUVs. There was a mixture of large mobile homes and caravans moved in to strategic locations, some quite high-end. A couple of tents were pitched, not small ones either. Then tables and chairs proliferated in clusters around the homes festooned with large Beat-Boxes. Very soon, the aroma of cooked food began to permeate...along with the clink of drink, glasses - and laughter. They were set up for the long-haul it seemed.

The gates were closed, relocked with new locks - and guarded. Nobody was going to come in without their say-so. And should any of them decide to venture out for any reason, there was always a sizeable, masculine presence that remained - in case of trouble from any locals.

***

But not everybody was laughing of course...in fact the opposite. Soon the owner of the pasture, the law and a few ramblers were at the gates remonstrating to open up and for the Travellers to clear off. It did not result in any violence but voices were raised with an implied threat or promise that should the locals continue to harass the travellers, concrete mixers would come out to really change the landscape with hardcore and proper parking areas.

The press got hold of this, which meant of course that so did the 'street-cleaner'...who, along with many others fumed at this banditry, perpetrated by those who it seemed had no respect for any rules. And of course the law would, might, eventually win through, but the process in achieving this often moved at a speed that made a glacier look like an Olympic sprinter.

***

This situation was not to be endured; Bob Shape was soon on the phone...to Mal.

'Do you know this farmer who has been invaded Mal?'

He knew of him, no more, although in fact had spoken to him once or twice at country fairs but he was reachable in terms of distance so Bob Shape suggested they venture that way together to see what they could do to help.

When they went, Bob Shape brought a drone along. When they approached he area it was obvious that many had gathered in and around the field in question...police, local press and a few spectators, so they moved to a lay-by several hundred yards away.

'Can't get in the usual way - both ends and gates heavily manned by the travellers. But look over there,' he said pointing to half-way down one side of the field...opposite to where all the the homes were set up. 'There's a large copse or small wood; I wonder what's on the other side - let's have a look,' he said as he launched the drone, sending it in the direction of the wooded area.

Later, they analysed the drone footage.

The field the Travellers had taken over was actually part of several fields and other enclosures that surrounded the wood.

'Quite a few Hectares there,' Bob said to Mal. 'Who's the farmer?'

'Jason Tuttle - and I do know he has quite a few cows...a lot more than I have.'

'This is interesting...just look close up at the video; see - you can just make out through the trees and foliage a path or track that goes from one side of the wood to the other...straight through it. He must know this but we'll remind him all the same because I have a plan. If you can come back with me and Mr Tuttle, we can turn the tables on the Travellers; they probably won't know about the wood...and its path.'

'Sure, and I'll get my brother to hold the fort while we're at it.'

A lovely day for mischief

Just as the weather was perfect on the day of the travellers' invasion, so it was equally gorgeous as Bob and Mal positioned themselves up near the area where there was still media and public interest in the illegal occupation of the farmer's field, both ends remaining well-guarded as the legal wheels moved slowly.

***

From an advantage point the two of them watched and waited. Once again the Travellers had wasted no time in taking advantage of the fine weather...tables and chairs, sun-loungers, magazines and the odd football appeared...and predictably, BBQs. Hardly a care in the world...

Bob looked at his watch and nodded to Mal; they then turned and focussed their eyes upon the edge of the wood opposite the parked caravans across the open space, where, if one looked closely, one might be able to discern an opening in the trees.

At the same time, one may have also been able to detect different sounds emanating from within the wood, but not from twittering, chirping birds - and perhaps becoming louder...the sound of larger creatures approaching.

Sure enough, and without any fanfare, farmer Jason Tuttle emerged from an opening in the copse at the head of some of his cows. He kept walking and the cows kept coming, more and more. At the same time another man, and this would be one of Mr Tuttle's sons, appeared by the perimeter fence on the other side across the green and very close to the caravans, making a call, a special call; he was 'calling the cows to grain' - and nothing was going to come in-between this horde of hungry beasts and their food on hearing the familiar voice calling them and who, almost as one, began to trot in the direction of the invitation.

The 'caller', armed with several buckets of feed and helped by other family members and farm-hands, spread out along the perimeter, also making a racket while emptying the grain feed over the fence.

It must have taken the Travellers all of about two minutes wondering what was going on before they realised what was afoot and springing into confused and noisy action. Voices were raised, with shouting and bellowing coming from the stunned but hapless sun-bathers as chaos reigned. Men, women, young and old, rushed around hither and thither in order to stem the tide - as King Knut had tried centuries ago with the sea - of these farmyard creatures, to prevent the cows rampaging and running amok through the motley collection of caravans and other vehicles. Sun-loungers and other house-hold goodies including TVs, tables and chairs were flattened as washing lines were trampled in into the ground.

And yet more cows were arriving...egged on by Mr Tuttle in a Pied-Piper, fatherly fashion.

***

Just to retrace reader...when shown the aerial footage and the suggestion made to him, Mr Tuttle had remarked that he always knew there was route through the small wood, but for people, not cows, so had never considered it as part of any solution to his current predicament.

'I've even used that path in the wood myself on occasion...but not for the movement of my animals. I was worried about them wandering away amongst the trees and losing them. It was always easier to go round the longer way round via the gate where I could keep my eye on them,' he had said. 'But of course, leading them by using grain as a bait, I suppose I could make it work and lead them through.' He was won over and decided to do just as Bob and Mal had suggested.

And so it came to pass.

***

Mal and Bob watched the unfolding carnage...tents were soon down as the cows trampled and uprooted the rigging ropes. This was shortly followed by two of the cows, no doubt irritated from having tent ropes tangled around their legs and hindering them, tried to shake them off, moving in a crazy manner...and then crashing into a Range Rover.

This was not all; watching the almost riotous events - and fearing for the safety of one of the caravans, one man tried to tow it away from the marauding herd, only for him to reverse it into a neighbours. It was like slapstick...sometimes hilarious. As the numbers of cows increased, with no sign of the carnage abating, so did the panic of the Travellers, to the end that it was 'all hands to the pump', resulting in those who were previously guarding the gates, leaving their posts to assist their fellow Travellers.

It was not long before the unguarded gates were open, with a message from Mr Tuttle to any Traveller who might listen:-

'This is my field and the cows are staying.'

Realising that to stay would only result in more damage, the Travellers hastily retrieved some scattered effects, hitched up an almost totalled Mini and limped off through the wide-open gate with cursing, threatening words.

Spectators peering over the gate had a ringside seat. And cheered.

***

'So what was the damage - what did you see,' Jason Tuttle asked, knowing what cows and other heavy beasts were capable of. They had filmed it all - with both air and ground shots.

Bob Shape and Mal looked at each other, almost answering in unison...

'We saw a smashed up Mini...really smashed up, probably 'totalled', two other damaged vehicles - one of them a battered Jag - with fairly new plates, a home that you won't want to live in for a while...its side was staved, both tents down....and left behind. No doubt there was more which we didn't see,' Mal added.

***

Embarrassingly for the Travellers, they actually attempted to invoke the assistance of the police who were not really interested. The leader of the Traveller family, Fred Goyshin remonstrated with the law...in vain. More curses followed, fists shaken. To rub it in, the groups of local and other spectators clapped as the intruders departed.

However...when they had all left and as Mr

Tuttle looked around his field, he was both shocked and angry to see what rubbish had been left behind. There indeed had been an attempt at laying a hard-standing, concrete parking area.

'It's as though they don't know the meaning, or the concept of dustbins and refuse collection or general cleanliness; it's absolutely disgusting! And why? I've had Travellers actually come and ask me if they could come and stay on my vacant fields...polite, with no trouble at all - well-behaved and tidy, so why couldn't this lot do the same, eh?'

'Well, I know that they aren't all like this thank God, however with this lot who are giving the rest a bad name, I have an idea...another idea,' said Mal.

***

So they proceeded to collect and bag every every last bit of rubbish they could find...every last discarded chicken leg, half-empty pickle jars, a discarded fat-covered frying pan and a few used toiletry items of which they could only guess their previous use...and shudder - soiled nappies being amongst all the rubbish.

All the rubbish dumped in the field by the Travellers was meticulously collected, bagged and itemised by the Tuttle family, ably assisted by many friends and members of the local population who were simply horrified at the way the countryside had been treated.

All collected.
All bagged.
Ready to go.

The Gravy on the potatoes...

Bob Shape and colleagues had tracked Mr Fred Goyshin and his travellers until they had taken up residence a few miles away on a lay-by that was part of a now defunct road but wasn't sure for how long.

As Shape wondered how they might be able to put their plan into action in what looked like such an exposed location with little cover - just some low bushes and saplings - farmer Jason Tuttle, the victim in this saga said that where ever they were - and to carry out 'the plan' - he could create a diversion with a pony & trap he had; this was important as they knew that the Travellers rarely left their homes unattended; there was usually somebody left behind in attendance.

'And see those few saplings behind where they've parked...?' Jason said...' ...well, on the other side is where the very old previous track used to run,'

'Hmm, once again, the countryside could serve us well,' Bob and Mal observed.

After a day or two of observation of the Travellers site, a pattern emerged of their routine of 'comings & goings'...and the next plan was put into operation.

***

A pony-and-trap clipped-clopped and trundled into the Travellers lay-by, its driver dressed up in an outrageous and real gaudy outfit - like a court jester of past times, although this one had a stove pipe firmly clenched between his teeth, a top-hat perched at an angle and sporting a huge smile as he tinkered with a banjo.

Additionally, he was also accompanied by three Border Collies, all sat obediently on the trap.

It did not take long. Amongst the Travellers the pony & trap was soon the centre of attraction; the weather favoured the mood, there was a light breeze with only a few wisps of white passing clouds and quite warm.

Caravan doors opened as curious faces peered out and for those already sat outside smoking, they paused in their deliberations, slowly getting to their feet to view this arrival in the lay-by. Children made a bee-line for the pony...which ensured the womenfolk followed.

'What's it called mister?' they cried, pointing at the pony, the attraction of children to animals universal.

'*Usain*,' answered the jovial man while plucking a few chords and laughing. The kids laughed too...a fast donkey; and the jester had also come prepared, dolling out a few sweets. The adults watched with suspicion at first then slowly migrated towards the attraction. They looked over the jester's trap and its motive force, *Usain*, without recognising the dressed-up owner...one of Mr Tuttle's cow-hands.

They talked about feed, traps, trailers, bells, accordions and of course dogs, which the kids could not stop patting, fondling and stroking.

Ten minutes passed. 'Sorry folks...gotta go now,' announced the court jester suddenly. 'Long way to go and *Usain'll* be getting hungry.'

The pony & trap moved off...considerably quicker than it had arrived...

***

The Travellers began to return to their previous activities; a minute or two later, screams and shouting emanated from one, then two, of the caravans. Men rushed to the source of the shrieks...

When the first of the women had stepped back inside their homes left unattended for the short duration of entertainment they had enjoyed with the jester, they were confronted by disaster; old stained divans and settees, litter-strewn carpets, beds and kitchens overflowing with rubbish accompanied with the inevitable and pungent, foul odour. Even the remnants of the concrete-laying found its way inside the caravans.

And pinned on each front door... "All yours, I believe...that you left behind."

By the time the organising elders had put two and two together....and how they had been duped, the jester and trap was well away by now but no chances were taken; two large tractors had suddenly turned up from the main road for a quick smoke, effectively sealing off the lay-by, by accident of course, thus preventing any Traveller vehicles wanting to go and give chase in a hurry.

As you can probably guess reader, Mr Shape and friends had made good use of those ten minutes of court-jester time, sneaking unobserved from the foilage on the blind-side into the open caravans to 'return' the rubbish...as the man on the trap was taking the Travellers' attention.

'Most enjoyment I've had for ages,' remarked Jason Tuttle.

'Me too,' replied the other two in unison.

Hardy & Sons

The Travellers choice of lawyers was a local firm who were well-known for taking the side of those they considered 'oppressed', such as some minority groups, claimants against police brutality and alleged Racism - all those up against what *Hardy& Sons* considered the Fascist State - and all authorities associated with it. It was usually the first port of call for those that generally sat on the left or on the anarchistic parts of the political spectrum.

And the firm had done well out it.

However, in the case of the targeted shop and the hospitalisation of its owner...and the current harassment of his wife, there were many who took a completely dim view of the whole saga, not least the use of tax-payer's cash for legal aid to the Travellers, the same Travellers that could afford to run cars like Mercs, Jags and other up-market vehicles, Range Rovers amongst them, to continue to make the shop owner's lives a misery.

The Travellers were now kicking up a rumpus, via *Hardy & Sons,* regarding their humiliating retreat from the farmer's property...witnessed by many.

The farmer Tuttle was furious...so too was Mal Munroe when told.

'We know someone who might be able to help...again,' Mal told him.

Mail

It had gathered behind the Brass-and-Glass doorway of *Hardy & Sons* on the floor as always - the mail. And as always the first job of the day...sort it all out as they were usually inundated, battles to be fought, injustices to be put right.

The staff were busy and the two sons who ably assisted their father in the running of the firm *Hardy & Sons* maintained keen eyes and ears for some juicy calls for help that might come their way, especially if backed up by somebody else's money, namely the public's.

The second son, Harry, went through the motions that morning of sifting the morning's post. A medium-sized envelope took his attention. At first, its contents just induced mild interest, a cover note fronting the package. However, and as he looked at what was behind the note, stopped him in his tracks; the typed note was accompanied by several photos...family photos; *his* family. His *young* family...

...and a picture of his house with his car parked in front.

...further pictures of his kids at the school gates.

...more shots of his wife and kids out shopping.

...and indeed, similar photos of his brother's family.

He read the note, then read it again...

"We too, dislike injustice...the injustice facing the shop-owners who tried to protect their business from pilferers...from those you are now representing. Please do not continue to represent these Travellers. You have a nice house, nice family...so advise not go to the police..."

A cold hand clutched his heart. So courteous the typed message...but it was the photos that emphasised the threat.

***

It was not long before his elder brother turned up in his office, agitated, a worried look on his face while holding up an identical package with identical contents, down to the last photo. He started ranting and raving...

'Who the hell is this...these people...?'

Hardy & Sons had faced threats before - phone calls, emails or just plain verbal abuse...but not like this, a situation that had suddenly placed their families directly in the firing line, down to almost intimate detail, as if 'they' - whoever 'they' were - knew their every step...as if they were *always present*.

'But they've made a mistake bro' because that house is not mine - or yours,' said the younger man pointing at another photo that came with the rest.

***

However, and what the 'elder' did not want to share with his younger brother was the fact that he certainly *did* recognise this 'other' house; it was the home of a widow with whom he had become quite friendly over the last year...perhaps too friendly. And it was his secret...or so he thought up until now.

'Let's speak to Dad...I know he's no fan of the police but even he might want to let them know about this,' said the younger, '...I mean, it's our families we're talking about.'

'No, no...not so hasty,' said the elder brother, fearing the collapse of his marriage should he be exposed.

They'd held a family war-council; voices were raised with much shouting but in the end...and also probably also due to their overall distrust of the police, *not* informing the law won the day, much to the quiet relief of the elder brother.

The Travellers were shocked, then enraged at the sudden drop of support and even resorted to their own verbal threats, while asking why? However, *Hardy & Sons* were not likely to change its mind and put their families at risk...

***

Not too long afterwards, the elder brother turned up to work late one morning sporting a huge shiner and a very scratched face; all he would say in response to the usual looks of concern was that he'd had a family argument - and that that was the end of the matter.
Yes...the wrong photo in the right place reader...

***

It was high fives when Mr Shape and friends - and including a certain Mrs 'Shopkeeper', met up.

'How did you do it?' they asked.

'All down to good intelligence,' Bob replied, silently thanking his lad Josh.

Policewoman Crushed

The policewoman had attempted to question a couple driving erratically and in response, they had driven at her slowly crushing her against her own police car...then drove off, running over her legs as she collapsed.

The two felons, a man and woman and both found to be on cocaine, were eventually traced and arrested. But now they were on bail after having promised to go into a special rehab regime after a short spell in an HM establishment.

That didn't last...they absconded and were out long, long before the unfortunate policewoman had gained proper use of her legs.

***

If you didn't know much about motorbikes you would never suspect that the machine that casually pulled up close to the cocaine couple we have just mentioned, was anything sinister...there were no visible markings on the adapted *Triumph*, no distinguishing colour schemes like a Kawasaki, no name, just a 'variable' plate - and as it was a Saturday afternoon on the high Street, it was busy.

No shots rang out as the high pressure CO_2 contraption mounted on the handlebar fizzed - twice - once for each of the cocaine pair who were just then casually ambling along the pavement, oblivious of their impending fate - these two who had crushed the policewoman. The man on the bike went for the girl first...through her neck, then her accomplice...again through the neck, wanting both to suffer - horribly.

She collapsed, clutching her throat, unable to scream. He, initially pausing at his girl's gasp and apparent and unexpected sagging to her knees, was next. As the man drove off, he vaguely recalled screams and shouts from passers-by but he wasn't worried...he hadn't actually stopped to carry out his deed...just slowed down right close to the pavement, along with a van adjacent to him, nicely timed - such was the traffic.

***

His primary task was the cocaine pair, however, his use of the Triumph he liked to keep to a minimum therefore he had lined up, from his intelligence sources, two other targets of opportunity on the same excursion that day, which resulted in a good tally; two more 'dopes' or dope pushers, were no more, courtesy of a hefty dose of ketamine. Both were easy and unsuspecting targets, each succumbing in a side street; he knew what they looked like and simply shouted 'Hi!' as he approached and drifting slowly by, enjoying the look of surprise on their faces. He paused briefly as he looked into target number one's eyes then further on, paused just to see the first one beginning to fold. He knew the outcome. This he repeated two minutes later with target number two.

***

The deaths of the couple was straight forward, they'd been either shot or stabbed, however, the police couldn't establish by what kind of weapon.

'Could have been something like an ice-pick kind of weapon - a quick strike, in, out, gone,' one detective offered.

'Yeah...but on the High street...? another offered.

Trouble was, no one appeared to have been that close to have carried out that kind of stabbing according to witnesses and the available CCTV. As for the other two other bodies discovered, the police considered it to have been yet another new drug experiment gone wrong...trying a new drug for new 'highs' - in this case ketamine. And just in case, the police looked far and wide for any signs of a dart, with no luck, nor were they expecting to find one,

'Too risky anyway...' it was thought, '...you could easily miss.'

Soon after these events, one of the messages the police received:-

'Two more off the streets....we didn't ask them to take cocaine...and nearly kill & cripple a policewoman.'

Police Matters

'Four! Four dead in the space of one hour....and all within half a mile from each other,' shouted the Chief Inspector. 'What's going on for God's sake?' He was not one to normally bellow but on this occasion, thus did the police inspector berate his staff, and then the world.

Both the Press and the Commissioner had been pressing him hard for answers...and for him to release suitable and soothing statements for the public's consumption from which to take heart.

However, when it transpired that in the following weeks, drug drops and associated business had almost disappeared from the streets, the public shrugged, the consensus being...'Well serves them right...and they're off the street, so no loss.'

***

The Chief Superintendent of the area, angered at the suggestion that somebody was doing what the police should have been doing - namely removing drug-pushers and dealers from the streets of his town, ordered a task force to be set up, to track down whoever was waging this war, whether it be rival gangs, vigilantes or just someone with a grudge? It even led to a suspicion that it was a rogue group of coppers...even an individual copper, carrying out the street 'cleaning'.

'We cannot have this...people settling scores or taking the law into their own hands; not on my patch!' he demanded, ignoring the irony that a result was a result - if it took the 'perps' off the street.

An Encounter

Oh, the vagaries of life! Only this morning had he been thinking of two women - the strange young girl who would suddenly turn up when he was on the park bench; the other was Julie of whom who he was wont to think of more and more these days while trying to ascertain where she lived.

And suddenly, Julie - there she was.

He was in town when he spotted her; a complete surprise to see her again after the months since their parting. She had left with no contact since: not a word. Bob was convinced at the time of their acrimonious parting - he would never forget that slap - that the whole episode had been a misunderstanding and that they had both overreacted. The incident often returned to his thoughts to torture him. And to compound this torture, for some reason that neither he, nor Josh could fathom, Josh had been unable to make his usual and reliable psychic connection to discover where she had moved to.

So he was thrilled to see her...but also apprehensive.

She was just twenty yards away walking in the opposite direction to him, completely unaware it seems of his presence.

'Julie?' he called out hopefully. She stopped and turned.

'Oh, oh Bob.' she answered, taken by surprise, hand to her mouth and then paused. 'Bob please don't, I don't want to get involved,' she added hesitantly. 'Please understand...' She had suddenly stopped mid-sentence, something had caught her attention out of

Bob's view. 'Please leave me alone; I can't explain right now...bye, I must go.'

The irony, 'Is it just me, another woman wanting to get away from me in a hurry?' he mumbled.

Bob wondered what it could have been that had abruptly curtailed Julie's response and had diverted her attention; he looked around to see. He wasn't quite sure but did he briefly catch sight of a departing figure who may, or may not have been, Julie's husband - her ex? It had been some time since he had last seen him so wasn't sure. But perhaps it was this that had frightened Julie away...she too may have caught a glimpse of her 'dearly beloved'.

Bob knew of her unhappy association at the hands of her bullying partner and remembered her attempts to hide her face behind dark glasses at work. He was also aware that they'd separated, that she was living on her own now although he did not know where.

He called out again. She looked over her shoulder while imploring, 'Please Bob, not now. Please go away.' Her words were troubled and she looked most unhappy. As was Bob now.

He was shocked. 'What on earth is going on.....?' he asked himself as he stopped and watched her vanish into another street. Now he was also torn; should he pursue or not, but decided against it, remembering that slap from the past. Dusk had produced an encroaching darkness upon the town so he turned and began to make his way back to the car-park. Before he reached the car-park he was strolling down a connecting alley, deep in thought on what had just transpired.

Seconds later, a voice. Bob turned...it was him; yes, the ex-husband...definitely.

'You, yes you...just stay away from my wife...' he said as somebody else grabbed Bob from behind pinning his arms. The husband came up close, 'If I ever see you within a mile of my wife, I'll have you sorted good and proper.' The words were followed by an explosion in his groin from a swift kick from behind by an unknown assailant. Bob crumpled to the ground in a heap.

'That'll stop him!' said a voice from behind, he wasn't sure whose. It took Bob a minute or so to recover, as he slowly stood up gasping at the pain while leaning against a fence for support; there was no way he could walk normally - just yet. He reflected; of all the times he had been 'out and about' putting the world to rights, he had come out on this day 'naked'...no tools, no kit - no special gear.

No protection.

A lesson here he thought as he took note - the husband had gloated as Bob Shape struggled to stand following the assault.

Julie had received a message on the incident, warning her off from any thoughts of any future liaison and of the consequences, loud and clear. If he could not have her then no one else could and Julie, knowing of his fondness for violence, was afraid for her one-time boss.

Which meant she cared.

***

The next day Julie's ex answered the door and being of the suspicious type, had first peeked through the blinds to see who was calling. It looked safe, an elderly chap wearing a long raincoat stood there expectantly. He didn't recognise him, didn't know him from Adam.

'What the hell does he want?' Julie's ex muttered to himself as he made his way to the front door, the worse for wear after a little celebration last night following the lesson he'd given to Julie's ex-boss.

The man at the door, attired casually but looking somewhat over-dressed in the husband's opinion, was above average height and sporting a slightly weathered, craggy face, conveying the impression of a life hard-lived. He looked almost like a street 'bum'.

'What?' he asked abruptly, displaying his usual wonderful bed-side manner – he knew how to make friends and influence people reader and not being able to help himself, followed up with, 'Bit over-dressed aren't we, it's not *that* cold,' while scrutinising the layers of clothing the old man was wearing.

But 'husband' was mildly surprised at the calm response; he always expected and liked, a spot of 'aggro' - an argument. He'd argue with an empty room if he could..

'About that...' the elderly gent replied quietly, 'You're absolutely right Sir, just let me take off my scarf, I am rather warm. Please forgive me...' he said gently, uttering the words slowly.

The softness off his tone in his reply surprised Julie's ex but the slow movement irritated him.

'Come on mate, what is it you want, why have you called? I don't have all day.' Julie's husband was almost transfixed, perhaps mesmerised now with the slow, deliberate and methodical manner in which the visitor quietly deployed, to undo his Mac, in order to gain access and free the scarf - that scarf he was intent on removing. It was during this movement that the old man had sneaked a look over his shoulder.

All clear.

Then with his Mac now open the old man took hold of one end of his scarf and said:-

'Remember yesterday...?'

'Eh...?' and before he knew it, the scarf was being pulled off the old man's neck and swung. Even in that short space of time, a millisecond perhaps as it arced towards him, Julie's ex realised this scarf was not behaving as a scarf should behave as it came off the neck. It looked more solid, heavier - and dangerous, as it swung round and crashed into the side of his head.

Indeed, at first glance, that's exactly what it had looked like...a scarf, but in fact it hid a narrow canvas bag containing a good collection of beach pebbles and sand, all held in a long seaman's' sock and all stitched within a colourful looking, proper scarf.

Julie's husband went down solidly, a couple of teeth flying as he fell back and crumpled inside his front door, senseless, but who would wake up in hospital with a broken jaw, broken cheek-bone, a black eye and general, severe facial bruising.

**

If you'd asked anybody who the man was at the front door you would have been told - that's if anyone had seen him - that he was not young, that he wore a pale green coat or Mac and sported a flat cap, a black one.

If you'd asked anybody else further along the avenue if they'd 'seen anything', they may have described a man 'of average height, with a mustard coloured coat and wearing an orange hat because as soon as Bob had left the house and turned the corner he flicked his switches as he passed through the plastic bus stop...always difficult to gauge and determine colours and material with the many reflections emanating from glass and plastic – don't we know already. His features and complexion returned and relaxed to a default position.

**

Robert Shape was content. Although not planned, it was another job done...*had* to be done. But would it be enough?

**

However...Julie's husband, when he had occasion to pontificate on his unfortunate encounter with the stranger at his door - *who the hell was he anyway?* - whilst recovering from his battering, slowly began to recall events; it was two words that now floated into his befuddled mind:-

"*Remember yesterday...?*"

He was sure that these were the words his assailant had spoken. And what had happened that certain *yesterday?* Was it connected to the satisfying warning he had administered to Julie's ex-boss? But this guy at the door was completely different - looked nothing like him. It was not him.

Was it?

But the two events must be connected...somehow, he thought. Definitely.

Remember yesterday?

It irritated him...those two words kept coming back - *"Remember yesterday"*. He was not likely to forget; he had finished up with a broken face which took the best part of two months to be put reasonably right again. Someone had to pay. He was sure Julie's ex-boss had a hand in this...he must have had someone else do the attack because it certainly wasn't the boss-Shape-whatshisname, because he would not forget a face. It hadn't been him.

But Julie's ex-husband was a fussy man when his pride came into the equation, but not too fussy about doling out punishment - especially when someone else was carrying out the deed; he would simply do it again, another beating, only harder this time, different - not the genitals but the face, just as his face had been battered, and take satisfaction in watching the proceedings.

So he had resorted to carrying out a little surveillance on Mr. Shape at cease work time and soon had a pattern of his moves which was rather boringly predictable - straight home...he already knew where Shape lived but was looking for any change in his routine - a change that would allow him with his 'heavies' alongside, to strike. Indeed, an opportunity did indeed occur, or at least, a change in the route; in fact it was a visit to a pub.

He parked round the back and was comforted to see his intended victim's car also there. This he made note of but realised that he couldn't be tailing this man everyday, so organised members of his heavy gang - there were two of them - to share the task at each cease-work time...and to let him know immediately should the man head for the pub - a pub with the convenient rear parking area away from prying eyes and cameras, as far as he could surmise.

This opportunity occurred quicker than he thought...Mr. Shape was on the move. As soon as he received the call, he set off to the pub, 'Must be his local,' he muttered.

Forewarned, Forearmed...

Bob Shape had learned an important lesson. Out of the blue, he had been attacked...by Julie's ex. How stupid of him not to have been expecting some sort of comeback from this jealous individual; Julie's treatment, her dark glasses was living proof of the man's temper.

So... he'd be ready next time.

To this end - and if ever he was to venture out on his own for whatever reason - he would do so attired appropriately, to expect the unexpected, something he was becoming quite used to. But he would be the first to admit though, that some of the automatic, mobile changes were quite tiring if selected and remained 'on' for any length of time, an irritation as a result of the constant distortion. Additionally, he was also mindful of the life of his body-worn battery that he had to take into consideration...he had to use it sparingly, only for 'when needed'.

However, he knew that Julie's ex was unlikely to stop the intimidation, which meant that at all times, being prepared.

'I don't need this; why can't he just let go and leave her alone?' Bob would often ask himself. He was already busy enough. 'And I don't really want to hurt him, after all...he's just a jealous idiot, nothing more, unless of course he tries to get all heavy with Julie again. *That* would change the situation.'

***

Following the recent encounters with Julie's ex, and yet another fleeting experience in town, albeit from across the street when Julie's ex had locked eyes and pointed at him...Bob Shape lost no time in finding out a little more about the man who simply could not 'let go', could not understand that his ex-wife no longer needed - or more wounding - that she wanted absolutely nothing further to do with him. All this had put Bob Shape in the firing line.

This was, albeit, a minor but irritating side issue for Bob Shape in his overall scheme of things...he had bigger fish to fry normally, did he not reader, so decided to deal with the problem forthwith. He began his own surveillance.

***

The scorned husband owned and operated a fairly successful business and employment advice company but Shape found out that his staff turnover was frequent which did not surprise him, knowing of the man's temperament.

Of the surveillance, it was the incident at the pub that provide the opportunity - he was just a little surprised when having parked his car there on one occasion and having to return to it quickly to pick up a journal he wanted to read over a drink before setting off home, an Alfa Romeo glided in to the car park. Shape knew immediately who it was; Julie's ex. He remembered he owned one, so why had he suddenly pitched up at the pub he asked himself? And he had a couple of passengers with him. Shape immediately drove off.

'Forewarned is Forearmed'.

Having begun his own monitoring of the Alfa Romeo, an easy vehicle to recognise with its distinctive car design and trade-mark grill, he had noticed without advertising the fact, that very same car, parked not too far away when he occasionally stepped out for lunch with colleagues; he would see it amongst a line of cars on the roadside. Occasionally too, at cease work it would be seen.

***

Julie's ex watched the 'workers' leaving the company...it was not a big outfit so it would not take long. Some parked within the company's premises driving straight out, some walking to the adjacent car park.

He waited, watching for his nemesis to appear. Couldn't see anybody...yet. Perhaps it was too early.

A tap at a window made him jump...somebody had approached from behind the line of parked cars while he'd been concentrating on looking straight ahead. The person at the window on the passenger's side was a woman, elderly...definitely not young.

'What?' barked Julie's ex. 'What do you want woman?' His voice ringing with annoyance. The lady motioned for the window to be lowered which he did - reluctantly, whilst trying to maintain an eye out for his Mr. Shape.

'Hello,' said a soft voice. Before he could respond, he was surprised when he realised he was staring at a torch that the woman had thrust towards him through the window. And in that split second he saw her lovely manicured nails, glittering, all of different colours, all belonging to the hand that held that torch.

'Wha...' was all he could splutter before the torch spat at him; he felt a sharp prick on his left shoulder which made him instinctively clutch at it with his other hand. 'Oi!' he shouted as he glanced back towards the woman who had already moved away to the rear 'Bitch! he hollered, turning to open his own door and go after her but somehow finding he was losing control over has hands while the dashboard seemed to stretch then shrink, becoming obscure; the world began to swim.

Then darkness.

***

The Police received an urgent call...that a motorist was seen completely drunk in the opinion of the caller...and had been like this for quite some time. Details, location, car model were given.

***

The police were soon standing around the Alfa Romeo, peering into it...

'Excuse me Sir..' but the policeman was wasting his time - the driver was completely out of it, noisily snoring away. Oblivious.

'Looks like drugs...can't smell any booze,' said one copper to the other after an initial look around. When the driver eventually resurfaced into the real world, still a little groggy, he simply could not convince the police, perhaps even himself, that he's been attacked by an on old lady. It did not help his case when he began to lash out, punching one officer and shouting obscenities, before he was restrained.

'Yep, drugs will do that to you,' came the Sergeant's response to the display he witnessed by the Alfa Romeo owner that day.

As for Julie's ex...he was totally baffled, and also in deep trouble.

***

Meanwhile, the 'lady' with the torch had returned to his own car, making sure that article by article, and using surreptitious moves as he made his way back, with all due precaution effecting a departure....carefully mingling amongst the throng. He 'restored' Robert Shape. A job well done he considered. The wig, the face, his colourful nails and of course the voice modulator - set to *soft-female*, worked perfectly. He hadn't wanted to cause any physical harm...only to warn him off even thought the poor sap didn't have a clue who the 'torch lady' might be.

Bob Shape soon found out that Julie's ex had been banned from driving as part of his sentence. This gave Bob Shape an opportunity; he was going to play 'the good guy'.

He made sure one morning to accidentally bump into him.

When this took place the ex was taken aback at first as Bob Shape spoke, sternly, brooking no argument.

'Look, I know what's happened between us in the past and knowing of your predicament right now...and of course for Julie's sake, I'd just like to bury the hatchet; should you need a lift anywhere, just call me - you know where I work. I'd like to help. Really. Just keep away from me.'

Bob Shape was playing his redemption card and hoped for two things, one, that it would get the ex off his back, and two, Julie might just get to hear of it.

***

For the ex...his initial instinct was usually one of rage but being on his own on this occasion, was now replaced with amazement; at first the he snarled as he tended to do in situations like this but the forcefulness of the tone Bob Shape used convinced the man - he had looked deadly serious and Julie's ex eventually came round and humbly accepted, was even grateful, especially when Bob Shape told him he wasn't chasing his ex, hadn't chased her, nor did he intend to.

Just yet...this part he kept quiet about.

They shook hands.

But he missed her...terribly.

Having the man out of the picture would enable Shape to concentrate on other matters which was just how he wanted it – and he really had matters to attend to.

Julie At The Library

She was placing the 'returned' books to their allocated shelves before wandering back to her work station near the back of the library, the education area, when she heard a voice, a voice she thought she recognised.

That voice was talking to her colleague Alan who manned the front desk. She was hidden from view but she slowly peeked round one of the racks to confirm if it was Josh or not. It sounded like him and when she looked, indeed it was - her ex-boss's son. However, she kept herself out of sight, not wanting her whereabouts to be known to Josh - and therefore to Bob.

Judging from the conversation she was overhearing for which she felt some guilt, he was enquiring about a book he'd ordered and 'was it in' yet? She too, often worked the desk but she never realised that Josh used the library and was glad to have not been manning it then. Apparently Josh's request had something to do with farms.

'Pass me a pen please Julie...' Alan had called out. '...mine's suddenly not working.' She reached into the pencil tin and pulled one out as he came to her table. 'I think the book he wants is actually due in today; I'll ask him if he can call back later...might be in by then.'

***

That pen hadn't worked either so she tried another, eventually finding, after several, one that did. Mental note - sort out the pens, which she began to do as soon as Alan had moved away. Libraries could be graveyards for ball-points.

As we remember reader, Julie never scribbled, absolutely not, no spider scrawl or doctor's scribble from her hand. On a series of small marker slips of paper on a small pad, she tried out all the ball-point pens, and there were many, trying out each pen and writing the same phrase each time. The words she used, and as Josh was very much in her mind, as was his dad, she found herself writing 'I miss you,' over and over. Only half of the pens seemed to work properly.

She tidied up the paper slips just as the book delivery arrived so began to register them, quickly finding Josh's book which she opened to register, making a mental note about the farming aspect.

However, all activity was interrupted when, and she had completely forgotten about this, the Fire Alarm went off - the weekly test - which made her jump, knocking her pencil tin over along with discarded paper slips going everywhere, all over her normally well-ordered desk top. The staff moved to their duly appointed places. Five minutes later the test was over. When the staff returned Julie started to clear up her desk then brought the new books to the front desk.

The possibility that Josh might turn up at any time put Julie on tenterhooks all afternoon so she stayed out of sight as much as she could, breathing a sigh of relief when Alan told her Josh had eventually collected it.

***

Later on, she considered her situation...that she shouldn't be hiding away or afraid of being seen by her ex-boss and yet she could not tell you why this was the case. Perhaps she was still feeling guilty about her knee-jerk reaction and what Bob no doubt construed as her evident rebuff when he had snatched a kiss from her.

Back then she had been startled, ruffled by his close proximity and affronted by his presumption. Now she regretted it. Or was it the fear that her husband might turn violent again? He had form, always overly jealous of any threat to his marital standing, even though they were now separated. There was always that hint of aggression associated with her husband in his dealings.

And now she learned of some fracas involving him and Bob; apparently blows were exchanged with Bob on the receiving end once more, although she could never understand how her husband, brute that he was, ended up in hospital A & E a few days later.

'A mindless, random attack,' the police had said, '...probably involving drugs.' She found that hard to believe because, although handy with his fists, her ex had never dabbled in drugs for as long as she had known him.

***

Her life since parting ways with Bob and *Shape Materials* had been one of dullness, of misery and partly of fear, of fear of her violent ex-husband and constantly looking over her shoulder. She was feeling not only forlorn but also unequipped to deal with the niceties and rules of romance; there had only been one man in her life...her ex-husband.

To make matters worse, an occasional picture would flash across her mind...Bob together, or even worse, in bed with, that siren Eleanor, Eleanor with her roving, beckoning eye and great, younger figure. He

278

wouldn't stand a chance against Eleanor's very female wiles and machinations.

And she was younger.

These thoughts were a torment.

The Ex and Eleanour

For Julie's ex, during his time trying to keep tabs on Mr. Shape while sat in the car, he'd had ample opportunity to see the comings and goings at *Shape Materials*. He wasn't deliberately on the lookout for talent but nor was he one to ignore any eye-catching ladies that passed by and sure enough, one particular female caught his attention as she walked to her parked car.

Quite striking, nice figure with a 'look at me' demeanour as she moved. This description fitted one woman perfectly who we have met already reader, and went by the name of *Eleanor* Shaw.

Long story told quickly...as she crossed the road he was able to weasel an introduction with a tried and tested method by deploying a wonderful smile coupled with a compliment - the kind of obvious and cheap compliment any self-respecting female must ignore, but Julie's ex was, as we already know, a blunt force when it came to bedside manners and human relationships. Equally, and naturally, Eleanor was of those who would never ignore and not respond to a compliment.

And so it came to pass...they very quickly became an item. Both were happy, however, and being who he was there was no way he was going to release his clutches and surrender his ex just yet...he felt he still had a score to settle.

It did not take long of course for knowledge of this romantic development to find its way into the company - and her boss. This in fact was music to the ears of Robert Shape; nor did he find it surprising as he already knew that the girl was one of those that demanded constant flattering and Julie's ex was the man to provide it. This news, he thought, might also go some way in reducing Julie's fear of him if she knew her ex was finally relinquishing his role as Alpha Male where she was concerned.

If only he know where she worked or lived...

Julie Ponders

Julie had thought again of Bob as she was wont to these days...increasingly, which had made her look to herself one evening, full length in the mirror - wearing nothing.

She viewed the reflection; thought she looked hideous. Some words from the past, courtesy of various sources, usually women's mags, came back to remind her...

"It's what a woman sees in the mirror that matters". In this case a full-length mirror, showing a horror story - or so she thought.

And how old was she now? Definitely not young. Straight from school, then part-time job, then the bad times - trapped with her Jeckyl-and-Hyde husband. And now here on her own in a new home; the age of fifty beckoned a few years hence. But surely, fifty is not old she told herself..isn't it the new 'forty'?

'Don't kid yourself lady,' said the demon sat on one shoulder. 'Doomed to lonely spinsterhood, watching reruns of 'I Love Lucy' on TV and old movies. Drinking sherry or wine every afternoon - Get used to it!'

'No no – not so, remember that kiss? Oh yes, he definitely wants you. Go get him,' said the voice on the other shoulder. 'And look, he's not young either!'

The ravages of time - the appendix surgery, the scar on her knee from a fall...and of course the wrinkles had taken their toll; she was a little heavier around the waist these days and one breast sagged just a tad more that the other.

'Nothing wrong with them,' said the nice voice. 'Stop worrying.'

Oh, if only she could turn the clock back to the certainty and confidence of her youth. But every time she thought like this - reminiscing of opportunities missed, tears would form. Different decisions would have been made...and she would definitely have collapsed into his embrace - an embrace that was offered and ready to be fulfilled...she had read the situation totally wrong and something she could never eradicate from her mind. It was because she was prepared because or her strict upbringing, to believe the worst in him instead of the best, being so used to her ex-husband and his sometimes brutal antics.

Where was he now? Had he flown, his patience and romantic inclinations only stretching so far? And who could blame him? But she had seen him, remember? Had spoken to him, and she, as before had sent the wrong signals!

'So where are you Robert,' she said to herself.

She had looked in the mirror once more after donning her underwear to cover some of her blemishes - and other 'pits and sagging parts'. Surely, he would run a mile - and she would be mortified.

'Who would want *this*?' she asked herself out loud staring at her image... 'WHO?' she asked again, while at the same time imagining Robert Shape having carnal pleasures with someone else, someone with a smooth skin and a taught, energetic body...and with no grey hair.

Could even the sexiest underwear transform her appearance into someone desirable, younger, she mused because, it has to be said, she was very traditional - no sexy flights of fancy with exciting underwear; her mind was just not like that? Knickers had to be full and white – or maybe pink, and that was that.

Her self-esteem was at rock-bottom - she wasn't getting any younger, the colour of her hair beginning to show the inevitable slide away from youthfulness. Perhaps it would need a man with a few gin and tonics inside him first. 'That would be my only chance,' she muttered ruefully. But *that* voice intruded once more...

'Don't be silly girl – you underestimate the power you have and remember, being young is a state of mind, it doesn't just depend on your body...so ignore my cousin demon.'

Desperate thoughts...could she make a first move...go to him and lay her private thoughts on the table and to clear the air? But this was simply not in her genes, her pride would not allow it, at least not yet. Too forward, be acting like a tramp...ladies of her ilk and upbringing did not behave like that. It was just the way she had been brought up.

But the Gods were smiling upon her, courtesy of the library – and fire alarm weekly test, a slip of paper...and of course, her beautiful handwriting.

***

Bob was pleased with Josh's increasing interest in the farm visits, an interest that would of course never replace his son's love of playing soccer but nevertheless, was an activity that was healthy and invigorating. A bonus was the addition of one-time-lout Karl; he and Josh had become firm friends. Another plus as far as Bob was concerned. And such innocent forgiveness from Josh.

But Josh was like that. It was in his nature, in his soul.

He was now deep into the husbandry of farm animals, realising from his library book that having animals was one thing but keeping them both safe and well every hour of the day and every day of the year, was quite another; they required constant attention during the day such as the feeding, protection from the elements, milking, even protection from other wild creatures - or simply just moving them. On Mr Munro's farm he also realised he was beginning to make attachments and favourites amongst some of the animals.

Three Words

'Mustn't lose that - might be important...'

A slip had fallen from the book Josh was handling. Bob bent down to retrieve it for him; on it there was writing, repeated several times in different inks and shades, some scratchy, the words being...

'*I miss you.*'

As soon as he saw the style, Bob instantly recognised its hand, its owner, the decorative strokes, the beautiful shapes and flow of each letter - even the serifs; words that could only have been penned by one person. Julie.

His heart leapt.

'Josh,' he called out, 'You remember Julie, was she in the library when you collected your book?' No, he hadn't seen her there; Bob showed him the slip.

'Unless of course she'd had the book out for herself, but that's definitely her handwriting, I'd recognise it anywhere Josh, so neat, so elegant. Beautiful.'

'You like her don't you Dad,' a rhetorical question. Bob realised he was blushing in front of his boy...just a little.

A visit to the library was called for; he'd wanted to know where she worked or lived for quite a while now and for some reason Josh's psychic skills were ineffective on this particular occasion.

'She's a blank Dad...nothing coming through at all...' he'd said when first asked. So this might be the breakthrough he needed. Then, typically Josh, '...probably because she might still be carrying that lump of Kryptonite in her handbag Dad, or even two lumps...that's why she doesn't register,' he said laughing out loud.

Bob chuckled too. He looked at Josh...so close to being snatched away from him by some thug.

'And she never answers her phone when I've tried to call...'

Each time Bob Shape cast his mind back to that fateful kiss...and that slap, his mind and feelings would churn because, he had to admit, he missed her...badly. He was also convinced that along with an abiding fear of her husband and how he might react, a fear that might extend to his own safety as well, that in fact she had feelings for him. Of this he was convinced.

She had been in a broken marriage but her husband's violent reach had already extended into her new life so Bob Shape felt that he had to quickly re-establish their friendship, whatever it took, whilst avoiding him. He was resolved.

As soon as he could, and finishing work a little early one day, Shape drove straight to the library, parked nearby and waited. He had to admit to himself of feeling guilty, apprehensive, even a little ashamed with himself for resorting to such an method in order to track Julie to her home, which in fact turned out to be not far away at all, a ten minute walk; indeed, she had walked to work. His heart had leapt when she emerged from the library and set off, Bob realising he would not need his car; he left it in the library car park and followed the lady of his dreams.

He watched her disappear through her front door, just two steps up from the pavement. Whatever the name of the street, which he hadn't taken note of, her house was No 23, while realising that the number was really unimportant.

Julie in control

Through the years of matrimony, the scolding, the put-downs and sneers of her ill-natured, sometime violent husband, one who demanded the flattery of constant abeyance, had produced a fear, a fear now ingrained in her mind. In truth, she should have moved a million miles away from him a long time ago.

That fear persisted and the sudden presence of Robert Shape on her doorstep induced panic as she knew her ex was relentless in his quest to intimidate her...especially where Shape was concerned.

'Oh Robert...' she gasped, startled. But before she could do anything, he firmly took her inside, out of sight from any prying eyes knowing of her fear and shut the door firmly behind them, a breeze of lavender following her - something he always remembered. 'Robert, Robert - you can't be here. You must go. He...'

He was having none of it this time. He stood up close to her pushing her gently but firmly against the wall. There was a little hesitancy from her, some resistance. 'Please Robert...'

Her wonderful fragrance, so close. How could he forget it. He took her hands in his...inviting her to sit in an armchair. But there was still resistance...

'Okay, okay. Please listen - and then I'll go, but let me say this so that there is absolutely no doubt with you...you must hear what I have to say.' He moved closer, knelt down in such a way she could not get up easily and slowly placed his hands on her chair - as gently as he could, looking directly into her eyes and speaking to her quietly, asked....

'Do you really want to hide away your lovely face and shining light from everybody, especially me Julie? To deny someone the pleasure - someone who dearly loves you - of not seeing you each day?

'Do you really want to deny yourself the tender embraces that could be yours, the soft caresses and the gentle kisses...the wonderful brief touches - do you want to deny yourself these?

'Do you forever want to lock yourself away so that each time you dress and undress, only you will see you and no one else will ever cast their hungry eyes over you - as I would - as I want to, to appreciate you as I do?' Now she began to flush.

'Will you not want someone...someone like me, who sees your vulnerability, your grace and beauty and inner softness, to be desiring you and wanting to excite you?

'And do you not want to love another, and be so loved in return, with passionate embraces and gentle cuddles, to be with someone who cannot live without you? Do you really want to remain shut away for the rest of your life, to be lonely...trying to escape from your past? I have seen your bruises behind the dark glasses; I know of these things which you should not hide, that you should not be ashamed of, because I love you Julie. And I think you love me.'

***

It was that voice again - from long ago...

'*Oh my Lord! Where were you when I was younger?*' said the devil voice sat on her shoulder. '*Did you hear all that Julie,*' it asked. '*Did you? Did you hear that? He loves you! For God's sake do something!*'

He'd noticed that she had coloured, her face first then her neck. Her mouth was moving, her lips quivering. She began to shake, her colour displaying some inner turmoil....and still she remained silent. Bob, just for a moment, registered her turmoil, thought that he might be wasting his time...whatever battles were taking place in her mind. He would try something...so he stood up:-

'May I...Big-Boys room please?' he asked, '...and when I come back, well...as you now know how I feel, I'll take my leave...you obviously feel unconvinced and uncomfortable with me here.'

A momentary reprieve...part of the plan...

When he turned to go to the bathroom he caught a brief glimpse of her face, a look he thought of alarm spreading across it.

Quick! said the demon on her shoulder....*Sort yourself out!*

***

He was away two minutes - enough time for her to 'prepare' - a rapid change of *some* garments and a spray here and there. Quick look in the mirror.

When he returned he noticed her altered appearance, her face had a look of agitation, flustered, as she stood adjacent to the divan, and was there a pervasive hint of her presence in the form of a fresh perfume spray - a clue perhaps?

But her mind was made up...there was no way he was going to leave, not if she could help it.

However, now she was in a panic...just a little; this was new territory for the lady and didn't know how to play it, even at her age. Deep breath...'I no longer need that voice on my shoulder,' she told herself.

Still, and like she was fresh from a convent, all trembling reluctance, wrapped in her sexual innocence like a budding rose and scarlet countenance, she looked into his eyes, inviting a first move while at the same time, almost afraid of it. What was he going to do?

He moved up closer to Julie. 'Shall I go?' he quietly asked, his mind already set on his reluctant course. But he was in for a shock.

'No, you had better not,' she whispered and moved to him, taking his hands in hers. He could feel her shaking. He took her to the couch...

***

Reader, we don't have to spell it out do we? Locked together, they had embraced and squeezed each other until it hurt. This was how they were for the remainder of the day and night apart from when they retired upstairs. All of her inhibitions, embarrassment, her shame and her prudence...all had melted away in his arms.

***

Both had been broken in their pasts - but the broken will always be able to love harder than most.

***

They had let loose with each other. Julie couldn't believe it as she lay there, the tingling, consuming passion with the exquisite moments she had never experienced before in her life. Now she just wanted to lay there in his arms forever. There had been an intensity of sensations the like of which she had never experienced before; the memory, the physical pleasures and sensations very recently enjoyed, lingered across her body. Now she was lost in ecstasy.

***

And later he told her of her Ex and Eleanor. She felt liberated.

'Thank you Eleanor!' she had said out loud, looking upwards. 'My guardian moves in mysterious ways,' and they both laughed as the light shone out from her eyes.

***

The events of that day resulted in, as you may have guessed - and to the delight of both Lynda and Josh - and certainly as far as Bob Shape was concerned - to Julie eventually moving in to join the family.

***

However, Robert Shape reflected...a niggling issue always at the back of his mind; following their evening of passion, he simply could not get Julie out of his mind and was worried, worried because he suddenly realised that as a result of the path he'd chosen - his mission - he could just as simply lose it all...at anytime...to lose Julie, to lose his family. If he was caught. The 'righting of wrongs' must finish but there were just a few loose ends to tie up...then he'd be done.

Meticulous as he had been in covering his tracks there was always the unexpected. Now just as he was experiencing happiness, these thoughts cast a black cloud over his mind.

At the same time, more unsettling news came...

Lynda upset

'Dad, I think Lynda is upset about something…' said Josh.

'How do you mean…how upset?' Josh went on to describe how he thought she'd been crying or weeping, had red eyes. Although Lynda would do anything, would die for Josh, she was, herself slow to open up on personal matters, matters on which Josh had no grasp or experience. Lynda almost mothered her brother knowing the way he was…and what he'd been through.

'Thanks son, I'll have a word.'

***

'Tell me my darling - come on, what's happened…why are you miserable eh, what's getting you down?' Bob asked. Lynda related with tears in her eyes…

In town recently on a Saturday Lynda had unfortunately encountered a nasty individual who had made a beeline for her and announced out loud…

'Well, well - it's the nice little girl with the nice little boobies,' he guffawed from several yards away. 'But not so l

ittle now…!' he added with a leer.

Thus did the bad *Penny,* the knucklehead son of Mallock, reacquaint himself to Lynda as he then muttered something to his companion who shared in the amusement as they laughed together.

She was shocked to see him; one did not forget this man in a hurry, his vacant, stupid stare, and now his leer. For one horrible moment Lynda told her Dad that she thought he was actually going to come up to her and molest her once more as he had tried to after the soccer game.

Penny had kept up the barrage of innuendo and lewd shouts and actually moved towards Lynda but was prevented from getting too close when she deftly moved into a shop.

This was a different Lynda to the one who had to ward off the grasping hands at the soccer match. A little older and mature now, she was shaping into a very attractive young woman...and as *Penny* had seen, was quite well endowed without it being obvious; there were no little *boobies* here.

The whole episode had unnerved the young lady; her instincts at the time were to give him a good slap, or a kick somewhere, but not wanting to draw attention to herself or the family, she had held back.

***

Robert Shape was furious; 'What *is* the matter with these people...with *this* family?' he asked in annoyance, while comforting his daughter. 'This idiot needs to be neutered...*they* need to be neutered Lynda, I will take care of this - and soon.'

And these people roam the streets...but not for much longer thought Bob Shape, who moved this man and his family right up the pecking order...the pecking order for retribution.

For removal.

He took out his phone. Something needed arranging and he would need some help for what he had in mind.

***

Shortly after his comforting and soothing of Lynda, and without drawing too much attention to himself, he walked round to the back of Mallock's garage looking for Karl. He spotted him out of the corner of his eye buffing up a vehicle in a separate bay.

Just the man, and exactly as he wanted him to be - on his own.

He put his finger to his lips and winked as he moved over towards him. Karl nodded acknowledgment - knew the score.

'Need your help Karl…' and went on to explain…

Karl nodded. This was one of those 'loose ends' Bob Shape had to attend to.

News... Some bad, some good...

He and Dave were together again, Bob lamenting on the recent development with the Mallocks and Lynda. Dave listened. Then he said...

'Would you like a run-down Bob...more snippets, more ammunition for you, you might say?'

'Go on then.'

'Yes we know...if there's trouble, guess who it might be – either directly or indirectly..?' Dave proceeded...a litany of low-level crime incidents, attributed most probably – to the Mallocks.

'So, no surprises there then.' Bob

'More on this family...' Dave continued. Bob listened....

***

'One of them is implicated in the barn fire last month...just gathering more evidence...

And the joy-riding - a tractor nicked from a farm – three cars and a van wrecked by it. Tractor left abandoned - set on fire just for good measure.

Who do think put soap suds in the village fountain. Purple colour, naturally. Light-prank you might think but oh no, a gallon of oil went is as well! Needed a special detergent to clear it all up. Cost quite a few pennies - a fortune in fact.

Casual violence in bus shelter reported.

Old man attacked outside his house – investigating someone creeping about in his garden...guess who had been creeping around – description fits...of *Penny*, the bad one.

'We'll have to turn into being Russian – rub some out Bob,' said Dave. Amazing how just one family can cause so much grief. And a million pounds a pop for a gang knife-crime murder investigation.

Bob wondered if repeated but lesser crimes actually contributed to the perception of lawlessness more so than the odd, or rare but vicious attacks. However, who would say that a burglary was a minor or lesser crime? Certainly not the victims. Crimes like these added up...and they were devastating to the victims concerned.

And the help you received from the law…? Get a crime number – and inform your insurance company!

***

However…it was not all bad news: Dave went on…'It was satisfying to read that the con-man accused of fleecing many vulnerable people was found dead in a skip following a drunken night out.

The company director who lived in a big mansion and who had syphoned off funds was hit by a lorry; was he pushed? Conflicting reports. Jury's out. Dave winked.

An 'eco' warrior who often caused mayhem on the highways and on building projects who had the habit of hiding up or staying in trees to evade the authorities – she was found hanging, dead.

From a tree, naturally.

Apparently her back-pack had snagged up round her neck and a stout branch on her way down. She had probably suffocated over a period of minutes according to the coroner. Her mates cried a foul because she was too experienced to make a mistake like that...she always used to throw down her bag before 'dismounting' they said.

'Hmm, someone's on our side then...'

***

Diamond thief...steals over a million pounds worth of rocks from a family-run jewellers, eventually gets caught; punishment? She serves a year in jail and fined a pittance. Where is she now? Found at the bottom of a village pond - weighed down with - guess what? Rocks in her bag. Real rocks. The irony.

'Don't think the Mallocks did that, Dave added.
Bob nodded. 'No, not their style.'
'The shape of justice Bob.' Bob remained silent.

***

More snippets flowed from Dave. Generally, and for the local incidents the Mallocks were prominent. Bob could see how - should this be repeated across the country - disproportionate effort and resources were required in dealing with them - the lawless few - not forgetting the misery caused amongst the mainly law-abiding.

***

Bob's work colleague, Vince, also bemoaned the general state of affairs in society, especially on crime; both him and Bob sharing and pontificating when the had their occasional work 'talks'...away from work of course, in a curry house.

As for Vince and the car-scammers? Bob would reveal what actually happened.

One day. A promise.

All this just added to Bob wanting to speed up dealing with the lovely Mallock tribe.

Three Down. On the Track…

Bob was now looking directly at Dave.

'Dave…welcome to your 'hit & run' crew; I present *"Mallock and Son"*. Pathetic aren't they?' Bob gestured to the two, tied together on the railway track. He knew they couldn't move…far - the live rail hummed its close proximity.

They were knotted, back to back. They looked up, still looking a tad dopey…sat on the railway sleepers, adjacent to the death rail.

'You'd better let us go right now otherwise you'll be in big trouble,' said Mallock in a tone, he hoped was charged with menace, but couldn't, due to his doped-up condition, the message half-hearted, groggy as he was, and failed to impress either of his captors; Bob well remembered that tone from the soccer game – an attempt at a snarl. Mallock followed up… 'Who are you, you bastards…'

Neither Mallock nor his son recognised the man who spoke, or his accomplice. They looked complete strangers…and yet, well, maybe not. There was something that tugged at Mallock's conscience, while the prodigal son was also trying to recall the a familiarity of the man who spoke - this man who held them at his mercy?

'Really? Do you know who my colleague is…?' replied the man who had spoken as Mallock and son continued to struggle against their bonds, one eye always on the rail.

'Dad, Dad…give them some…' The language descended into a rich mixture of expletives and an extensive range of profanities, some of which were even new to our man Shape. Therefore reader - I cannot repeat with pen on paper what in fact was uttered by these snivelling examples of humanity. It was not nice - it would not do.

'Oi...watch your language; there's a policeman present,' said Bob with a smile.

'Shut up you idiot!' shouted father to son. 'Just shut up!'

'But Dad, do something...the bloody train will be here soon...' Again, apologies reader, as other diabolical expletives were added.

'Did you hear that Dave, the language? My God, terrible - his English teacher must have done time. Probably in *Strangeways*,' Bob said in mock horror.

Mallock senior swore in return towards his offspring:-

'Shut up…keep your mouth shut,' was the polite version or rendering of what was said which I am using here for your tender ears.

'Please allow me to interrupt - and listen,' said Bob Shape sternly. 'This fine gentleman who is with me, my colleague and friend...well, you may have briefly caught a glimpse of his face just before you ran him and his daughter down a few years ago then slunk away like the snivelling cowards you were...*are*, leaving two broken bodies behind...in agony. Still sure you don't recognise him?'

A silence descended upon them. The Penny dropped, one physically.

Mallock's head slowly sank to his chest as his memory stirred and recognition came. Then suddenly Junior Mallock burst out, hopefully seeing a chance...

'It was an acci…' gulped the son before being cut off, realising that the game was up.

'For Chrissake shut up will you, you idiot,' repeated Mallock. Another pause. After several seconds the father was about to say something when Mallock Junior cut in:-

'It was an accident - it was an accident I promise, honest - they were too close to the road. It was an accident. It was not my fault…' he wailed. 'I wasn't used to the car…'

Now this was news to both the men who stood over them.

Dave's mouth dropped, a gasp escaping.

'So…it wasn't you driving the car then,' he said as a statement as he looked at Mallock before returning his gaze to the son… 'It was *you*!'

Dave moved towards him; the son flinched away, however, a restraining arm came from Bob which interrupted Dave's move as Bob whispered to him, 'It's okay Dave, we've got this - we've not done with these two just yet and I don't want *you* electrocuting yourself.'

***

Bob Shape was now absorbing this fresh information and how he had felt when Karl had told him of his suspicions with Mallock's damaged car, the name-tag…or part of a name tag - '*Carr*' and the full name - *Carradine* - David *Carradine*. When Karl had told him during their session on the park bench Bob had felt a measure of satisfaction, vindication even. And of course that it had been the son *Penny* who was actually driving.

This was additional satisfaction for him.

***

Of all the many times they had met at the pub, he realised that he knew little of his friend and hadn't even asked his friend's surname initially - Dave was *Dave* and always seemed preoccupied which Bob was not really surprised about considering his occupation and his seemingly ongoing and underlying medical issues.

And then when Dave had told him, how witless of him not to have made the connection with the name-tag. He now felt that he'd let his friend down in some way and for being slow on the uptake. The poor man had survived devastating, life-threatening injuries which it seemed was playing havoc with his life...to this day.

And into the bargain, he had lost his daughter

***

His attention returned to the two miserable characters they were watching over, sat on the sleepers, both realising now who they were dealing with. And why they were there – on a railway track.

'Hey, you two, look at me!' It was then that Bob Shape flicked a switch as he looked directly at the Mallocks, his face making some subtle changes over a period of a few seconds. It didn't take long for recognition to sink in...

'Oh shit - Dad, *Dad*! It's him! It's the man from- '

'Yes! I bloody well know who it is you stupid ignoramus, but if he doesn't stop this nonsense I will personally see to it that he will suffer,' he snarled with renewed confidence as the effects of the drug wore off, while looking at both of the men who held them captive.

But then he paused as another penny dropped, knowing the significance now of the railway. 'This is all down to you and that football match you blasted twerp.'

Mallock also began to recognise that they really were in trouble; his confidence began to ebb. Then a cold hand clutched his heart; he was sure he could hear a train. He became still. This stillness transmitted to his son.

Another pause... 'Dad! I can feel the rail, I CAN FEEL THE RAIL. IT'S COMING DAD! - THE TRAIN'S COMING!' he said panicking.

This made Bob look up along the railway line both ways; they were situated on a curve partially obscured by a copse of poplars in one direction so that any train would not be travelling at high speed on a bend but at the same time, any 'visuals' along the track by the driver would be impeded slightly plus the fact there was a degree of embankment. Any driver would be at a disadvantage from this direction. The other direction was quite clear.

More feeble struggles by father and son followed, to no avail.

'Actually, I feel sorry for the train driver, don't you?' commented Bob looking at Dave, who nodded. However, Bob Shape noticed that his friend appeared anxious - to be in some torment as if the current situation and the new revelation about who was driving the car was beginning to overwhelm him. He leant in close and whispered, 'You okay Dave?' Bob was worried about him...he looked pale. Dave answered, also in a hurried but muffled whisper;-

'Yes, yes - I'm okay...I'm okay.' Then:-

More shouting from Mallock the younger...

'Dad! I can feel the rail, I CAN FEEL THE RAIL VIBRATIONS...IT'S COMING DAD, THE TRAIN'S COMING!' His words once more descended into a total rant and railing of blasphemies as even Mallock Senior began to look worried...he could detect a very mild vibration - as if the track was faintly singing, heralding the arrival of certain death.

'Don't touch that bloody rail!' shouted Dad Mallock at his son.

'He's right...I think I can hear it too,' said one of the standing men calmly to the other.

'Yep, looks like it, said the other,' nodding. 'But I wonder if it will be as painful as being hit by a car..?' The son broke down and began to wail.

'It's a shame really, it'll be too quick for them...in the blink of an eye and all that. No suffering; instant 'lights out'. All in all, too good for them.'

'Agreed...' said the other...the conversation very much within earshot of the two men on the ground. 'And I'm sure it's getting louder...yes, definitely, definitely getting louder.' Turning to the two on the ground, 'Any last thoughts gentlemen...while you can *actually* still think - while you still have a head connected to your shoulders?'

The two, father and son, were now struggling and straining to look over their shoulders towards the direction of the expected train while crying, gasping and muttering as they lost the battle against their restraints. Then:-

'My God! What's that awful smell...?' exclaimed one of observers, pointedly looking at *Penny* Mallock. One of those on the ground had lost control of both his bowels and bladder it seemed. Yes, it was Mallock the younger who was now crying in fits and loud sobs.

In the distance, they caught a glimpse of the train near the trees. From its shape and colour it looked like one of the local commuters, with only three coaches and not travelling too fast.

'Ah, there it is. Do you think it might stop in time?' asked Bob casually. 'It's not going fast. You could be lucky lads,' he said to the two captives who seemed to have aged suddenly and considerably over the last few minutes.

'Not sure,' said Dave, also casually. 'But perhaps we should go now?'

'Good batting think-man.' Bob.

The two on the ground started to scream and shout while tussling with each other and their bonds. *Penny* the son was doing most of the screaming, *Mallock* just shouting.

Beforehand – the events leading up...

Before they had arrived at the track, Bob and Dave had concocted a plan...with a little help from Karl, a plan that would hopefully lead to the 'removal' of at least two of the *Mallock* brood, namely father and son, by a third party - the train - without any direct involvement in their demise. This was to lure them to where they were now - the railway track.

But of course it was one thing to know what you wanted to do, but putting it into action was another. This had been achieved by Shape, with help from Dave using a laced dart on *Mallock* senior who, lured to the back of the garage on some pretence and well out of sight of others, had collapsed into Karl's arms.

'*Penny*, quick!' Karl had cried out, '...something wrong with your dad!' Within seconds *Penny* duly came running to be met by another dart dispensed by Shape, and who quickly succumbed as had his dad, now both out cold. Rapidly, the three of them - Bob, Dave and Karl - bundled father and son tied up together into the back of Dave's *Ranger* and vanished quietly leaving Karl behind looking after the garage.

Whilst the two were out cold, Dave had produced a tablet of oxycodone, poured water into the mouth of Mallock Junior and as the body made its natural reflex action to swallow, dropped the tablet into his mouth.

And here they were – at the track.

***

The two men, neither of whom wanted to witness a mess, a bloodbath, moved away from the track as they released a chord and quickly headed towards the *Ranger* parked behind a hedge.

***

The two Mallocks were effectively hooked up to the track while bound together, adjacent to the live rail. During their futile struggles they had been very careful not to stray too much with the rail so close, humming with lethal power and energy.

Now they watched - seeing the release of the master chord effected by Dave who definitely knew his knots, as a signal that it might herald a reprieve of sorts - but no, its release only freed them from the track; they were still tightly bound to each other without much freedom for their hard-fettered feet and arms, the train approaching.

The train came into view to them all...horror was now writ large on the faces of father and son. It seemed to be going way to fast...

Two seconds later a look of horror also appeared on the face of the train driver...as he saw two men ahead, hopping about together as one, over the track.

But no worries he thought - the driver who was no novice, estimated that he could comfortably stop in time. Brakes were slammed on. Drinks were spilled in the train...baggage fell over and curses were uttered.

Unfortunately, the driver's estimation of stopping distances was not shared by father and son who only saw certain and instant death looming, just seconds away. Heads removed from shoulders. Legs severed. Doom.

***

Had you been close enough to hear, above the screeching brakes of the clattering train, the last words possibly uttered in desperation by Mallock senior were, 'Bollocks to the live rail son!' - or words to that effect because the driver witnessed in front of him a blinding flash as two people seemed to be ejected upwards and off the track to the side.

The mad scramble to free themselves and escape what they thought was certain death courtesy of the train had failed - spectacularly. Literally from the frying pan into the fire.

And then stillness...as both the train – and the bodies of the two men - came to complete rest, the train many yards from a gruesome sight. Some smoke from the men's clothing was visible, noticed the driver. He had to admit that he did not want to look too closely but even from his cabin he could see that they were dead. And could even see the surprised look on Mallock senior's face – and the the shear look of horror on the distorted face of the son. After a period of a few seconds, he clambered down while pulling out his phone.

As he made the call he looked around. Apart from a few houses, an estate not too far away and the trees, he and the train were alone. There was nobody else in sight.

Police Matters

There were those amongst the 'Rank & File' who doubted the wisdom of a task force being set up to tackle the burgeoning death rate amongst the Criminal Element...namely the druggies, rapists and perverts - it would only divert resources away from investigations of burglaries, fraud, violence and and other murders, but hey-ho, the Chief Superintendent must have his way.

He desperately wanted to find out how sensitive info was leaking out from their own intelligence in such a manner that those on the receiving end of the so-called 'Street Cleaner" for some, or 'Knight in Shining Armour' for others, were more or less pin-pointed - names, locations and specific details that only the police should know, therefore there would be a sweeping internal trawl for leaks. Additionally and more to the point, the Chief wanted to double-down on effort and recheck for other clues on who might be this elusive killer.

Indeed, the Chief was well aware of the name given to whoever it was doing the so-called 'street cleaning' and bumping off the bad guys', as did the rank and file. And the way the police were messaged post-event, also irked him.

***

The neighbouring forces were similarly frustrated with lack of progress, Chief Superintendent Yvonne Rimmel amongst them, however, she had her ear closer to the ground and could understand the public's almost tacit support for the nick-named 'Mr Cleaner', occasionally wondering in this case if a woman may be involved somewhere along the line. Unlikely she thought. Another aspect to the deaths was the absence of any noise...no shots heard, no gunfire sounds, no yelling or screams prior to the deeds, no chasing or running; one moment they were going about life...or their business, the next, they were dying. It all seemed to be conducted silently, clinically. A very quiet assassin.

As for descriptions...so far these varied but generally described a male...by gait, by walk and movement and by size. Occasionally the words 'with a limp', were used to describe the man's movement - that's if it was indeed a man. Description of his clothes also varied as one would probably expect - normally hoods or base-ball caps were the 'de-rigour' - but there were no hoods, only an occasional cap.

Nor could anybody pinpoint an age that fitted all the reports. It varied...from young all the way through to 'doddering old git' or tramp-like, a vagrant; scarred features were mentioned, or some sort of disfigurement. No two descriptions were alike.

Chief Rimmel thought that short of catching this vigilante 'cleaner' in the act they were not going to be successful in apprehending the man - and for the Chief, she was sure it was a man.

'We have a theatre in town don't we...let's make enquiries there. In fact in the neighbouring towns too, and check out any 'joke' shops while we're at it. Our felon seems to be a master of disguise so we'll start with them.' She was well aware that they'd probably already trodden these paths in the earlier days of the investigation but it would do no harm to go over old ground...she knew from experience that results came from unexpected sources - a combination of methodical slog and ridiculous chance.

Thus the Chief at a briefing to her staff - and ordering more patrols - by both foot and by car.

They needed a breakthrough. And they thought they had one...

Heart Attack

After releasing the chord the two men quickly set off towards the *Ranger* parked on a track by a dilapidated shack, an old barn lean-to, nicely out of sight from the world and near the road that had brought them there.

They had briefly stopped to watch the outcome of the struggle of father and son on the track knowing that in all probability the train would stop in time, however, the satisfaction of witnessing their actual final dance with death resulted in Dave, still bitter from finally finding out who had actually mowed him down and his precious daughter literally from the horses mouth, giving a thumbs up to Bob in silent acknowledgement of a debt now paid.

Shape...he hadn't informed Dave what might happen if the Mallocks had survived – if they'd not been hit by the train. Was there a plan 'B'? Well yes, there was. There was no way he was going to let them get away if the train, or live rail, hadn't done the job; he had other means in reserve. Just in case. He's tell him in the car...

***

As they approached the Ranger, and just before they clambered in, Dave faltered…

'What's up Dave?' Bob asked, concern in his voice. Something was wrong. They had both paused.

'Suddenly don't feel too well Bob...but let's get in, need to sit down,' he said quietly. 'It's probably my ticker...the doctor did warn me.'

'Hospital then – sharpish!' said Bob Shape. 'I'll drive. C'mon.'

'No Bob, NO. Look...something I want to tell you, been wanting to tell you these last few days, weeks...' he said in almost desperate whispers, 'Just listen,' and proceeded to tell him that he knew he was living on borrowed time and therefore, knowing of his friend's mission in life and his part in it, with the short time he had left, he had made certain preparations and provisions, including having written a letter. In the letter...

"To whom it may concern" etc., setting out a few details and the fact that it was he, and he alone who was responsible for the sources of intelligences and the spate of killings of the criminal element...that *he* was the *Street Cleaner.*

No one else.

And additionally... that the two bodies on the track were in fact *his* 'hit & run' killers.

'They would obviously want some sort of proof of that but - I don't care...and that letter is in the glove compartment Bob. It also details my burial requests.

'Bob, promise me you won't do anything stupid. You have a living family, a life to live. I just want to go - to join my daughter, God bless her. She's down there in the ground, all on her own Bob...she needs me there with her.' A sob escaped him, tears cascading off his cheeks - a sight that no matter how hard he tried to contain himself, Bob too, fell to weeping. Dave mustered a little strength and continued, 'I knew this time would come so everything is prepared, everything...did it awhile ago.'

However, now that he knew who had actually been driving the 'hit & run' and who had confessed to it on the track which he hadn't known before, he had to hurriedly scrawl a note about which he laboured, before adding it to the letter.

Bob could see his friend now drifting away, fading as he began to double over. He managed to whisper, 'Please do not try and save me. And please *don't* keep up the good work - another promise for me. Promise,' his voice was now a whisper, fading to almost nothing but he looked up into his friend's eyes and smiled. 'Must go now - you must get out of here, save yourself. Just leave me, leave me; I know where I'm going...to see her...'

His last words....as his head sank.

Bob realised he was now weeping heavily. He gently lent Dave forward onto the steering wheel and took a few moments to assess the situation and looked around. Indeed, he must leave quickly.

In all his 'activities' he had always been scrupulous with the wearing of gloves - not your normal kind either, reader. He also knew that shortly the train and track would be swarming with the emergency services. Indeed, he could hear faint sounds of sirens in the distance already.

Definitely time to go.

He set off across a field, hugging the hedges and small paths as he knew that in all likely-hood any vehicles responding to the inevitable call from the train driver would take the same road they had recently used.

***

On his way back Shape had gone over what his friend had said...that because of the letter, he, Robert Shape, should be 'home free' and that any suspicions would now be transferred to Dave. Once his car was found and searched.

Robert Shape had not expected this turn of events. It was a liberation. Could it be true?

But he was irritated. In all the time since he and Dave had struck up their friendship, he realised, sadly, that he had known too little about his friend...the man who had played a vital part in helping him in his quest to 'clean the streets'...his mission. As for the burial; no doubt he would find out where soon enough once all the hoo-ha had died down. He certainly intended to pay his respects as soon as he could.

Ah, his mission; did somebody else not remind him about pursuing a mission? Oh yes, that young woman on the park bench. He briefly smiled as he recalled their meetings. 'I wonder what she's doing right now?' he thought to himself.

Anyway, there was work to be done, enquiries to be made about his departed friend.

***

Later, he reflected...

What a man...poor sod, thought Bob. It was then that he realised that Dave had for a moment looked happy, knowing he was going to a better place, to be with his daughter, but shockingly, Bob realised he did not know her name...Dave had never told him, in fact Dave was almost secretive about his family and personal details. This left a sadness in his heart, not knowing anything about her, even her name, except to know she had been buried. Somewhere.

He would endeavour to find out. But who would know? When he thought about this he wasn't sure who to approach, nor could he remember her name being mentioned in the press when the incident had occurred. Then he thought of Josh and his friendly connection to PC Proctor, a man who might be able to help.

Anyway, there was work to be done and inquiries to be made...

Breakthrough

'Boss...sorry, Ma'am, have you heard...been called in - Mr Mallock and his son - both dead. Found dead on the railway track not far from the school sports ground.'

'Beg your pardon, *on* the railway track did you say? This is not a joke I hope,' replied Chief Superintendent Rimmel then realised immediately that the message had been imparted with due gravity.

'Beside the track Ma'am, actually. First indications...looks like they were electrocuted.'

'Right, thanks, please keep me posted – now I have a few calls to make.'

***

Hmm, if true, good news and bad news. She well knew that the Mallocks were habitual criminals - always a pain in the proverbial, so good news that they were now 'off the scene', finished.

The bad news? She instinctively felt that it was probably a meaning in the *method* of dispatch - a message perhaps which meant somebody else is out there settling scores - or could this be the result of a 'turf war?

'Also found Oxycodone tablets on one of them,' added the messenger.

'Oxycodone, oh really?' She remembered during a brief trip to the U.S. - Oxycodone was also called the 'Hill-billy Heroin'. Quite dangerous if you don't know what you are doing. 'Please check his home, his garage - we've always known he used it as a front for his drug activities. Didn't know that they were 'users' though.'

If there was one person who was not surprised with the news about the Mallocks, it was Karl.

'It does not surprise me one little bit,' he had confided to Bob Shape days later, 'Always knew he was bad.'

***

Then shortly after this excitement and potential breakthrough...

'More news boss.' As the police had widened their search from the railway track, they had subsequently found the Ranger belonging to 'one of their own' – David Carradine, along with the letter. Other items were recovered...false 'tache, some spray paint, funny shoes and wigs.

Rimmel went quiet for a few seconds, this was a shock. 'Well well well, fancy that. Was he on our radar?' she asked.

A killer, no, wrong word – an *assassin* amongst them and yet no one had the slightest clue, knew or suspected. She was worried that executive management was losing track on essentials - the essentials of the good 'tried & tested' basic behavioural norms and patterns amongst the force; how do you keep an eye out for, or identify the rogues that slip through the net, she wondered? David Carradine...hmm, practically from left-field...unexpected. If truth be known, she was actually a little disappointed that it was one of her own...how much more satisfying if it had been a real villain's villain - a thug from the known criminal ranks.

However, along with many others in the force, he would certainly have had access to the tools and intelligence with which to pin-point his targets and carry out the actions, with access to drugs and firearms. But no firearms had been used as far as she knew. This she put to the team…

'He must have been using something else. Ideas anyone?'

None were forthcoming.

At the same time, she was struggling with the thought of Carradine - all by himself - managing to subdue two adults, two crooks from God knows where, and then haul them into his pick-up and then transfer them onto the railway track. Yes, they must have been sedated somehow.

Must have tied them up together of course when they were out cold; but how could he get them onto the track, avoiding the deadly rail without killing them in the first place – the train driver was adamant that he had seen the two men very much alive and very close together? Carradine must have had help; it was known of course for coppers to 'call in' the odd favour now and then from various sources and contacts…but, well – there was no one else in the frame…and street crime was down after all. She'd let it rest at that…for now.

***

'Josh, I'm trying to find some details on a *David Carradine* – a copper, the one in the papers.' Bob Shape didn't expand on the reason why he wanted to know. He went on, 'He was a victim of a hit-and-run driver a few years ago, he and his daughter. Can you suss out any info on the incident for me please.'

It was a few days later when Josh had been chatting to Karl at the farm…a memory. It had just entered his mind, had literally 'popped into it'. This was the dream - the dream he had while he was in the coma...that dream he had told his Dad about - of the appearance of the young girl, a complete stranger to him who had come into his hospital room alongside his family. Now he remembered...she had said something when they were around his bed.

'Dad, I didn't know who she was, but I remember now she said that like me, she was hurt.' Bob looked up, now mildly interested.

'Go on...what else did she say, like *why* she was visiting you, or anything?'

'She looked very sad Dad...very miserable.'

'Poor girl,' Robert Shape responded, 'but it was a dream Josh...maybe due to all the drugs they had pumped into you and all that? Josh, let's contact the copper you are friendly with, you know - the drunk episode. What was his name now? I'll see if I can get some more details...'

'PC Proctor Dad; here's his card.'

'I should have known you would have remembered,' said Shape rolling his eyes. Then, as an afterthought, 'Can you remember what your dream-girl looked like Josh...tall, short - colour of her hair..? Was there anybody else there in your dream with us?' Shape was thinking of his dearly beloved wife - she could fit the bill...bit of a stretch perhaps.

'Not really Dad, although when you were around the bed you all talked together as if you knew each other, like friends. Sorry, why?'

'Nothing Josh.' He wasn't going down *that* road his imagination was driving along. There was a pause. In the back of his mind...his dear wife Sarah from long ago. You never know, the mind plays clever tricks - past memories hidden deep in the psyche. Then...

'But aha, ah yes, hang on Dad...I do remember about her head...she had a red ribbon in her hair at the back.'

Like a pig-tail maybe...?

Don't be silly Robert, he said to himself. But this little tit-bit of information inserted itself in his mind... a red ribbon in her hair at the back.' *Like a pig-tail maybe...?* Just a coincidence. Surely.

***

In fact, over the months following the drunk incident and whenever their paths crossed, the policeman would always take the time to say 'hello' to Josh, swap glib pleasantries and then possibly talk about soccer or police cars therefore Bob wondered if Proctor might be the man to approach, if approached in the right manner, to provide further information on Carradine. He had to be careful on account of not wanting to be sucked into, or be drawn into the now on-going investigation into his friend's demise, secretly grateful to him for his deliberate act of, by confession, pointing the finger at himself.

And surely, thought he, that the police must know about Carradine - who his friends were, and therefore also know about himself and their drinking habits; somebody must have seen them together.

But there again, the fact that the killer turned out to be one of their own might relax the scope of the investigation; they had their man, a man who, along with his daughter, had suffered at the hands of low-life criminals, thus feeding a desire for revenge. He may also have felt that not enough effort or resource had been allocated towards finding the callous, cowardly, unfeeling bastards. Who knows? And with his on-going and serious medical condition, he may have felt he had nothing to lose.

He was striking back...while he still could. He had taken revenge on the killers.

***

Did he do it on his own though? Chief Inspector Rimmel for one, had not been convinced...at least not convinced at all that only *one* person was responsible for the carnage amongst the criminal element, at least not initially.

As the evidence mounted, and because there were no other names, no other obvious suspects in the frame, she was persuaded that indeed, Carradine had committed most, if not all, the crimes laid against his door.

But the irony...a killer, working for himself, for whatever reasons, had actually reduced, to a considerable degree, crime on her patch.

A Knock On The Door

Robert Shape was not surprised when the police 'came knocking', initially by an email request to the company. Inevitably they had found contacts amongst Carradine's effects and of his interest in technology that may aid the police and Law & Order generally, in matters such as none violent restraints, and one of the contacts listed in Carradine's home had been *Shape Materials*.

Both Bob Shape and Vince took part in the session and it was essentially, to clear up loose ends and that yes, they had had contacts and messages from him...all recorded naturally, and offered to hand over any tapes while also offering to conduct - at any time - the police around their premised to show what 'Gucci' kit might be in their hands...one day.

They departed – both parties satisfied.

***

What both Bob and Vince did not know that during their trawl of the house, the police had found plenty of other evidence - press clippings and other articles relating to the devastating events of the 'hit & run' when it had occurred, with raging and frustrating comments added in the margins by Carradine. There were numerous net searches and some notes on the many 'perps' who became victims of 'the cleaner'

***

And then there was Julie...his love; the woman in whose arms he would lay each night now, her tender touches sweeping away all his worries of the day.

She of course knew nothing at all about Bob's 'mission' and about his other life. Or about the role his friend Dave played in it. She would no doubt read or hear the news of the railway incident in due course. However, and just as before, he realised he would have to take a reckoning of his own personal situation which had been given as escape route back to normality, courtesy of Dave if matters turned out good for Robert Shape.

He would curtail his mission.

A Headstone and Flowers

'Josh, should you see your friendly policeman any time, PC Proctor was it - would you be able to find out if he knows where Carradine, that copper who's in all the papers right now, what the funeral arrangements might be...where he's being buried?'

It transpired that, notwithstanding the special circumstances - after all, Carradine was a multiple killer was he not - several policemen, friends and colleagues would attend the burial service, Proctor amongst them. As he reflected and feeling a little selfish about it all - so engrossed was Bob Shape on his own 'mission' - he belatedly realised that David Carradine was more than likely to be interred in the same cemetery and perhaps close by his daughter. But where?

The information came back...

'So...at St. Cuthberts Church then?' Bob said to Josh. 'Don't forget son, the debt I owe him for all the info he passed my way,' he added, Bob touching the side of his nose.'

Of course, Josh may have helped but would have had no idea *who* was actually keeping the streets clean.

A Visit to the Cemetery

'Julie my love, do you remember my friend 'Dave' from when you were at the company?' She did. 'I suppose you know what he did then?' She knew that too - it was the main news and in all the papers.

'The infamous *Street Cleaner*? Shame they caught him, shame he's gone.' she had responded. He liked that.

He told her that 'a friend is a friend' and that he was going to pay his respects - as he had told Dave he would.

'Yes you must,' a pleasing and kind encouragement from the love of his life.

Reader - he didn't realise what he was in for...

It did not take long for Bob Shape to find the grave of David Carradine. He spotted the new clean and polished black marble headstone from afar, set to one side of the cemetery, close to the boundary.

If you were to ask him beforehand what he might say to his departed friend, he wouldn't have been able to tell you...that he'd had no idea what words he might utter at the graveside of their fairly long acquaintance, besides, he knew that he was too easily moved to tears in such surroundings, not the strong stoical type on these occasions. Notwithstanding the fact how he had dished out death "to those that deserved it", at times like this, by a grave, he was a proper wimp, he would admit.

He had heard too from the police grapevine and perhaps not unexpected, that he was going to 'take up residence' alongside his daughter. Bob could see that coming - and why not? He had thought this likely in any case - he had no other family as far as he knew.

Then of course..; at last, he would find out her name. As he approached he could see that yes, they were indeed together as per his wishes - with a single and combined headstone; he moved closer:-

DAVID CARRADINE
Born...1980
Died ...2021
Sadly missed by those that knew him

and *Father* to *Stella*

STELLA CARRADINE

Borne...2004
Died...2017

STELLA – YOU WERE TAKEN TOO SOON
...SO MISSED
'Your life a blessing, your memory a treasure.'
Death leaves a heartache no one can heal, love leaves a memory no one can steal.
...now together again - forever.

***

Bob Shape stood and stared, heart in his mouth... Oh my God - another Stella!

'What a coincidence...' Two of them − not so rare a name after all thought he. His gaze now took in the complete surrounds of the 'Father & Daughter' grave. It was then he noticed a quite small, enclosed photo in a frame sunk into the ground on its own prop and adjacent to the headstone which drew his attention. He knew that this practice of displaying photos by the graves of the those interred was becoming increasingly popular.

'Oh, must be a picture of the poor girl,' he mumbled. Because of its size he had to crouch down and lean in towards it to get a clearer view. 'I wonder what she looked like...' then froze.

It was the girl on the bench!

Stella? ***STELLA!***

OH...MY...GOD! Surely not *MY* Stella − *MY* Stella from the park bench! No, no...it cannot be. Bob Shape was in shock as he stared at the headstone, re-reading it over and over and looking back at the picture.

He was transfixed. Yes, that girlie smile on her lips and that joy in her face; it was definitely her. This revelation took his breath away, brought him to complete stillness.

'Oh no *Stella*...oh no - surely not *you*...my girl on the bench? Oh please God, no...it can't be,' he moaned as he looked upwards.' Besides, he'd spoken to her had he not...! He remained stunned for several moments as it all sank in and as he attempted to process his thoughts.

But then he realised it had to be her, her mysterious and sudden appearances...and equally, her departures. For moments he was in shock then spent nearly half an hour muttering, talking, weeping as it sank in...for the two of them, for her and for his friend: both taken before their time was up.

So that was it - now he knew. Now he knew why Dave was tremendously affected by those crimes involving a loved one, especially a daughter...beginning with his own, and perhaps why he had an attachment to Bob and his family following their near-disaster after the soccer match.

***

And *Stella*...that lovely, bubbly, bright, scatty-brained girl on the park bench, Dave's daughter, now lying with her father.

'He knew all along that one day he was going to join her did he not, that he had subsequently planned it all this way,' he muttered to himself. 'Nice one my friend.'

The headstone had been refashioned and updated.

He remained visibly upset, trying to keep control of his emotions as he recalled those 'visits' in the park. 'And now I must get some flowers; their graves need flowers.' he mumbled, now unconsciously ambling towards the exit. He would pick up flowers from *Love with Petals* and on the return, pass by the park and seek out *that* bench just once more.

***

However, at the flower shop he paused. He found that he could not pick out flowers quickly...he had to linger awhile, thinking. He wouldn't be able to tell you why at first but on reflection realised that he remained quite upset and shaken by her passing, while Dave's demise was not unexpected but he never thought for one moment, nor had made any connection that the girl that had sat beside him in the park had anything to do with his friend, so felt a tribute, a thought - with some flowers was required after all – and quite simply, very little of his mission could have been accomplished without Dave's aid. His mind was in a jumble as he pondered.

'Can I help you Sir?' asked one of the shop assistants who had observed him stood motionless and in deep thought. This shook him out of his temporary mental paralysis - he was still coming to grips with the shock at the grave.

'So sorry, miles away...I'm looking for something bright and cheerful - perhaps like this one,' he said as he moved towards and homed in on a yellow plant - a Sunflower.

'Oh yes,' the assistant responded adding... 'Wonderful flowers, quite distinctive; we have a variety of Sunflowers...' But Bob Shape was quite taken by the one that had first attracted his attention; it would do nicely. It was a *Firecracker* – the assistant said, quite a suitable and appropriate plant he thought to fit his memory of *Stella*. He also added another gorgeous flower he'd spotted whilst looking around - a rose; the assistant told him it was of the *Explorer* variety...a beautiful deep red. You couldn't miss it...it stood out.

Bob Shape came away from *Love with Petals* happy with his choice.

He'd added the rose to compliment his selection - as far as he could remember *Stella* had sported bright red ribbons when they had met on the bench. Pleased with the result, he set off to the park.

The park was deserted. On arrival at the bench he sat down placing the fresh bunch of flowers alongside him and began to weep once more...freely.

***

But who was the Stella he had met? An unhappy spirit? A restless spirit waiting for her father to come and join her, to come and see her again. In that case then, it must have been a ghost.

But 'I don't believe in Ghosts or weird, unexplained things like that, do I?'

Really? So what about Josh then, he asked himself...Josh with his unexplainable and wonderful mental capabilities that were beyond comprehension - almost like magic? Yes...there really are strange things in this world.

'Did I see a ghost? No, I didn't imagine it...she was there. Even Karl saw her, he suddenly remembered. And we spoke. We laughed together.

'I hope you are at peace now Stella,' he said out loud. But that was fine...the place was deserted - they and the park bench were all alone with nobody else about to witness his melancholy; tears were on his cheeks, a deathly hush had descended upon the scene as he looked about for other people - nobody; he would have been embarrassed to be seen like this, practically crying, sat there, chin on his chest.

And then he heard a tinkle of laughter like the sound of little bells...of gaiety, yes definitely, he *had* heard it. Was it *her* and *her laughter?* Startled, he stood up and looked around, but no, all was quiet - he was still alone. He was lost in sadness and misery as he sprawled out on the bench, thinking about *Stella* - if indeed it had been her.

Then a gentle breeze blew across behind him caressing his neck and shoulders, soothing his arm like the soft human touch of someone's hand, accompanied with a rustle and a soft, serene voice...a voice almost lost in the breath of the gentle breeze. Again startled, he looked around but as before, there was nobody and yet he could swear that there was a presence quite near, close to him.

'*Stella*?' He shouted. Silence. Just as he was resuming his position he heard it again - the tinkle of bells from 'over there' as *Stella* used to say, 'I come from *over there*,' she had said in the past, not pointing to anywhere specific. He looked in the direction of 'over there' where she may have indicated in the past:-

And there she was, quite away off by a gate...beaming, smiling and waving her arms at him as she faded from view, as she had always done in the past.

He shouted, '*Stella*!' as he waved in return but she was gone now, completely faded. However, he only felt pure joy. 'Oh *Stella* - she's happy at last.' He cried again but was now smiling at the same time. Then he laughed, and laughed, Bob now exhilarated.

When he bent down to pick up his flowers to leave...they were not there - they'd gone. Vanished.

'What's going on here...?' he muttered to himself, paused, then relaxed. He looked around. There was no sign of them...but he knew where they might be.

***

Robert Shape hadn't mentioned to Julie about the strange young girl who would suddenly turn up at the park bench during Bob's lunch hour probably because they'd parted before these events occurred; he couldn't remember. And would she believe him?

***

On his return Julie looked up. 'How...' then saw his face; she could tell he'd been upset. 'Oh my love, are you alright?' concern written over her face. They embraced. 'Please tell me...' After several seconds...

'Something I've never told you about Julie...and this part of the story comes first - of a young girl on a park bench...you have to hear the story in the right order.'

***

Bob Shape then related what had transpired - how he was captivated by a young girl who would suddenly turn up almost out of the blue...how intrigued he was with her excited and unusual babble, how she had changed with each visit. He had been quite astonished, baffled even, by her open and obvious innocence, totally unafraid of talking to a complete stranger...and of the bizarre mention of 'missions'.

Then the rest of the tale, the hit and run, Dave's illness - and of his visit to the grave that morning.

'But...but *how* Robert? It's scary. Surely it cannot be the same girl...? It can't be...it's creepy.'

***

Julie was reduced to tears too; they were holding onto each other. Julie was absolutely absorbed and shaken by the events. She said softly:-

'Oh the poor girl...poor girl – and poor David too. You must show me the bench; *I must see it*. I just don't know what to say.'

Nearly forgetting, the told her about the flowers he'd bought with the distinctive Rose and Sunflower - not that he'd bought flowers, but how they'd disappeared. 'Where did they go to - someone steal them?' A look of horror on her face. 'Shall we get another bunch when we go?'

He shook his head, 'We probably won't need to,' he said with a knowing look as he squeezed her hand.

At the bench…

Julie became very quiet when they stood by the bench; she took Bob's arm, a sobering tranquillity and stillness about them. 'On this very bench..?' she asked, looking around. 'It has a feel about it,' she murmured.

He nodded, and seeing her searching glances, 'And...no, you won't find them here...the flowers.'

Then they set off to the cemetery.

***

As they approached the grave Julie pointed out that somebody else had already placed flowers on the grave but at a glance, Bob Shape could see straight away the distinctive *Explore* and *Firecracker* within the bunch lying adjacent to the the Headstone.

He smiled to himself. 'Nicely Done *Stella,*' he thought...because *he knew*...

Julie gasped, she too, noticing and pointing at the distinctive flowers as Robert Shape was nodding. 'Your flowers…? Oh my God. I can't believe it Robert. How…? Oh *Stella*…?'

'Yes my love – something, or somebody, must have moved them from the bench to here. I wonder who?'

'Oh no, you're not telling me…' as she put a hand to her mouth, 'I'm a little scared,' she said as she took his arm. It was time for tears again by the grave...Julie was having a quiet weep.

'Oh Robert, let's go home now – I just want to curl up in your arms tonight and cry.'

This she did. In fact they both wept that night at the sadness of it all - and of course at the happiness of two spirits - now reunited.

***

On their return, both Lynda and Josh realised that the returning pair had undergone an experience, the sorrow on their faces was manifestly evident. They had remained silent knowing of the sensitive nature of their visit. Then bob said:-

'I shall tell you both about it sometime soon, I promise – a sad but at the same time, a wonderfully uplifting story,' he told them.

***

That evening, they became lost in each other's comforting embrace and passion, with softness and tender touches, mixed with both sadness and happiness as they recalled the day's events.

Printed in Great Britain
by Amazon